JENNIFER L ADAMS

UNDER THE CYGNET MOON

UNDER THE CYGNET MOON

ISBN 979-8-9930762-0-1 (ebook)

ISBN 979-8-9930762-1-8 (paperback)

ISBN 979-8-9930762-2-5 (hardback)

First Edition October 2025

Published by Sylvan Lake Press

3101 N Central Ave Suite 183 #6661

Phoenix, AZ 85012

info@sylvanlakepress.com

authorjenniferladams.com

Cover Design by: Miblart

Editing by: Enchanted Ink Publishing

Map Design by: Jennifer L Adams

Author Photo by: Livecopyphoto

For Sylvie
I love you to the Moon and Stars

Celestial
Summit

Stormspir
Mountain

Serelia

Verdant
Forest

Emberreach

Valor

Unknown
Lands

Realm

Shadowed Isles

Veilkeep

of Serendith

CHAPTER 1

Elara

To Elara, the palace was a prison—elegant, gilded, and suffocating. She held her breath and hugged the wall, her bare shoulder brushing against the smooth plaster as she crept through her eerily silent home. The midmorning sunlight poured through massive arched windows lining the hall, illuminating dust motes like trapped stars.

Sneaking around in the daytime was far more difficult than she'd expected. Another nobleman sauntered past, offered her a curt nod, and ignored her otherwise. Relief rushed through her as she let the forced smile fall from her face, then ground her teeth. The last two men to cross her path had stalled her, stealing away her precious minutes with their fawning. She waited for this one to disappear around the corner before she kept moving.

As her heels clicked along the polished marble floor, she winced at each echo. Her shimmering skirts tangled around her legs, threatening to trip her, but wearing anything simpler would have drawn even more attention. A princess en route to the queen's tea service was the perfect disguise for hiding in plain sight.

1

Elara's heart pounded as she reached her true destination. Before her, a tapestry covered the wall from ceiling to knee, displaying a serene scene of a mother picnicking with her two toddlers. Few others in the palace knew that the embroidered meadow concealed a door.

Years ago, one of her guards had shown her the network of secret tunnels hidden behind the palace walls and beneath its foundations. The adventure had been a game at first—a way for the guard, Jalin, to flirt with the young princess. When their dalliance ended, exploring the tunnels alone became an idle habit. Now, the passageways held the key to her plan.

She craned her neck to each side to check for onlookers before she slid her arm behind the heavy fabric of the tapestry. Her fingertips found cold metal, and the latch clicked. Glancing down the hall one last time, she pushed the inset wooden door open and climbed inside.

Raw stacked stones and dirt replaced cream-colored plaster and gleaming marble. Even the air changed, a cool dampness settling over her cheeks and neck. Her eyes fought to adjust to the sudden darkness that swallowed her as the door clicked shut behind her. She placed the palm of her hand against the closest wall and followed it until she found the first bend in her path. The floor sloped upward, earth transitioning into stone, until the ceiling met her hair. *Almost there.* She hiked up her skirts and began crawling on hands and knees. She tried not to think about the silky cobwebs that stuck to her skin. *This better be worth it.*

For days she'd argued with her father, King Reginald Evensong, begging him to present her to the Council of Magi as the heir to the Serendithian throne. The announcement would signal to Elara, and her people, that she was ready to leave her books behind and learn how to rule at her father's side.

Her mind wandered back to their argument this morning. She'd approached his study and found the door ajar. She paused, curiosity overcoming courtesy, and leaned in to listen. Peering through the narrow gap, she watched her father facing a figure clothed in cobalt blue. The stranger's hands gripped the edge of the king's desk, knuckles white.

"If you think for one second I would agree to those terms . . ." the king hissed.

"Fool," said the man. "You think you have a choice, old friend?"

"She's my daughter—"

Elara rapped her knuckles against the weathered oak with a firm *tap, tap, tap*, interrupting the conversation. She bristled. She'd seen that look on her father's face before. Every time the king discussed her personal life without her present, fury bloomed in her chest. The strange man turned to leave, locking eyes with her. He squinted, his eyes a warm golden brown, but his gaze icy.

"Your Highness," he muttered, bobbing his gray head as he brushed past her.

A shiver danced down her spine.

"Elara," her father said, gesturing to a chair in front of his desk. The king's face was red, but his smile for her was genuine, causing the soft skin at the corners of his eyes to crinkle. "Your timing couldn't be better." He chuckled. His laughter, soft and familiar, thawed her indignation—but only a little.

"Who was that?" she asked, taking a seat before him.

"Lord Eamon Stormrider," the king replied. "He and his son have traveled from Veilkeep for the council gathering."

"What were you arguing about?"

He waved a hand, brushing her off. "What can I do for you, dearest?"

Elara dropped the matter, prioritizing her own agenda. The king had enough secrets that this one wasn't enough to distract her from her goal.

"You already know," she said with a frustrated sigh. "I want to attend the council meetings with you this year. It's time I take my place at your side." Elara sat forward in her chair, squaring her shoulders and puffing out her chest.

"You are young, with ample time ahead for learning."

"Father, please." Her hands balled into fists in her lap. "I'm ready now." She should have started attending the gathering two years ago, when she turned eighteen. Instead, her father had insisted that she wait and focus on her studies instead.

You are ready only when I say so. Her father's harsh words echoed in the back of her mind, stinging her more than the rough stones beneath her knees.

E LARA SHIFTED HER WEIGHT, trying to get the blood flowing through her legs. Her kneeling position, while uncomfortable and unbefitting of a princess, was necessary. Wincing at the sensation of pins and needles running down her limbs as she moved, she turned her attention back to the council meeting below. She leaned forward, closing one eye to sharpen her view as she continued spying through a tiny hole in the stone wall.

Below her, the great hall buzzed with rare purpose. The Council of Magi only convened once a year before the final harvest, settling into the capital, Valoria, for several weeks to share news of the different cities throughout the kingdom. The lords and ladies of Serendith were accompanied by talented mages and a select few trusted advisors; together, they formed the full council that served the monarchy.

Elara huffed. She'd been eavesdropping for an hour, and nothing of note had happened. *I should be in there, next to Father.* She pressed her forehead to the stone so hard it throbbed. Her pain was a small price to pay for information.

The gathering had begun with old friends embracing and the council elders showing off their prized sons and daughters, who would assume their council seats this year. Then, as often happened when the king hosted a royal event, rare and strong wines flowed. So, too, did the news of the realm.

With palates whetted and lips looser, the council members asked the king for various things—food, supplies, favorable trade agreements. Her father addressed each request with calculated diplomacy.

The casual, friendly atmosphere shifted. Conversations quieted. Laughter silenced. Chairs scraped against the floor as the magi took their seats. Several of them squirmed in their high-backed chairs. Others sat like statues, with their shoulders stiff and necks straight.

The reason for the soured mood strolled through the entrance to the great hall.

Lord Stormrider.

The man loomed over the other guests in the room as he strode onto the central circular dais that was framed by long, curved tables. He looked at the empty throne, and from her hidden perch above, Elara swore she caught a trace of longing in his gaze.

"Eamon!" the king called, making his way over to his throne. "Welcome, my friend." He clapped a hand onto Lord Stormrider's back. The king sat on the throne and waited, nothing in his expression hinting at their earlier disagreement.

"Your Majesty," Stormrider grumbled, bowing so low the ends of his long gray hair brushed the floor. He rose and gestured to a young man behind him. "May I present to you my son, Captain Caelan Stormrider. Should the stars align, he will serve on this council in years to come."

Elara blinked. Something was missing from his tone: pride. She recognized its absence—she'd seen it lacking in her father's eyes too many times to count. *If he'd only give me a chance, I wouldn't be cramped in this stars-damned tunnel.*

Elara tried to drag forward any memories of the Stormriders. They came from Veilkeep, which was at the southernmost tip of the Shadowed Isles. The Stormriders used to dwell in the

Valorian court until Elara's family, the Evensongs, had ousted them generations ago. The reasons were murky, the resentment less so.

The Shadowed Isles were the ancestral home to both the Moiren and Nimireth. The blue garments suggested the Stormriders were descendants of the former.

Hopefully. She shuddered at the idea of illusionists in the palace.

"Sorcerers," her mother, Queen Evadne Evensong, had once called them. The Moiren controlled water with their magic, but the Nimireth twisted reality with theirs. Unlike the other bloodlines that made up the Council of Magi, illusionists had lacked representation for decades, their power taboo.

The younger Stormrider, Caelan, bowed to the king before finding a place to sit. His tanned skin provided a stark contrast to his unruly dirty-blond curls, which seemed to have a life of their own. His clothes were the same cobalt fabric that his father sported. Despite his wealthy attire and polished manners, there was a roguish air about him, with his unkempt hair and stubbled face.

Caelan's expression brightened as he leaned in to whisper to his neighbor, a striking young woman in a gray gown. Her silky platinum hair cascaded down her shoulders, framing her sharp cheekbones and delicate nose. She tried to suppress her laughter by covering her mouth with a slender hand. Caelan grinned and caressed her arm with easy affection.

Elara rolled her eyes. *I've heard rumors about you.*

Caelan had been a frequent topic of conversation at her mother's teas. He was a notorious rake, leaving a trail of brokenhearted noblewomen in his wake.

Other conversations filled the air as the woman continued blushing and giggling. Elara's ears homed in on a particular phrase across the room, drawing her attention away from Caelan and his latest victim.

"My family continues to lose our essence affinity," said a woman with rich brown skin. "It is worse with each generation. We must find a solution," she begged the king.

Elara had never seen her at court, but the amber dress meant she was from Emberreach.

"If you'd open your minds to our devices," another voice said, "we wouldn't need to worry about essence at all." This magi Elara knew. Lord Malcom Ashfall hailed from the Celestial Summit in the Stormspire Mountains and was a Son of the Sky—an energist who could create and manipulate electricity. That power was so rare that the northernmost cities had evolved to rely on technology instead of magic for their survival.

"Bah! We don't trust your *artifices*—they are dangerous, not to mention blasphemous." The woman slammed her fist onto the table.

Elara flinched. The artifices were devices inspired by ancient artifacts imbued with essence. As natural-born essence affinities had become less common, some turned to those devices to harness power.

Such things were illegal in Valoria, but the king often made unsavory deals with leaders of other cities to skirt the law. The queen herself had gifted Elara and her sister a pair of enchanted jewelry boxes one winter solstice. When opened, they each played a special song, much to the delight of the two little girls.

What other artifices could be out there? The possibilities seemed endless. And dangerous. If weaponized . . .

The king needed to tread carefully and measure his response. The royal family's power came from their alliances, not magic.

Soft scuffling noises filled the small space around Elara, pulling her attention away from the debate below. A warm fuzzy body scurried past her leg and into her scrunched-up skirts. She yelped at the small rat; the noise echoed. She swiped one hand toward the tiny creature and clapped the other over her mouth.

She waited and prayed to the stars above that she wasn't discovered.

No footsteps. No alarm.

A few heartbeats later, the rat was gone. Elara peered through the hole and let her hand fall away from her face. Caelan stared up in her direction, his golden gaze fixed on hers.

Impossible. Despite herself, a blush warmed her cheeks as she locked eyes with him briefly before he shifted his attention back to the king.

The council discussion had transitioned to preparing for the last harvest before winter.

Damn. I missed it. She would have to research the artifices in the library—and riffle through her father's notes—later.

For now, she crawled, her knees and hips complaining at the movement. When she could stand again, she stifled a groan, dusted off her skirts, and began the journey out of the damp tunnel.

A heavy weight settled in her chest as she prepared to trade her fleeting freedom for the stuffy formality of court. She exited the tunnel, straightening her skirts and smoothing her black hair, and returned to her gilded cage.

Chapter 2

Caelan

L IGHTNING FLASHED OUTSIDE THE massive windows of the makeshift training room. The subsequent thunder shook the leaded glass, adding a metallic clanging to the roar of the storm. Caelan held a hand over his head, attuning his essence and summoning a light shower to cool himself off. Water cascaded over him, soaking his hair and running down his face, bare shoulders, and chest. With a reverent sigh, he shook his wet hair out, relishing the sensation of the cool droplets on his skin.

Caelan and his father had wasted the morning sun sitting through the first of what promised to be many tedious council meetings. Now, instead of training outdoors on proper grounds, the two men were crammed into a room together to avoid the nasty weather. Someone had moved all the fine furniture aside and covered it with ghostly white sheets.

As if that will protect it, he thought, shaking his head.

"Ready for round two?" Lord Stormrider asked. Caelan and his father had just finished the first sparring match of the day—both a bit stiff after the voyage from the Shadowed Isles. The journey had been long but enjoyable. They'd cruised by the coast, admiring scenic cliffs. Caelan loved the fresh salty air filling his lungs and the sun warming his face—the fleeting freedom of the sea.

"Always, old man," Caelan replied with a grin. He'd lost the first match within minutes, but training together was one of the few things they shared without outright resentment. Most of the time. It beat formal dinners, and he'd take training over council meetings any day—though he craved the boisterous late-night court parties to come.

Caelan picked up his short sword, flipping it across the back of his hand before securing his grip around the hilt. His favored weapon—aside from his magic—it was adorned with a bronze pommel, the stag's head inset into the metal gleaming faintly in the dim light.

"Show-off," his father muttered, falling back into his preferred fighting stance. His face showed no hint of amusement.

Caelan knew his father enjoyed the training, but the elder Stormrider always approached it with intense focus.

Caelan assessed his opponent—pressing forward and raising his sword—then shifted into a defensive stance to counter his father's aggressive posture. *Typical*, he thought, blowing a strand of sand-colored hair out of his face. He took a deep breath. *One, two . . .*

"Go!" Caelan said, starting the match. The two men stepped sideways in perfect synchrony. Their years of fighting together were evident in the way they started each match with this dance. A step to the side each. A step backward for one, while the other inched forward to fill the void. Caelan waited, knowing that his father would strike first. He tilted his head to the side, his eyes following the twitch of his father's lips as a small cruel smile spread across his face.

"Come and get me, boy," Lord Stormrider said.

Caelan faltered. *Teasing?*

His mind churned, wondering what had prompted this unsettling shift in his father's behavior. It must have been a ploy to distract him. Caelan struck first.

The screech of steel hitting steel filled the air as Caelan's sword bit into his father's. His father pressed his forearm guard into his blade and used his full weight to force Caelan back a few paces. Another flash of lightning illuminated the room, casting colorful light through the stained glass windows. It caught Caelan off guard, allowing his father to gain the upper hand.

"What do I always say?" his father asked, beads of sweat forming on his weathered brow.

"Expect the unexpected," Caelan grunted. He found his footing and prepared to parry once more. Then raindrops plopped onto his forehead and nose. He refused to look up. Despite the afternoon storm raging outside, he knew it wasn't a roof leak.

The sparkle in his father's eyes gave him away—he was playing dirty, conjuring rain inside to mimic the stormy weather outside. The fight dragged on, with neither side gaining an advantage. Caelan was young and agile, but his father possessed the strength and wisdom of experience.

Just as Caelan was about to call for an end to the match, a geyser of water shot from his father's palm and struck him directly in the chest. He fell backward, slamming his tailbone onto the hard marble and gasping for air, only to be met with the searing pain of water filling his throat and lungs. He tried to roll away, but the torrent grew until it engulfed his entire body with water.

No. Please. Fear, plain and visceral, clawed at his mind. As much as he wanted to believe that he was safe, he couldn't convince his body that his father wouldn't kill him.

Helpless, drowning, he curled into a ball and prayed for the torment to end. When it finally did, he convulsed before vomiting up a vile combination of water and bile. He coughed and heaved, fighting to get air into his lungs. Sweet oxygen filled his chest. Black spots flickered at the edge of his vision but faded as his breathing stabilized.

Stunned, Caelan traced the intricate gold-leaf patterns on the ceiling with his eyes, his mind reeling as he tried to make sense of what had just happened. His father would occasionally conjure rain or ill-placed puddles during their sessions, but he'd never used essence to attack during training.

Not since . . .

Caelan held his hand out in front of his face, examining the scarred flesh that bubbled across his palm and onto the back of his hand. Even now, a shiver ran down his spine, the phantom pain of his skin melting a reminder of his lost innocence. The unwelcome memory forced its way to the forefront of his mind.

Caelan had been a boy, no older than twelve—running around the manor at Veilkeep, chasing girls and distracting them from their chores. His father had summoned him for an extra training session at dusk. A gap-toothed smile spread across his face upon discovering a boy his own age standing next to his father.

"This is Rurik," his father said. "He's here to help with your training."

Lord Stormrider whispered into Rurik's ear, and the boy's mouth fell open, his amber eyes becoming saucers. Caelan could almost smell the acrid fear rolling off him—his father often had that effect on people.

As soon as Caelan stepped forward, arm outstretched to shake Rurik's hand, the dark-haired boy cowered. At Lord Stormrider's gaze, sharp as daggers, Rurik held out a shaking hand, palm up. A ball of fire flared into being, burning bright against the darkening sky.

An Embrathi.

"You must learn to defend yourself from every form of magic," Lord Stormrider said. "Fire, as your elemental opposite, is the most logical place to start."

Caelan fought the urge to run as that same fear that had overcome Rurik began crawling under his own skin, filling his veins with ice. Instead of fleeing, he gathered every ounce of his courage and stood his ground. He went into a defensive stance, a practiced movement that was as familiar as his own heartbeat. He gave Rurik a slight nod.

Hit me.

The blast was blinding, and Caelan shielded his eyes against the light. Pain seared through his hand before he could quench the flames with his own magic. His water soothed the blistered flesh, but not his frightened spirit.

"Father, please!" he called out, cradling his injured hand.

"Again," Lord Stormrider commanded, not satisfied that his lesson had been learned.

Any semblance of trust between Caelan and his father had gone up in smoke that day.

"Get up," Lord Stormrider snapped, bringing Caelan back to the present. "We're in the den of our oldest enemies. Who knows what they have in store for us? You must be prepared for anything." He reached down, offering an outstretched hand to his son.

Caelan took it, clambering to his feet, his limbs heavy. His father was right—the Evensongs couldn't be trusted. They were betrayers. Liars. He'd grown up on bedtime stories about their deceit and how they'd turned Serendith against the Stormriders, exiling his ancestors from Valoria. Lord Stormrider had spent his life rebuilding their political power, just so Caelan would have a seat on the Council of Magi. Maybe even more.

"Sit," Lord Stormrider ordered, sauntering across the room to a table.

Caelan glared at him but obeyed, collapsing into a chair across from his father.

"You know why we're here," his father said, pouring himself a glass of crimson wine. He didn't offer any to his son.

Caelan nodded, folding his arms across his aching chest. "I know." His throat burned as he croaked out the words.

"What do you think of the girl?"

"Never met her. Just seen a portrait," Caelan said. "Does it matter what I think?" He raised an eyebrow.

"No. But it will be easier for you if you can remain . . . unattached." Lord Stormrider took a deep swig of the wine.

Caelan nodded again, chest tightening. "I know. When?"

"The end of the week." His father's mouth became a tight line.

Caelan's heart skipped a beat. *So soon. I'd hoped to have more time before . . .*

"Understood, sir. Anything else?"

His father leaned forward, causing his chair to creak. "You are the key to our success. I'm counting on you." He paused, his eyes searching Caelan's face for any sign of weakness. "Will you stand with me, son?"

Caelan schooled his features, ensuring that his father found nothing there to criticize. He couldn't stomach the look of disappointment that he'd grown so familiar with over the years. "You can count on me, Father. I won't let you down."

Caelan waited, the clinking of his father's wineglass against the table the only other sound in the room. When he finished, Lord Stormrider strode out of the room and closed the heavy door behind him, leaving Caelan utterly alone.

Caelan's hands shook as he snatched his sword from the floor, the wet metal ice-cold against his skin. With a desperate heave, he hurled it at the drenched silhouettes of the ghostly furniture. The clatter of steel echoed in the empty room. But it wasn't loud enough to drown out the scream trapped in Caelan's mind.

CHAPTER 3

Elara

T HE MORNING AFTER THE first council meetings, Elara rushed down one of the servants' stairwells, tucked away behind a pillar of hewn granite. Dressed in loose trousers and her favorite pair of short leather boots, she piled her hair atop her head and pulled a ribbon from between her lips to secure the dark strands. She'd finished dressing by grabbing an apron off a hook to tie around her waist and adding thin leather gloves to one of its large pockets.

As she headed out the door to meet her sister in one of the dozens of gardens on the palace grounds, a timid servant waved her down and offered her a hat to protect her from the harsh sunlight.

"Thank you." Elara smiled at the young girl, who beamed up at her before scurrying off.

Tucking the wide-brimmed hat under her arm, she stepped into the bright morning sun. She closed her eyes and let the light wash over her face, breathing in the crisp autumn air.

Today was a cleanup day—gardening was one of her younger sister's favorite pastimes, and Elara didn't mind indulging her.

Thalia already crouched in a flower bed, shoving fistfuls of yellow and brown leaves into a worn sack. She was radiant, even in her simple gardening dress, her cheeks flushed under her own floppy hat.

Elara kneeled beside her, placing a gentle hand on her sister's shoulder. "What wrong have those leaves done to you to deserve such treatment?"

"Not turning into a proper mulch fast enough?" Thalia deadpanned.

"Well, splendid morning to you too," Elara said, laughing.

"I mean, if you want a hug—" Thalia wiggled her filthy gloved fingers at Elara.

"No thanks." Elara grinned, content to take up her spot next to her best friend and clear her mind of yesterday's events. Her mind whirled with the tiny bits of information she'd gleaned—wondering about her father's latest scheme, the artifices, the younger Stormrider . . .

Her joints still ached with pain from crawling through the tunnels. Elara stretched, then scooped up leaves and shoved them into the sack before yanking a few spiky weeds from the soil. The rich, earthy smell of wet soil mingled with the musty scent of decaying leaves, the aroma heavy in the air. The blooming flowers brought the landscape to life, their vibrant petals outstretched. In a few months, only the hardy perennial varieties would stand a chance at surviving the upcoming frost.

After several minutes' work, sweat beaded on her brow. She dragged a mostly clean forearm across her damp forehead before replacing her hat.

"You're awfully . . . enthusiastic this morning," Thalia said. When Elara didn't respond, Thalia huffed and tried again. "What's wrong?"

Elara stared down at her gloves. "Father wouldn't let me attend the first council meeting with him," she whispered.

"Ah." Thalia nodded. "I'm sorry." She leaned over and wrapped an arm around Elara's shoulders, careful not to soil her clothes. "You just have to trust him, Elara. Father will know when you're ready."

"He'll never see I'm ready if he never pays attention," Elara pointed out. A flare of jealousy ran through her, and she shoved it down. It wasn't Thalia's fault that their father often favored her, leaving Elara to her tutors while he indulged in her little sister's many hobbies.

"You're just overthinking it!" Thalia grabbed a pair of shears and began pruning some of the creeping phlox spilling over the short stone wall of the garden bed. The powdery-blue flowers on its tendrils had already shriveled. "He does love you, you know. You don't have to play 'perfect princess' forever," she whispered.

Elara shook her head, eyes resting on the beautiful peachy-white rose blooms of a desdemona bush. Thalia didn't understand the responsibility of being the heir or the pressure Elara faced. Legacy pressed on her like a stone, fueling her desire to restore their name.

Elara had seen enough from shadowed alcoves and peering through keyholes to know that their family's name no longer inspired reverence. Her father's debts, his whispered bargains—it all added up. She didn't yet know what the consequences would be.

While she didn't agree with the king's methods, Elara still loved and respected him. She simply wanted the opportunity to show him, and the world, a better way.

"I thought older sisters were the ones who are supposed to give advice," Elara said.

"Not when they're as annoying as you," Thalia teased. "But I love you anyway."

Elara shook her head again, the corners of her lips tugging up into a small smile. She loved Thalia more than anything. The sisters shared everything, rarely failing to find a solution to a problem together. Elara always took care of Thalia, cleaning her scraped knees and giving her kisses, brushing her tears away with a steady hand.

"I love you too. Even if you're a know-it-all," Elara replied, grabbing a second pair of shears and attacking another bush.

After a few more minutes of silent work, Thalia stilled, a telling gleam in her eye. "Wait! If you weren't at the council meeting or Mother's tea, then where were you?"

Now Elara grinned, her smile stretching lazily across her cheeks.

"You were in the tunnels, weren't you?" Thalia asked skeptically.

Elara nodded, and Thalia crossed her legs, settling into a more comfortable position. She propped her elbows on her knees and placed her fists under her chin. "Tell me everything!"

Elara laughed, shaking her head. "You were supposed to distract me, not interrogate me."

Thalia pouted for a moment, but she couldn't help but break into a wide grin that showed off her pearly-white teeth. Surrendering, Elara recounted what she'd witnessed in her father's office and overheard at the council meeting.

"What's Father up to now?" Thalia asked, blue eyes narrowing.

"Nothing good," Elara muttered. She shuddered at the thought of another of his schemes further damaging their family's reputation. While their birthright as the only remaining bloodline with any ties to the Serathi had allowed Elara's ancestors to claim the throne after the Shattering, the Evensongs' hold on the royal seat in Valoria was tenuous at best.

The king had spent the last decade borrowing money and goods from each of the noble houses across the continent. And worse than that, he often traded in secrets and dangerous promises—like allowing the artifices to be sold in the capital. In Serendith, where essence was waning, a promise was law—a promise was power.

The noble families were as greedy as they were vicious, clawing and grasping for power wherever they could. The last war—the Shattering—had left Serendith fractured politically. Allies betrayed one another. After the druids—the featured villains in most nursery rhymes—had been defeated, the once-united human forces had broken into factions. They'd retreated to the ancestral seats of their essence affinities. Only the Council of Magi had held the fragile peace together for the last four hundred years.

Now, whispers of skirmishes at the edges of Valoria and other cities, along with several years of poor harvests, left her people agitated and hungry. Based on what she'd gleaned yesterday, Elara wondered if the damage was also metaphysical. According to her father's notes—which she had lifted from his desk after the meeting—essence was bleeding from the realm, limiting the magical energies available to humans and leaving a void to be filled with other forms of power.

"Tell me more about the younger Stormrider," Thalia said, changing the subject to something more lighthearted. "Is he as handsome as they say?"

Elara resisted the urge to pelt her sister with dirt clods. "I didn't really get a good look at him." She shrugged and pretended to be interested in a worm writhing in the soil.

"Sure." Thalia rolled her eyes but didn't press any further.

Elara let the relief wash over her. She wasn't ready to discuss handsome strangers with her little sister—especially not when she was worried about what schemes that stranger's father was cooking up with hers.

P ANTING FROM THE HEAT, Elara trudged down the corridor, brushing dirt and debris from her trousers. Sticky with sweat and ready to relax in the bath before tea with her mother—a real one this time—she turned the corner to head toward her chambers and—

Smack.

She slammed into a thick wall of flesh.

"Ow!" she cried, stumbling back.

"Watch it!" a deep male voice scolded. He turned to face her.

Elara blinked up at him. *Caelan Stormrider.*

"Oh," he murmured, brows lifting. "I beg your pardon, Miss . . . ?"

His eyes traced her face, which was filthy, before he reached up and plucked a stray leaf from her tousled hair. Her cheeks warmed, and her heart fluttered before she cleared her throat.

"Elara Evensong. And you're Caelan Stormrider."

Caelan's mouth slackened before his lips curved into a cocky smile. His gaze traced her figure from her dark hair to the tips of her boots and back up again. His brow arched at her trousers, and she shifted from one foot to the other under his scrutiny.

"Your Highness," he said, dipping into a low bow. He grasped her hand, and sparks danced up her arm. Golden eyes flicked to hers. "Captain Caelan Stormrider at your service, Princess."

Elara rolled her eyes at the way he emphasized their titles.

"Are you hurt?" he asked, though with no trace of genuine concern.

"I'm fine," she snapped.

"Indeed, you are." Caelan grinned.

Charming. But, indeed, he was. He was taller than her by a few inches with that mop of curly sand-colored hair, and his skin was tanned by either the journey across the narrow sea from Veilkeep or from a lifetime of sailing. Elara's own skin was fair—no amount of time gardening or riding would make up for the rest of the time she spent inside the palace.

She scowled. She had no desire to become entangled with the Stormriders. The elder had a rumored fondness for battle and cruelty, the younger for drinking and women. She had no interest in being charmed by him—or anyone else, for that matter. Her mind was set on tidying up her family's political affairs before she considered anything as frivolous as romance.

"If you'll excuse me." Elara shoved past him with her shoulder.

Caelan snatched her arm with a firm grip. "Wait," he whispered, his tone serious. "We should . . . talk."

Talk about what? Panic flooded Elara's system. He'd reacted to her yell during the council meeting. *Does he know?* Her arm throbbed under his fingers.

She looked up at him, her eyes narrow and her frown deepening. Her cheeks became even hotter, this time with anger bubbling beneath the skin. "Does that work on all the other girls?" she spat, glaring at her trapped arm. "Let. Go."

Caelan sighed and released her, holding his gloved palms up in surrender.

It took every ounce of self-control to keep from sprinting away from him. As soon as she rounded a corner and was out of his sight, she stopped. She placed a hand over her chest—her heart was pounding. Elara took a long breath, trying to calm herself.

Handsome, she thought, rubbing the tender spot on her arm, which was sure to bruise. *And cruel.*

CHAPTER 4

Caelan

C AELAN TOOK A LONG swig of purple wine from his crystal
goblet. He scanned the dining hall, stifling a yawn. The
long wooden table stretched across the massive space, seating at
least sixty self-important people. The others ate and laughed,
celebrating the first week of the council gathering. Caelan had
no appetite. Not after that training session—and subsequent
conversation with his father—several days ago. His throat still
burned, and he would have collapsed into his too-soft bed and
slept for a few days if his presence hadn't been required at more
dreaded meetings.

Drowning on dry land will do that to you. He drank again, trying
his best not to wince at both the sting and the taste. The wines
favored at the Valorian court were cloyingly sweet compared to the
crisp, dry vintages native to Veilkeep.

At least the princess had given Caelan a minor distraction from
his pain. *So beautiful*, he thought, picturing her raven hair and
sapphire eyes. *And odd.* He smirked to himself at the thought
of whatever she had been doing that had left her so filthy. That,

along with her obvious disinterest in him, made her all the more intriguing. Caelan's charms seldom proved ineffective, especially with single young noblewomen.

Caelan leaned back and remembered the first time he'd sailed across the narrow sea that separated the Shadowed Isles from the rest of the continent. He'd been a boy of eleven years, swinging from the ship's rigging and learning terrible manners and colorful language from the crew. They taught him well, for beneath his polished exterior was the mouth of a seasoned sailor who could make just about anyone blush.

Now Caelan was here as a future magi—heir to his father's legacy, a twenty-five-year-old man with a boy's heart. He longed to travel the continent, to see the fabled ruins of the Verdant Forest with his own eyes and explore the unknown lands to the south. So much of the world he hadn't seen, had barely been able to dream of visiting.

Instead, he pouted in this dining hall, drinking disgusting wine and listening to the richest families in Serendith bicker. Tomorrow night, this suffocating palace would trap him, perpetually drowning him once more.

"Hey there, stranger."

The soft, slurred voice drew him out of his thoughts. Caelan glanced over as Lady Seraphine Greythorn slid into the chair next to his.

"Where are we going tonight?" she asked, beaming at him, green eyes glistening with mischief.

Caelan waved, summoning a servant to bring her a goblet of her own, although, judging by the twinkling in her eyes and the way she'd slurred her greeting, she didn't need any further libations.

"Water for my friend," he ordered when the attendant appeared.

"You're no fun, *friend*," she whined, swatting him affectionately on the arm. "I'm fine," she argued, even as she knocked around her silverware with the long sleeves of her violet gown and nearly toppled out of her seat upon turning. Caelan gripped her wrist and held her steady until she settled, reclining.

"I don't doubt it," he said, chuckling. "Let's get a little water in you—and some bread to soak up whatever's sloshing around in your stomach—before we go."

With Seraphine's meal attended to, the pair withdrew from the dining hall before the dessert service. Caelan tugged the hood of her cloak up over her head, concealing her bright hair and obscuring her face.

"I don't know why you bother," she muttered. "We both know I don't need protecting." A wicked grin spread across her face, and she held up a hand, conjuring a purple mist that swirled around her delicate fingertips. "Besides, if I was going to disguise myself, I can do much better than a raggedy old cloak," she teased. With a flourish, her purple smoke puffed into her face, transforming her emerald eyes into sapphire ones. A wisp of blond hair sticking out from under the cloak shifted into a raven curl, and her tanned skin lightened. "She is beautiful, you know. You could do a lot worse," Seraphine said.

Caelan stared at Princess Elara's face. "Not funny, Sera."

She giggled and dropped the illusion, returning to her normal self. He slung his arm around her and guided her down the hall. Sera was right—she didn't need his protection—but he wanted to at least pretend that he was doing her some good by keeping their relationship hidden. His disrepute had yet to taint her after all these years, and he intended to keep it that way.

They ambled down a deserted hall lined with alternating panels of ivory and obsidian, in search of a particular drawing room. Caelan had had enough of the sickly sweet drinks mixed with vapid conversation and craved company more fitting to his particular tastes. The Valorian court's pristine facade hid more than intriguing political webs, including his father's own spies. At this moment, what mattered most to Caelan was that it concealed a notorious network of illicit gatherings.

One last turn brought Caelan and Sera to their destination. The sound of Caelan's knuckles against the door—two quick taps, a beat of silence, and then three drawn-out knocks—cut through the silence. A guard, opening the door but facing away, grunted, "Drop it!" to someone inside. "Password?" he asked, sounding annoyed and turning to face them. When his eyes locked with Caelan's, panic filled his voice. "S-sorry, Captain Stormrider! Please, right this way," he said, bowing his head.

Caelan grinned. "Don't fret, Geoffrey," he said, patting the familiar palace guard on the shoulder. "Besides, isn't it still 'Ember's Breeches'?"

The sturdy man sagged in relief. "Indeed, sir. Please enjoy yourselves. Oh, and"—Geoffrey leaned in to whisper into Caelan's ear—"I'd avoid the red stuff tonight if I were you."

Caelan nodded and tugged Sera through the threshold.

A thick red haze shrouded the dim room, the air tinged with the smell of turpentine. A puff of the pungent smoke wafted into his nostrils as a nearby woman blew rings from her pipe.

Aether.

Caelan coughed and navigated away from the smokers indulging near the doorway. The "red stuff," also known as "aether" or "stardust," was one of the newest commodities to come out of Emberreach's mines. Its public purpose was medicinal, of course, but when inhaled or ingested in more substantial quantities, it offered a blissful escape from reality. The perfect remedy to ease Caelan's troubled mind.

Ignoring the guard's warning, Caelan grabbed a fluted glass of sparkling red liquid as he settled into a plush loveseat at the back of the room. The emerald-green velvet crunched beneath him as he sank into the cushions. Sera took her cloak off, tossed it to the nearest servant, and joined the throng on the dance floor. The crowd swayed to the lilting notes of a lone harp as gilded candelabras cast their flickering shadows onto the indigo wallpaper.

Caelan tilted his head back, downed his drink, and propped one foot up on the low table in front of the couch. Enjoying a prime view, he observed several couples who had separated from the flock of over two dozen party guests. He shook his head at a magi lounging in a chair while a woman half his age perched on his lap, caressing his whiskered, weathered face with her smooth fingers. *Typical.* Like a coin, everyone at court had two faces—the polished one they showed to the world, and a tarnished backside reserved for more private settings.

The dancing and mingling figures blurred at the edges of Caelan's vision. Warmth pressed against his side, and a slender hand traced the inner seam of his trousers. He brushed it off and crossed his legs, reaching for another drink—whiskey this time—from a servant's silver platter as it floated by. Before he could even take a sip, he swallowed hard and placed his glass back onto the tray with a clatter, realizing why the doorman had told him not to drink the red stuff.

She's here. He'd been to dozens of parties over the years during his court visits but had never seen a royal attend one.

Princess Elara, arms folded and eyes narrowed, stood by a table laden with fluffy pastries and fine meats. A smile brightened her expression as a young royal guard approached, slipping a book and a pile of papers into her waiting hands.

With his hand on her shoulder, the guard grinned, his teeth gleaming in the dim light. Caelan noted that the touch lingered a little longer than appropriate. The guard wandered off, maybe to fetch some drinks, and the princess continued to observe the crowd. Her lovely face twisted, her brow furrowing with worry.

She approached a cowering servant girl cornered by an enraged noblewoman and two gentlemen. Elara's face was a mask of calm, but her hands were balled into tight fists at her sides.

"Sincerest apologies," the servant said with a sniffle. The young girl trembled, tears spilling down her face. "It was a simple mistake."

Caelan shook his head, trying to clear the aether's haze enough to compose himself and focus on their conversation.

"Simple? Is it?" one of the men sneered. "You ruined my wife's gown with red wine. That fabric is worth more than you'll make in a lifetime, you useless girl!"

"I'm so sorry," the girl squeaked out.

Caelan grimaced. The girl couldn't have been older than ten and she had no business serving drinks at a party like this. He resisted the urge to help, instead wanting to see what Elara would do.

"There now, that wasn't so hard, was it?" said the afflicted woman. "What should we do with her?" she asked her companions. The vicious look on her face suggested the violence she had in mind.

"Hush now," Elara said to the tearful girl, "you did nothing wrong. It was an accident." She turned to face the others. "You should be ashamed of yourselves," she hissed.

The second man, the one who hadn't yet said a word, raised his arm and prepared to strike the girl. Elara stepped in front of him just in time to block the blow with her shoulder.

Caelan's heart pounded and he gripped the edge of the couch.

"Stars! Who do you think you—" the man roared at her, shaking out his hand. They both straightened, Elara's gaze sharp and unwavering as she stared him down, her blue eyes like steel. His hand, already raised to strike her again, trembled with rage as her royal guard's voice cut through the air, interrupting the impending blow.

"Your Highness," the guard said, drawing the man's attention and giving him a panicked look.

The man stared back at Elara, dumbfounded. "I-I am so sorry, Your Highness," he stammered, bowing deeply as he backed away from her.

"Indeed, you should be," Elara responded. "Now, tell me, what gives you the right to assault my staff?" She folded her arms across her chest, a frown etching itself onto her face as she waited.

"A misunderstanding, Princess," the first man said, his voice smooth as silk despite the tension in the air. "We would never presume to punish the servant. It's just that—"

"It's just that you planned on beating this poor girl senseless—or worse," Elara said. "I witnessed it personally."

Caelan sat up straighter, impressed by her boldness—by her care for the girl. Even in his own household, servants were mistreated, and he hated it. Hated to see innocents suffer. More curious was the fact that a princess—an Evensong nonetheless—would risk her own safety to help.

"Please forgive us, Your Highness," said the woman, deflating. Their actions were defenseless, and they knew it.

"Jalin, escort our guest here to his lodging for the evening. I'm sure a night in a cell will mend his temper."

The guard nodded, then shoved the man out of the room.

"Come," Elara said, offering her hand to the girl. "Do you like cake?"

The servant's little mouth plopped open, and her eyes were wide as saucers as she put her tiny hand into the princess's.

Caelan shifted in his seat, eyes following the odd pair as they exited together. The stories he'd been told about Elara's family warred with what he'd just witnessed. The Evensongs were cruel, cunning. Not kind or protective.

Maybe she's different, he thought. *No.* He shook his head and gestured to the woman who had shown an interest in him. She walked over, hips swaying, and sat on his lap. He licked the palm of her hand, coating his tongue with powdery red crystals. He didn't have time to think—not with his father's plan already set in motion. He let the red haze carry him away and into the beautiful stranger's warm embrace.

CHAPTER 5

Elara

A SHARP RAP ON her door startled Elara, pulling her from the task of transcribing her father's notes. Jalin had retrieved them while Elara was trapped at her mother's tea and slipped them to her during his shift in the red parlor last night.

They weren't as helpful as hearing the information firsthand from the tunnels. Her father's notes were sparse, much of his work living only in his mind. But they were better than nothing and didn't require her to sit cramped in the dark.

"Come in," she called, tucking her work into the back of her desk drawer.

The queen opened the door and the scent of roses wafted into the room as she entered. Elara loved that perfume.

"How are you feeling, darling?" her mother asked, sitting in a plush chair near the glowing fireplace.

"I'm fine, Mother." Elara sighed and leaned back in her own chair. Her heart pinched with guilt. She'd lied to her mother, feigning illness the first day of the council meetings. "But thank you for coming to check on me," she added, tone softer.

"You were so quiet at tea this morning. Then you disappeared all afternoon," the queen pressed, raising a delicate eyebrow.

Elara shrugged. "I found an interesting book." It wasn't a lie. Jalin had also found her a tome about the artifices. She'd have to ask Thalia to help her translate it tomorrow, since she'd yet to make any sense of it on her own and her little sister had a knack for languages.

"Were you with that guard again?" The queen's tone turned teasing, a knowing smile spreading across her face and revealing the dimples in her cheeks.

Resisting the urge to toss a pillow from the bed at her mother's smug look, Elara shook her head. "Has Father said anything about how the council meetings are going so far?" she asked.

Her mother sighed and examined her perfectly manicured nails. "The usual: the elementalists are arguing with the Children of the Sky, who would rather secure their trade agreements and flee to the mountains than debate with the Embrathi."

"And?" Elara leaned forward, hoping her mother would share more.

The queen never attended the council meetings, preferring gossip and games to politics, but she had a sharp mind and the king's ear. Elara realized over the years that the queen's influence was hidden, not absent.

"I know you wanted to attend the meetings this year. You just need to be—"

"Patient. I know." She slumped back into her chair, deflated.

"It's all right for you to be frustrated with him."

The tension in Elara's neck eased. It was a relief to have someone understand her frustration and to feel that she wasn't alone.

"Do you want me to speak with him?" her mother offered.

Elara shook her head again. She didn't want her mother to influence him. She needed to convince the king she was ready on her own.

The pair sat in silence as the fire crackled and popped. The queen stood, her gown rustling softly, and approached Elara.

"You look pale, my love. Let's go riding in the morning. Enjoy the fresh air." Her mother brushed her cheek and tucked a curl behind Elara's ear.

"Sleep well." She pressed her lips to Elara's forehead and turned to leave.

"I love you," Elara whispered as the door groaned shut behind her mother.

T HE SMELL OF SMOKE pulled Elara from sleep. Eyes flying open, she rolled out of bed and rushed to the window. She gripped the age-roughened stone of the windowsill as she leaned forward in apprehension. The stained glass window, once vibrant, was already dulling with soot as flames blazed below.

The wagons of hay standing outside the inner wall of the palace were now engulfed as a dozen servants attempted to douse the fire with buckets of water. A strange flicker of movement drew Elara's eye over to the main gate. Several figures navigated the narrow archway with their torches. Had they set the fires on purpose? Or was it an accident? In the black of night, she couldn't see whose colors they wore; they were merely shadows creeping through the courtyard of her family's home.

Elara realized she had little time. If they were intruders, it wouldn't take long for them to reach her chambers, or those of her parents, or . . . Thalia. She had to reach her little sister, and the king's chambers, before the enemy did.

She heard a cacophony of movement from down the hall—metal and voices and bodies clashing together and echoing through the stone hallways. A deafening *thud, thud* sounded just outside her chamber's wooden doors. The sound was quick, yet sickening, and she had a feeling it meant her two guards were dead. Elara's chest tightened, and her heartbeat thundered in her ears as adrenaline began coursing through her veins.

Swallowing her terror, she stumbled to the back of her room, almost tripping on the hem of her long nightgown. Her bare feet protested against the scratchy threadbare rug at the edge of her chambers. She shivered, either from the chill or from fear. The large four-poster bed served as a barrier between herself and the door. Her eyes swept the space, searching for anything she could use to protect herself, and her sharp letter opener taunted her from the desk across the room. She'd never reach it in time.

Elara braced herself, squaring her jaw and shoulders, and did the only thing she could at that moment.

She waited.

Smoldering embers crackled in her hearth.

Then the doors burst open with such force that Elara almost lost her footing and her nerve. The first few moments were a blur. Two soldiers marched through the threshold, followed closely by two more. In the dying glow from her fireplace, she recognized their armor: scale mail over deep blue tunics with a serpentine crest across the breastplate. These men were from the Shadowed Isles.

Stormrider's men.

The soldier in front eyed her, his mouth curling into a grin behind his helm. "We're here to collect on your father's debt, Princess," he said. He cocked his head to one side, assessing her like a predator. His eyes traced the outline of her body through her sheer nightgown before resting on her face. Chuckling, he sauntered over to her while the others waited by the door. He placed a hand on her shoulder, trying to coax her out from behind the bed with surprising gentleness. Something about him was familiar, but she didn't have time to ponder it.

No.

Elara flew into action, ignoring the logical part of her brain that knew she could never best these men in a fight. She bolted to her desk, snatched the letter opener, and jabbed it into the man's side. It was useless. His armor deflected the feeble attack, the force of the blow causing him to take a small step away from her while she tumbled into her desk chair. The wood buckled under her weight, and she slammed onto the floor.

Heart pounding and fiery adrenaline licking through her veins, Elara reached into the fireplace, trying to find anything she could use to defend herself. Her hand closed around hot embers. She didn't feel her flesh burning, but she could smell it. She threw the embers at the soldier's head, hoping to distract him long enough for her to find a proper weapon.

With a flick of his wrist, he stopped the embers midair with a burst of water.

A Moiren.

Elara's heart raced. She stared at the doused embers as they fell to the floor in front of her.

The watermage strode toward her and hauled her up by her waist. She hit him over and over, clawing at his helm.

"Let go of me!" she hissed.

One of the other soldiers restrained her from behind, wrapping his arms around her arms and torso. She kicked at his shins until cool steel grazed her throat.

"Enough," the watermage growled. "Trust me, you'll want to come with us. He has your family."

At the mention of her loved ones, she finally stilled, the blood rushing from her face. Her frenzied panic calmed enough for her logic to return. If her family had already been captured, the safest thing she could do now was to surrender.

The watermage removed his sword from her neck, leaving a thin slice that trickled blood onto her nightgown. She ignored the sting of the cut, but the pain of defeat swelled in her heart.

The soldiers flanked her, preventing any further ill-fated attempts at escape. They didn't even bother to bind her wrists. The stench that surrounded her was overwhelming—iron, sweat, singed hair, and the burnt flesh of her own hand. Dried blood flaked off the back of the helmet in front of her. Elara gulped down her dread.

As the soldiers escorted her through the dark hallway, she chanced a glance backward to the slumped figures on either side of her doorway. Both appeared bloodied, motionless, but she dared to hope.

"Are Jalin and Kaz dead?"

"Who?" the watermage responded.

"My guards," she clarified, only now realizing she'd spoken aloud. "Are they dead?"

"Just unconscious," he mused.

Jalin and Kaz had always been more than guards to Elara. They were more like older brothers—protectors, confidants, and avid tricksters who always knew how to lift her spirits. Once, Jalin had been even more than a friend . . .

They're alive. A long exhale escaped her lips, and some of the pressure lifted off her chest. But not all of it.

While the men bumped and nudged her along, Elara worried for her sister. At just sixteen, Thalia was four years younger than Elara and the truest embodiment of a Serendithian princess: educated, poised, and kind. She was also weak—which was exactly how Elara felt now, being herded like a helpless animal through her own home.

Rage replaced her worry. *How could Father let this happen?* Elara's mind brimmed with questions. Why these men had come for *her* as revenge against the king's penchant for failing to follow through on his many promises was beyond her.

While she was heir to the throne, she had no essence affinity. Her political education afforded her confidence that she was more useful dead, so that one of the noble families with greater magical abilities could step in to rule. As this thought hit her, panic fluttered in her belly. She prayed to the stars that she was not being escorted to her own execution.

Elara's bare feet chafed on the hard polished floor as they shuffled along. The plush runner of the sweeping staircase provided a small relief as they ambled up to the throne room. Elara jumped when one of the soldier's shoulders brushed against a vase, sending it crashing to the marble steps. The watermage looked at the shattered pieces of sharp porcelain and then to her feet. He shrugged. She seethed, tiptoeing through the debris as they continued to climb.

They finally reached the throne room, and the watermage signaled for the men to stop. She nearly smacked into his backside. He turned to face her, hand raised. When she flinched away from him, he chuckled and cupped her chin. After staring at her for several breaths, he brushed her sweat-dampened hair out of her face.

Elara's face flushed in anger at the tender gesture. She snatched her chin out of his grasp and swatted at his hand. That only made him laugh harder. The doors to the throne room inched open as her thoughts whirled.

Are they here?

Are they alive? I am, so they have to be, right?

Will I have to fight?

Can I?

She held her breath as the doors opened wide. What she saw flooded her with relief and horror.

Lord Stormrider sat upon her father's throne atop the dais at the back of the massive room, the sight of him there turning her stomach sour. Strategically placed soldiers guarded the platform's front and the room's remaining borders. The stunning blond woman from the council meeting was at his right hand, wearing a violet gown. The edges of her face shimmered, and purple smoke curled around her fingertips.

A Nimireth.

The sorceress held Elara's family captive. They kneeled facing away from the throne. Their eyes glowed an eerie white—unseeing. Elara scanned them for injuries, relieved that they appeared unharmed. Thalia's soft brown hair hung loose, tousled. Her mother—imperious and cold with her subjects, joyous and dazzling with friends and family, always doting on her daughters—had been reduced to a motionless statue at Lord Stormrider's feet. And the king . . . Her proud father's once-sharp jaw hung slack.

The sorceress had rendered them helpless, taking away their ability to experience their true surroundings, imprisoning them in a vision. Elara prayed again that her loved ones were entranced in a calm, if debilitating, darkness and not something more sinister.

"Welcome!" Lord Stormrider's booming voice drew her attention away from her family. He smiled politely but with no lightness in his eyes. His shoulders sagged with exhaustion, no doubt the weight of planning and executing the invasion fatiguing him. The work to prepare for this moment would have taken months: courting spies, researching weaknesses, plotting out every move.

Elara hated him for all of it. The dreadful things she'd heard whispered at court about the Stormriders' reputation now came to life in front of her.

How dangerous rumors can be, she thought, *especially when they are true.*

Elara said nothing as she glared at him, fighting the urge to bare her teeth. Her jaw ached from clenching it so hard, trying to exude a confidence she didn't feel. Her eyes stung, but she blinked the moisture away.

"Do you know why I am here, Princess?" he asked, as though addressing a young child.

She shook her head.

"Your father and I had a deal. Unfortunately, he was . . . unable to fulfill his obligations."

Elara nodded, eyes misting over. She gazed at her father, allowing herself to memorize the lines of his face in case this was the last time she would ever see him. "This wouldn't be the first time," she whispered.

Lord Stormrider laughed. "Indeed," he said. "His actions have affected many other nobles within the kingdom in the same manner. We are tired of being disappointed. After all, what is a king worth without his word?"

Or magic, Elara thought.

She cleared her throat. "What do you want?" she asked with false boldness, proud that her voice didn't shake.

A lazy grin formed on his face. "I'm here to help you maintain control of the kingdom, of course. While your family is . . . indisposed."

"If you're here to overthrow my father, why are we still alive?" Elara braced herself against his answer, imagining the worst—picturing her family slaughtered in front of her.

His eyebrows rose. "Clever girl," he crooned. "You, my dear, are alive because I have a proposal for you. In exchange for your family's lives, you will wed my son."

CHAPTER 6

Elara

E LARA FROZE. A ROARING, wavelike sound filled her
ears as the room spun, making her nauseous and
disoriented. *Marry . . . Caelan Stormrider?* Exhausted from the
earlier struggle, she fought to stay conscious, every muscle
screaming for relief as her body longed to collapse. She took a shaky
breath, her heart heavy in her chest.

"Your Highness, may I introduce my son, Captain Caelan
Stormrider," Lord Stormrider said.

Elara scanned the throne room, searching for the man she'd
bumped into a few days prior. Then her gaze followed the direction
of Lord Stormrider's outstretched hand.

The Moiren?

The soldier beside her removed his helm and shook out his
sweaty hair. The same sandy-blond curls she'd admired during the
first council meeting were now coated with sweat, soot, and blood.
He smirked before kneeling in front of her in a mock proposal.
When he reached for her hand, she crossed her arms in front of her
chest.

"You," she hissed. Her heart dropped.

"In the flesh, Princess."

When she refused to give him her hand, Caelan rose. He gave a cursory bow with a flourish, taunting her. He flashed her another infuriating smile before turning to face his father.

Elara's face burned. She had thought him *handsome*, for stars' sake—and now? He had attacked her. Humiliated her. His father held her family captive. The weight of it all threatened to send her crumbling to her knees.

"Why?" she asked, voice hollow.

"Consider the gravity of your situation before asking questions, Your Highness." Lord Stormrider turned to his mage.

"Wait," Elara said as one of the soldiers grasped her arm, holding her in place. Her eyes locked on the sorceress, who clicked her tongue, the sound grating on Elara's tender nerves. With a wave of the Nimireth's hand, smoky tendrils curled around the queen's face, and tears began trickling from her unseeing eyes.

An icy fist gripped Elara's heart. Her world tilted on its axis, and she was helpless to stop it.

"Stop! Please—don't hurt them," she begged.

"Of course not. Not physically, at least," the sorceress purred.

"If you want my cooperation," Elara hissed at Lord Stormrider, "you will keep your Nimireth in check. Do not harm my family—physically or otherwise."

"That's enough, Seraphine."

The blond woman pouted, then obeyed. The queen's tears ceased.

Elara released the breath she'd been holding and the last of her adrenaline faded. *I have to keep them safe*, she thought. *No matter what.*

"Well, Your Highness?" Lord Stormrider leaned forward, interlacing his fingers under his chin.

Elara swallowed a lump in her throat. "I accept your proposal. I will marry your son in exchange for my family's safety."

What have I done? she thought, mind racing. *I bought us all time. I can figure this out.*

A muscle in Lord Stormrider's cheek twitched. "I'm pleased to hear that, Princess. One last thing: tell no one of what transpired tonight." He nodded at the soldiers to escort her out.

"Sleep well, Princess," Caelan called as her captors marched her out of the throne room.

She refused to look back. Before they reached the threshold, her vision blurred, the pain in her heart and hand throbbing. Her knees buckled. The soldiers tried to catch her swaying form before she hit the floor, the world around her slipping away.

A SHARP *TAP, TAP, tap* on glass pulled Elara from sleep. The soft rays of first morning light filtered through her window. She sat upright, rubbing her eyes, and crawled out of bed to investigate. A raven perched on the outer sill, clacking its massive beak against a pane of crimson glass in the lower corner. Instead of flying away as she approached, it tilted its head and blinked a beady, intelligent eye at her. She turned away from the strange bird, unsettled, and went to sit at her desk. The chair was missing. Soot stains and burn marks freckled the floor where embers had fallen. Memories rushed back to her.

The broken chair.

The fire near the gate.

The proposal.

Elara inspected her room, noting that whoever had cleaned it last night had left little evidence of what had transpired. She had collapsed in the throne room, which meant someone had carried her to her chamber and tucked her back into bed, then tidied up. She shuddered.

I was hoping it was just a nightmare.

Elara raked her hands through her hair. She glanced again at the burn marks near her feet, then paused. She held her right hand out to examine it. There was no blister, no redness, not even a hint of the searing pain she'd felt just hours before when she'd plunged her hand into the hearth. Her knuckles and fingernails were unscathed despite her frantic scratching and hitting against Caelan's impenetrable armor.

After hunting for her hand mirror, Elara kneeled by her bedside table to make use of the faint light emanating from a small lantern there. She examined her reflection. *It was real.* Her black hair was a tangled mess, and her pale face was grimy. Dried blood, dark and crusty, stained her neck and trailed down onto her torn linen nightgown. She touched the skin where the blood began. It was smooth. No cut. No scab. She shook her head. There was no way she'd escaped that fight without a single scratch.

Unless . . .

She dropped the mirror onto her bedside table and sat on the edge of her bed, hugging her knees into her chest and leaning against the carved oak headboard. Sleep had given her a temporary reprieve from her racing thoughts. Now that she was alone, exhausted, and overwhelmed, she had to face them.

Elara tried to deal with one problem at a time. Starting with the proposal. She pressed her forehead against her kneecaps and groaned. She'd agreed to marry Caelan Stormrider. *Maybe it's worth it*, she thought. Maybe if her sister lived, if her father and mother still drew breath, the rest of her—her pride, her future, her crown—could rot for all she cared. As long as they were safe, nothing else truly mattered.

A soft knock at her chamber door interrupted her thoughts. Elara would know that sound anywhere.

"Come in, Iris," she called out. Her favorite maid bustled into the room with a cheery smile.

"Morning, Elara!" Iris chirped. "Exciting day, isn't it?"

"What do you mean?" Elara asked slowly.

"You don't have to play coy with me, dear," Iris said. "All the servants are talking about it!"

Elara blinked at her, confused.

Iris placed her hands on her wide hips and pursed her wrinkled lips. "Well now, Elara, I know it's a big change, but you should be at least a little pleased."

"What did you hear?" Elara asked, her tone harsher than she'd intended.

"Why, you're engaged, aren't you? To that handsome young Captain Stormrider." Iris beamed.

Lord Stormrider's order to keep the coup a secret rattled in the back of Elara's mind. *Play along. Find out how much she knows.*

"Right. I'm thrilled," she said, rolling her eyes. Iris was well aware of Elara's strong aversion to the concept of marriage. She aimed to be a queen in her own capacity, not just a king's wife, and definitely not a pawn in some political alliance.

"That's the spirit," Iris said, winking.

"What else did you hear about what . . . happened last night?"

"Just that there was an accident—some hay out front caught fire. Probably another drunken guard milling about with his pipe, if you ask me," she scoffed. "The king really should do something about the stardust dens." She glanced warily at Elara. "My apologies!"

"It's all right, Iris. I don't like them any more than you do." Elara shrugged. The red parlors were a shameful fraction of the black market her father had allowed to pollute the capital. First aether, now the artifices. The king meant well; keeping the council happy was the best way to ensure peace and protect the crown. She shook her head and unfolded herself, standing.

Iris continued chattering. "Not to worry though, dear. We'll have everything cleaned up in no time. We must make a good impression, after all!"

Bile rose to the back of Elara's throat. Stormrider's men had worked fast to cover up their coup in a single night, by clearing the physical evidence and apparently feeding the palace rumor mill.

"Now, let's get you ready for breakfast," Iris said as she finally looked at Elara in the full daylight. "Stars above, Elara! What happened to you?"

"Nothing," Elara said. Lord Stormrider had warned her—threatened her—not to talk about the coup. Besides, the fewer people who were aware of the truth, the more she could safeguard her family. If the wrong nobles found out the royal family was compromised, she'd have more enemies to contend with.

Iris shook her head. "Come now, I may be losing my eyesight, but I know that's blood on your neck and smock."

Elara sighed. "I think I was sleepwalking in the garden again. Nerves, I suppose. Must have scratched myself on something. I'm fine, Iris. Can you please draw me a bath?" She hoped the lie would stick, seeing as she had sleepwalked several times as a child.

Iris looked skeptical but didn't press. "Of course! We ought to lock you in here at night," she teased before hastening to the adjacent washroom.

AFTER A LONG SOAK in the clawfoot tub that left her fingertips wrinkled, Elara sat on a stool at her vanity. Iris combed out her tangled hair. Compared to their usual playful chatting, the silence grated on Elara's taut nerves. She tugged at a drawer and reached inside. A tiny box coated with a thick layer of dust hid within. Picking it up and brushing her hand across its lid, she revealed polished mahogany and a pattern of etched gold swirls. With a gentle click, she opened the enchanted jewelry box, and her mother's favorite lullaby filled the room.

"I haven't heard that thing play in ages," Iris said.

Elara hummed along to the tune. Despite its beauty, there was a sense of melancholy in the piece. Appropriate, considering her present situation. She wondered about the agreement between her father and Lord Stormrider and how it might have soured. Her best guess was that Lord Stormrider had proposed the marriage alliance and the king had refused. Her heart squeezed at that. She felt a mix of pride and anger toward her father for not agreeing to the matter outright. *Maybe this is all my fault.*

Whatever the deal, it had gotten them all into this mess. Had the king confided in her, maybe she could have prevented this situation. She couldn't shake the feeling that she should have seen this coming from the first moment she laid eyes on Lord Stormrider sulking in her father's office.

Iris began twisting and pinning curls into an intricate updo. Elara let her smudge kohl around her eyes, as well as place some blush on her cheeks and a cherry shade of stain on her lips. Elara coughed when she inhaled some of the fine powder Iris brushed on her skin.

Iris stepped back, pleased with her handiwork. Elara held her own gaze in the mirror and waited for Iris to leave and fetch her gown. The makeup made her look more herself and less like a walking corpse. Despite the blush and powder, her skin was sallow. She ran her fingertips over the smooth flesh of her neck where her wound should have been, still finding nothing. Sapphire eyes above crescent-moon shadows stared back at her.

Iris had selected a silky coral gown for her day dress, and a burgundy gown that had been called up for dinner hung nearby. Elara felt ridiculous getting dressed up, as if she were meeting essential friends of the crown. As Iris fussed over the ties of the dress, Elara felt her entire world imploding. She wanted to scream, shattering the palace's windows to taste fresh air.

To be free.

There has to be another way. They didn't want her. Just power. Legitimacy. A wedding was just one way to accomplish that. Couldn't she offer something else instead? A treaty? A trade agreement? Maybe she didn't have to wear the chains to keep them from tightening around her family.

"You can do this," she told her reflection once she was alone. She could face Lord Stormrider and negotiate to get her family out of this mess—without having to marry the man who'd humiliated her. She gulped, remembering the power and strength with which he'd subdued her.

Thoughts of her helpless parents and sister filled her heart with a heavy ache, tears welling up in her eyes as she drew on her inner resolve. She couldn't afford to fail—not after begging her father for a chance to prove herself for so long. Now she had no choice.

She would find a way to save them all.

CHAPTER 7

Caelan

S ERA STROKED CAELAN'S WILD hair, pushing the long curls away from his forehead. He traced circles on her bare shoulder with his finger, the two of them nestled together in his bed. His eyes lingered on her form, covered by a light linen sheet that revealed just enough to make him sigh. This might be their last time together.

Even if his betrothal to the princess was only a political gambit, he knew it would be hurtful to both women to continue his relationship with Sera. If he could even call it a relationship. The two of them had been friends since childhood, when his father had taken her on as his ward after her parents died. They'd spent their long days together, irritating their tutors and each mastering their own magic.

To the rest of Veilkeep, Lady Seraphine Greythorn was a talented and terrifying Nimireth. She had the rare ability to isolate a person in their own mind and make them see whatever she wanted. But to Caelan, she was simply Sera.

Shaking his head to himself, he twirled a tendril of her platinum-blond hair, marveling at how the messy-haired, knock-kneed girl who'd once projected the night sky onto the stable ceiling could now bring even the king to his knees.

Caelan trailed his fingertips down her arm absentmindedly. "I'm going to miss this," he said.

"You know," she purred, "we don't have to stop." She pressed a featherlight kiss to his chest, her gaze darkening as her eyes found his.

He shook his head in dissent. "You know I have no interest in keeping a mistress. It's not—"

" 'Fair to me or to her,' " she recited, deepening her voice to mimic his. "You can't blame me for trying." She sighed, stretching her arms over her head.

Caelan chuckled. "No, I suppose I can't."

I don't want her to stop trying.

They were each other's first. Many women had followed her, and she was equally popular with the courtiers, but they always found their way back to each other. She felt like his home.

This will be my home now, he thought, picking at the silver embroidery of the plush comforter.

The first time he had seen the palace, it waited for him like a sleeping beast, with its window eyes and spikelike spires for horns. It had looked ready to wake and swallow him whole at any moment. *It's about to.* He couldn't believe that he was going to be married, that he would one day be the king of Serendith. When his father had come to him with the plan, Caelan had thought it impossible.

The Evensongs and the Stormriders hated each other, and he was actually glad for that historic animosity. If the Evensongs hadn't banished his ancestors to the Shadowed Isles, he never would have met Sera. His great-grandparents had made an alliance with the native Nimireth who'd founded Veilkeep, where the illusionists and, now, many other Moiren lived together and thrived. Caelan had been grateful—for the most part—to train with some of the most talented elementalists in the world. The lack of magic in Valoria felt as foreign as the wine.

This new, albeit ill-gotten, alliance had the potential to alter the continent's destiny, if Caelan proved himself a worthy king. But he would miss his freedom. Veilkeep. The sea. He may never see the Celestial Summit, where lightning kissed the mountaintops. Or the scattered ruins of the druid civilization hidden deep within the Verdant Forest. He longed to spend more winters in the Molten City—Emberreach—forging blades with his friend Rurik. Being king meant everyone else traveled to you once a year for the council gathering.

This palace would soon become his prison.

Caelan wished, more than anything, that he could run away with Sera and leave the stifling expectations of this life behind, abandon his mission and start a new adventure in one of those mythical places. He could ready a ship for departure this afternoon; she could pack their belongings for the journey.

He shuddered at the prospect of his father discovering the betrayal. *What he would do to Sera . . . and to Elara.*

The princess wasn't what he'd expected. She was brave and headstrong. *And an Evensong*, he reminded himself. *Pretty, but not to be trusted.*

"You're thinking about her, aren't you?" Sera whispered, her breath sending goose bumps across his shoulder.

He nodded, unable to lie to her.

"Do you like her?"

"I don't know," he answered honestly. "She's . . . interesting. You should've seen her try to fight back during the coup. She's got guts, that's for sure."

Elara was bold. And kind. He recalled her fierce protection of the vulnerable servant girl and her genuine concern for the well-being of her guards. He'd had no doubt she would agree to the engagement to protect her family, whose lives now hung in the balance.

"Good," Sera said. "She'll need them."

He nodded again. "Let's just hope that she's made of tougher stuff than you and me," he whispered. "Once my father has an idea in his head, there's no turning back."

Many years ago, losing Caelan's mother had profoundly impacted his father, transforming him into a hardened and uncompromising man. He possessed an unyielding ambition and a complete disregard for others—his ruthlessness was legendary, and he was impossible to satisfy. The throne was his goal, and he'd let nothing, and no one, stand in his way.

You have your role to play. Caelan heard his father's voice in his thoughts. And so he would play his part. They all would.

Sera shivered and sniffled. Caelan wrapped his arms around her, nuzzling her hair and inhaling the light heather scent.

"Hey, it's going to be all right. We'll make it through this," he said to reassure her—and himself.

BY MORNING, THE PALACE looked unscathed. Lord Stormrider's men had erased all signs of the invasion, clearing Elara's room and dealing with the torched hay wagons. Everything had gone according to plan. The fire had served as a helpful distraction for any on-shift servants, while the king's palace guards had been subdued and now resided in the dungeons. The news of their engagement swirled around every conversation. Lord Stormrider had fed the council a tale of the king absconding to the countryside to care for his sick wife and daughter.

Caelan's agenda for today involved the morning review with the soldiers who'd replaced the king's guards and meeting with Sera to clean up other loose ends. She waited outside his chambers for him, dressed in a simple purple gown so dark it was almost black, her expression stormy.

"Ready?" he asked.

"Never," Sera muttered, folding her arms across her chest. "Not for assignments like this." While she took tremendous pride in her skills as a Nimireth, she rarely used her magic for anything more than party tricks or, as was the case today, tasks given to her by Lord Stormrider. She would have refused this one given the chance.

"I know," Caelan said, gently placing a hand on her shoulder. "But it has to be done."

A flicker of anguish crossed her face, her upper lip curling back from her white teeth. "I know. I just wish someone else would do it."

He looked her in the eye, serious now. "You know what the alternative is."

"Death." She nodded, sorrow settling over her features.

The pair descended to the dungeon, where the king's guards and a handful of unfortunate servants were imprisoned. They were all witnesses.

You have two options, Lord Stormrider had told them. *You can kill them, or you can conceal their memories. I don't care which one you choose.* Caelan shuddered at the cold brutality of his father's orders.

Caelan lifted a lantern to light their final descent. Sera slipped on one of the stone steps, sending pebbles clattering down the staircase. The tiny rocks echoed around them, along with Sera's whispered curses. He gripped her arm to steady her, and she wrapped her fingers around his bicep.

The first set of iron bars loomed before them, the rusty metal groaning under the weight of years. One of Elara's guards was inside, his shallow breathing audible in the otherwise quiet space. Caelan recalled the names the princess had mentioned—it was either Jalin or Kaz. He held the lantern up to his own face.

"Come forward," he commanded. "We are here to release you, but my friend here has something to give you first." He tried to keep his tone warm, inviting even. "Are you Jalin? Or Kaz?"

This got the prisoner's attention, and he shuffled to his feet, almost slipping on the wet floor. The rhythmic *drip, drip, drip* of water against stone in the back of the cell was maddening. With a sharp flick of his wrist, Caelan held the droplets midair, silencing the water.

"I'm Kaz," the prisoner breathed. "You're letting me out?"

Sera nodded. "Yes. The princess is very concerned about you." Her smile was sharp, a thin line of displeasure.

Caelan grimaced, hoping that she wouldn't scare the prisoner. He didn't want this to be any harder than it needed to be. Thankfully, the darkness softened the harshness in her expression. The prisoner warily approached the cell door.

"Give me your hand," Sera said, extending her own hand, palm up, through the bars.

Caelan tensed, preparing to fight if the prisoner tried anything. But Kaz obeyed her, gingerly placing his filthy hand in hers.

Sera curled her fingers around Kaz's hand. With her other hand, she gripped a large amethyst pendant that hung from a silver chain around her neck. The amulet had been a gift from Lord Stormrider. It was a relic—an ancient artifact imbued with essence—one that twisted and amplified her natural power so that she could conceal someone's memories. She closed her eyes, and a warm light emanated from the stone clutched in her hand. Kaz's eyes widened, then glowed violet.

Caelan waited in the silence, sweat beading on the back of his neck despite the chill in the air and in his bones.

After a minute, Sera dropped Kaz's hand, and he slumped forward onto his knees. With her task complete, a familiar wave of exhaustion washed over her, leaving her trembling. Caelan caught her before she fell too. All magic had its limitations, and its price.

"I'm fine," she hissed, shoving him away.

Caelan looked at the row of cells ahead of them. *This is going to be a long day.* Her amulet drained her of her energy, but the cruelty of the task itself ate away at her soul.

"Promise me something, Caelan," Sera said. "When you are king, never ask me to do this again."

CHAPTER 8

Elara

T HE OUTSIDE AIR HAD a hint of crispness to it. Intermittent shade from the trees offered coolness, and the breeze sent a shiver down Elara's spine. The last heat of the summer was finally starting to fade, giving way to autumn. This summer had been a sweltering one, brutal and drought-ridden. The crops had suffered, and so had the king's popularity. The queen frequently toured the poorest areas of Valoria to distribute rations. Elara had begged to go, but her father had forbidden it. Despite her mother's efforts, the servants whispered about the unrest creeping through the city. A king who could not keep even his closest subjects fed was a failure. Now her father might not get the chance to fix it.

Elara walked the palace grounds, as she did every evening. Now, instead of Thalia, her new guards—two of the soldiers who'd assisted Caelan during last night's invasion—accompanied her.

"When can I speak with Lord Stormrider?" she turned to the older of her new guards. She'd spent the day trying—and failing—to see Lord Stormrider.

"Soon." The gray-haired man didn't even look her in the eye.

Elara huffed at his answer—the same he'd been uttering all day. "Do you ever say anything else?"

The younger guard snickered. He appeared to be about the same age as Kaz, judging by the fine lines around his eyes.

"What about you? Do you speak?"

His lips pulled into a thin line at the scathing look from his peer.

"Please," she tried again, her voice softening. "Can you at least tell me your names?"

"I'm Felix," the younger one said, running a hand through his red hair. "This is Silas." He jabbed his thumb at the other guard.

Silas grunted.

Elara sighed. *I hope Jalin and Kaz are all right.*

The trio passed the front gate, where the burned hay and damaged wagons had already been cleared away. The gardeners she passed whistled as they scraped at the ground, removing various weeds from the beds. Her chest tightened with the memory of doing the same with Thalia just a few days ago.

Other servants bustled about finishing their usual daily tasks and errands. None showed any sign that anything was amiss. *So strange,* she thought. *Surely some of them witnessed the invasion.* Lord Stormrider's men had replaced the king's guards overnight. Absent were the Stormriders' blue tunics and scale mail—they donned the emerald green and swan crest of Elara's house. She recognized none of them.

A short distance away, a guard had paused his patrolling to chat with one of the many servants who was scurrying around. He was tall, broad-shouldered, and had an air of command about him. A subtle dignity, the way he held his head, the precise set of his shoulders—all proclaimed his high rank. And those blond curls . . . He turned toward Elara and caught her staring.

Caelan. Of course it was. He offered her a gallant wave before returning to his conversation. *Stars help me.* She flushed and ground her teeth.

Her guards continued ambling along the gravel path until she stopped at a bed filled with desdemona bushes—the same ones she and her sister had last tended. She pretended to enjoy the fragrant blooms and tried to eavesdrop on Caelan.

"Hello there," Caelan purred from behind her.

She jumped and whirled around to face him. "Hello." Warmth spread from her neck to her chest, her rage simmering.

"Enjoying your evening stroll?" he asked.

Elara glowered at him.

"What?" he said, raising his hands out to his sides, palms up. An unusual scar marred one of his hands—a reminder that, despite his charm, he was a warrior. Elara held her own hand behind her back, hiding her missing injury from last night.

"You want to ask me about my walk? Or the weather? What do you expect from me?" She was seething by the end of her last question.

"I expect my future wife to be cordial with me," he growled back, frowning.

"Future wife? I want nothing to do with you!" She crossed her arms over her chest.

"You don't have a choice, darling."

"Just because we're engaged doesn't mean I have to like you, *darling*."

"Pity," he said, shrugging. "There's a long line of women—and men—who would kill to be with me." He gave her another lazy, irksome smile.

Elara bristled. "Well, I'm not one of them. Look, I will keep up appearances for the sake of my family, but make no mistake—I don't want you." Bile roiled in her stomach.

"We shall see." He titled his head, a deep chuckle escaping his throat. "I look forward to our dinner tonight, Princess."

Elara balked. "Dinner?" she whispered, glancing around to ensure they weren't overheard. "You invade my home, capture my family, and torture my mother in front of me; and now you expect me to have dinner with you?"

"Technically, I only helped with the first part."

"You—"

"Careful, Princess." He jerked his chin toward a gardener pushing a squeaky wheelbarrow nearby.

Elara's frown deepened, her teeth aching from clenching her jaw.

"See you tonight!" Caelan offered her a low mocking bow before he turned on his heel and strolled off, the gravel crunching loudly under his heavy boots.

Elara, in her frustration, yanked a bloom from the nearby bush. Thorns pierced her skin, and blood dripped onto the stony path. She dropped the flower and crushed it beneath her feet as she stomped away. Her hand tingled as her skin knit itself together. She curled it into a fist, hoping that the guards hadn't noticed.

The most logical explanation of the phenomenon was also the most uncomfortable one. The royal family came from a long line of Serathi, gifted with the affinity for healing essence. When the Evensongs rose to power after the Shattering, rumors claimed they were immortal, their lasting youth a testament to their stars-blessed bloodline. But none of the royal family had healed so much as a splinter with magic in four generations.

Fewer Serendithian children showed signs of essence affinity with each generation. Those who did often only possessed minor talents, parlor tricks. Gifts like Caelan's—and perhaps his father's—were rare and dangerous. Even the most powerful magi on the council could only light a candle or serve as a glorified lightning rod. Elara had never seen magic like Caelan's, or the sorceress's, before.

The memory of her mother's eyes filled her with dread, a sense of powerlessness creeping in as she thought back to her fight with Caelan. If similar mages existed elsewhere, the crown was in more danger than she'd ever imagined. The power linked to a name could only last for a short duration amidst warriors who could manipulate the elements. And being a Serathi wouldn't help her fight them off. If anything, it made her more of a target.

Her gaze followed Caelan's back until his figure vanished into the palace's shadow. She hadn't the faintest idea what his angle was. She tilted her head back to savor the salmon-and-azure sky, the first bright stars twinkling, and a sliver of crescent moon peeking through the clouds.

What do you plan to do with me?

ELARA FORCED HERSELF INTO the dining room in her burgundy ball gown, every step bringing her closer to her enemy. The gold embroidery on the dress weighed enough that she had to kick the full skirts out of her path with each careful step. A footman pulled out her chair at the long mahogany table. Lord Stormrider sat in her father's usual seat at the head of the table, setting Elara's teeth on edge. Caelan sat at his right hand, directly across from Elara. Next to him was the sorceress. Elara avoided the woman's piercing gaze, not wanting to anger her and further endanger her family.

She swallowed hard. She could endure dining with them if it meant she'd finally have the opportunity to negotiate—to change her fate.

Glowing candelabras filled the room with flickering buttery light, serving as centerpieces for the feast before them: chicken, bread, fish, lamb, and more. Tendrils of steam wafted off the spread, making Elara's mouth water despite the growing pit in her stomach. The footmen and guards lining the perimeter of the room were statuesque in their stillness, their presence a silent threat along the walls.

Her heart leapt when she recognized Jalin and Kaz in their ranks, but the relief faded almost as quickly as it came. They didn't meet her gaze—not even a flicker of recognition. Jalin's jaw was clenched, a cord of tension visible in his neck, and Kaz stared through her like she was a ghost. *What's wrong with them?*

Her family was conspicuously absent. *Where are they? Are they still in the palace?* Servants plated the first course in silence, the only sound the clinking of silverware against porcelain dishes. Elara sat stiff-backed, every muscle wound tight. Despite being surrounded by people, she felt utterly alone.

"You look stunning in that color, Your Highness," Caelan crooned before taking a long drink from his wine goblet.

"Thank you, but if you think you can win my affection with silly compliments, you are sorely mistaken," Elara replied coolly before turning her attention to Lord Stormrider. "Where is my family?"

"The king took your mother and sister to your country estate." He reached over and patted Elara's forearm. Her skin crawled under his touch. "I'm sorry they were both taken ill so suddenly, and right after the wonderful news of your engagement. A shame." He shook his head. "Ah, well, we will simply have to celebrate for them. After all, your father was so pleased."

Elara schooled her features into an expression of nonchalance. "And I suppose you have graciously volunteered to run the remaining council meetings in his absence?"

Lord Stormrider beamed at her. "Indeed, as well as hosting all of your engagement festivities. Such wonderful timing, to have all the noble families already gathered together."

Elara gulped. "Festivities?" she asked.

"A ball to celebrate our engagement, along with a tournament," Caelan said, dipping a piece of meat into sauce and swirling it.

Elara felt a powerful urge to smack that smug expression off his handsome face.

"And don't forget your appearance at the festival," the sorceress said with sweet venom. "We hope you'll take part in each of your obligations to ensure your family rests and fully recovers during their time away."

Elara glowered at the thinly veiled threat, then composed herself. She turned back to Lord Stormrider. "I understand that you and my father were in the midst of a negotiation when my mother and sister fell ill."

"Yes, well, that is not your concern, my dear."

"I would be happy to assist you in fulfilling that arrangement, without the need for an engagement. If you would consider—"

"It's too late for that," Lord Stormrider snapped at her, clearly annoyed at her bluntness. "You should focus on celebrating your joyful engagement. And be grateful that you didn't fall ill too," he said through gritted teeth.

Elara nodded, her breathing shallow beneath her fitted corset as her heart sank. "How can I trust that my family will be well cared for at the country house?" she asked carefully.

"I swear it." Caelan leaned forward, surprising her. "We want this to be a peaceful, advantageous arrangement for both of our families." He stared intently into Elara's eyes, his voice dripping with sincerity. "I give you my word that no harm will come to your family or any of our subjects."

Elara's heart pounded. *"Our" subjects.* There was a partial answer to her questions. *Lord Stormrider wants his son on the throne. And I was right. Father must have declined an arrangement involving me.*

Elara held Caelan's golden eyes. Despite her fears, she nodded at him. "Very well." *Look docile. Easy to control.*

She tried to bolster confidence in her decision with the fact that she was securing her family's lives. Bargaining was a game of leverage, and she had none. Lord Stormrider had her family, the palace, and her future in his hands. So she let them believe she'd surrendered.

Elara remained silent the rest of the night as her fellow diners discussed plans for the upcoming events. Caelan never took his eyes off her. It unsettled her—the intensity of his stare, the way he seemed to absorb every detail of her. She took a drink from her goblet, observing the intricate pattern on the table runner. Caelan's reputation preceded him, and not in a flattering way. Elara had heard his name come up at several of her mother's teas. One story in particular came to mind.

"There now, Lady Isoldea, you will find another suitable match," the queen had said in a rare moment of empathy for someone other than her daughters. Isoldea had grown up at court alongside Elara and Thalia, though she was quiet and reserved. A beautiful, if naive, young woman, she cried into her tea, sniffling over the rogue who had lured her away from her fiancé, only to abandon her. Hers was a common story at court—and one that Elara had always been eager to avoid.

Not only was he a social rake, but Caelan was clearly a skilled Moiren and one of the most powerful men in all of Serendith. His was not power like what her family had—a power which had to be bargained for and thus so easily lost. His was ancient, primal power. Elara imagined she had only witnessed a tiny fraction of it during their encounter, and her palms dampened with sweat.

Caelan's gaze caressed her neck, and a tiny line formed between his brows, causing her fingers to fly to her throat.

"Excuse me," he mumbled, not waiting for a footman to pull out his chair. He shoved away from the table and cut a sharp path out of the room.

Lord Stormrider frowned at his son's back. Elara seized the distraction as an opportunity. She glanced hopefully at Kaz and Jalin. "Help me," she mouthed. Blank stares, as if she were a stranger to them, haunted their faces. Elara stole a look at Lady Seraphine. The sorceress met her gaze and gave an almost imperceptible nod. The guards had been silenced with some sort of magic.

Elara slumped back against her chair. She was a prisoner in her own home, alone, completely powerless. Except for one thing—Lord Stormrider wanted her name, her bloodline, her throne for his son. All she had to do was convince him they were his for the taking.

CHAPTER 9

Elara

E LARA APPROACHED THE DOOR to the great hall. She had spent months hoping for this moment, a lifetime preparing for it, and a week dreading it. Today marked her first official council meeting. Her heart pounded in her ears as she steeled herself to give the performance of a lifetime.

To distract the council from her anxiety, she wore an uncharacteristically gaudy dress, studded with colorful gemstones and paired with her ugliest, most extravagant tiara. She looked like a walking rainbow—ridiculous, but dazzling. The perfect misdirection—something else for the nobles to gossip about alongside the formal announcement of the princess's engagement to a prominent noble family.

Silas and Felix—who were escorting her to the meeting—slowed, forcing Elara to do the same. Casting her gaze across the throng of courtiers, she noticed the two gentlemen from the red parlor gliding toward her. They halted in front of her, bowing deeply.

"Lovely to see you again, Your Highness."

"Yes—and under much better . . . circumstances. Do forgive our ghastly behavior." The one who'd struck her took her hand, pressing his lips to her knuckles.

His touch made her skin prickle. She resisted the urge to pull away. To survive in this court—and have any chance at finding her family—she needed allies, no matter how unsavory.

"Of course," she said, inclining her head. "The red parlors seem to bring out the worst of us, don't they?" She smiled warmly.

"Indeed. Thank you, Your Highness." With a final peck on her hand, the pair scurried off, back into the fray.

Elara looked up to find Caelan marching toward her. He dismissed her guards with a wave, then rested a rough hand on Elara's shoulder. She tensed as he pulled her closer.

He leaned in close, whispering into her ear, his breath a feather brushing her neck. "Be careful in there, Princess. We wouldn't want anyone to suspect there's trouble between us."

"Then you might want to stop manhandling me in crowded hallways," she hissed, her voice tight with anger. "The courtiers might have missed the coup, but they won't miss this." She shook his hand off her shoulder. "I will do my best. I want them to believe in us." Elara knew how important it was for the council to think her family strong, in control.

Caelan waited until the last of the chattering noblemen disappeared around the corner. Then, in the sudden silence, he wrapped his hands around her waist. With a shove, he forced her back against the cold, hard wall, arms caging her. The rich, heady scent of cedar and amber, with an underlying bite of pepper, filled her nostrils. He leaned in, his body pressing against hers, crowding her space entirely. Fear, raw and visceral, choked her, mingling with a sense of dizzying anticipation.

"Perfect," he purred. "Since we both know you're an impeccable liar."

A shaky "Wh-what do you mean?" escaped her lips, her heart pounding against his chest.

"I saw the blood. I know I cut you here." He traced his fingers over her throat, and Elara gulped, her eyes widening. "I noticed during our dinner. And your hands," he said as he wrapped his fingers around her wrist, pulling her hand in between their faces and sneering at the smoothness of her skin. "No one else walked away from that fight as cleanly as you did." He gestured to some yellow-edged bruises and thin pink scratches on his own face. "I know what you are, *Serathi*, even if the rest of the world doesn't."

Stars above, he knows. Elara's own skin displayed the evidence of the truth, leaving her no plausible denial.

"Caelan," she gasped, shock stealing her breath. "Please, I can explain."

"Don't bother, darling," he growled. "I guess we are just two liars tangled together. Keep your secrets, and I'll keep mine."

"Listen," she pleaded. She tried to shove back against him but only succeeded at bringing their bodies impossibly closer together. "I have no idea how, or what exactly, I did that night. A Serathi hasn't been born in my family for generations." Her fingers touched her neck. "This had never happened to me before."

Caelan pinched her chin painfully and tilted her head upward. Hot tears pooled in her eyes, threatening to spill over onto her cheeks. Her bottom lip quivered with the effort of holding back a sob. She was completely at his mercy. He held her gaze, eyes searching. After another moment of her squirming, he finally released her and stepped back.

"You really didn't know, did you?" he asked, folding his arms and raising an eyebrow.

Elara shook her head vigorously. "No."

"Does anyone else know?"

"Just you," she whispered.

"Good," he said. "Keep it that way. We can talk about it more later." Caelan offered her his arm to escort her into the great hall.

"I need a moment," she said, taking a deep breath to steady herself and gather her courage. Her corset bit into her flesh as she hunched forward, head down and hands braced on the thick fabric covering her knees.

"Whenever you're ready, Princess," he said, leaning casually against the wall.

She tried her hardest to ignore him while she composed herself. After her unshed tears evaporated and her heartbeat returned to its normal rhythm, she straightened.

"I'm ready." When he offered her his arm once more, she hesitated, then took it.

As they entered the great hall, the height of the vaulted ceiling overwhelming compared to her cramped perch in the tunnel, the Council of Magi rose from their seats. Representatives from each noble family formed a circle around the dais at the center of the room. Each house wore colors specific to their ancestral essence affinity—a sea of cobalt blue, amber, scarlet, and her own emerald green. Elara's stomach churned with a sickening anxiety, twisting itself into tight knots. Although these nobles served her, today they could not save her.

Elara had dreamed of this moment for years, begging her father to let her attend. Now that she was here, her dream became her nightmare.

Lord Stormrider sat at the head of a curved table. His intense gaze made her heart pound, and she offered him a tight forced smile. She and Caelan proceeded to the center of the room, and Elara nodded at several people she recognized—her family's strongest allies, who staunchly fought to maintain unity across a nation that often felt like it was held together with smoke.

Caelan helped her up the few steps to the platform—no easy feat given the weight of her dress—kissed her hand like a proper gentleman, and sat beside his father and representatives from other elemental houses. That simple display stirred up hushed conversations throughout the room. Whispers buzzed back and forth, creating a chaotic energy that caused droplets of sweat to bead at the nape of Elara's neck.

Elara clapped her hands, the sharp sound cutting through the anticipation of the dozens of magi, her gaze locking with each one in turn. Silence fell over them, heavy and expectant.

"Welcome," she began, her voice bold despite the fear threatening to swallow her. "I formally open this seventh Council of Magi of the gathering season. May the stars guide us."

"May the stars guide us," the audience recited back in unison.

"Before I hand the meeting over to Lord Stormrider, I have an announcement to make." Elara took a steadying breath, noticing several people lean forward in their seats. "The king has expressed his dearest wishes to bond together the Evensong and Stormrider families. Therefore, I am pleased to announce my betrothal to Captain Caelan Stormrider."

A communal gasp echoed through the room.

Then, mercifully, the magi rose, and a thunderous applause filled the hall. The elementalists clapped Caelan on the shoulder and shook his hand, pride evident in their expressions. Elara noticed one magi whose amber eyes gleamed—the woman from Emberreach. Carved into a volcano's caverns, the subterranean city was home to the few remaining Embrathi and Tharven—gifted flamewards and stonesmiths. Together with the Moiren and the Sylari, the four clans formed a loose alliance of elementalists. Uniting the Stormriders with the crown would elevate the Moiren without ruffling many feathers.

The match was astute, leaving Elara feeling guilty about questioning her father's genuine reasons—protecting her—for his initial refusal. Before she could dwell on it further, Caelan climbed up next to her and grasped her hand in his, raising them up above their heads in triumph.

He informed the magi of the approaching festivities celebrating the engagement. Elara didn't hear a word of it over the roaring in her ears. She was nothing more than a pawn. A prop. A prize. She had waited her entire life to be presented to this audience as heir to the Serendithian throne.

I was meant to be the future queen, she thought, *not a future king's bride*. She plastered a smile on her face, bright and brittle, concentrating on staying conscious. The energy in the room crackled and surged, a palpable wave threatening to pull her under. She squeezed Caelan's hand as hard as she could, forcing him to pause his speech for a split second and look at her.

The spectators likely witnessed a man gazing fondly at his fiancée. Elara prayed that Caelan saw a desperate woman who needed out. He finished his sentence so that none of the magi realized his speech was cut short. He escorted Elara back to the door with a grace that exceeded her expectations. She was nearly panting as the two of them exited the great hall. The moment they were alone, Elara's legs gave way, sending her crashing to the marble floor with a sharp *crack* and searing pain in her kneecaps. Caelan caught her as she fell, his hands wrapping around her upper body just before her head hit the ground.

"Are you all right?" he asked, voice thick with worry.

So confusing, she thought. Elara reeled from the ever-changing turns in his demeanor.

He kneeled in front of her, positioning himself so that they were face-to-face, his hands on her shoulders.

Elara was still struggling to catch her breath. Her hands gripped bunches of her gown, her knuckles turning white, fingers threatening to tear the delicate fabric. She looked into his eyes, aware of the tears rimming her own.

"What do you think?" she spat. Shame rippled through her—she couldn't even make it through one meeting. How was she supposed to convince the council of her strength? How could she keep her family safe?

"Don't worry, I'll make a suitable excuse for you," Caelan whispered.

Elara shook her head but didn't protest. She held Caelan's golden eyes, staring at her with concern.

I can use that.

I can use him.

Caelan would be the key to keeping her magic hidden, freeing her family, and stopping the wedding. Elara would play her part: the sweet solemn bride-to-be. But she would not be idle—she would watch, listen, and learn. She would find Caelan's weaknesses—his insecurities, his desires. And if there was even a flicker of decency in him, a single ember of rebellion or doubt, she would find it and stoke it until he burned for her.

CHAPTER 10

Elara

E LARA HAD NEVER BEEN much of a flirt, but like any skill, she figured she could learn it. For her education in mastering the art of playful banter and charming smiles, she turned to her most faithful allies—books. The worn leather of the tomes pressed against her chest offered a familiar comfort. Several days after the disaster of a council meeting, she was browsing the shelves of the palace's immodest library for her favorite romance novels.

A chill permeated the air around the shelves. They no longer held the cozy scent of aged paper and binding glue, instead smelling faintly of dust and neglect. The servants had turned their attention to preparing for the tournament and the ball celebrating her engagement. With the last manual stacked on top of the teetering tower in her arms, a sudden, sharp pain tugged at her heartstrings.

Once, she had dared hope she might fall in love. In the distant future, when she was ready, she would have become engaged of her own accord. Even with a politically motivated marriage, she would have chosen her partner and at least gotten to know him first.

Under more conventional circumstances, she would have been able to ask her mother for advice and support, or giggle with Thalia as she mocked her awkward attempts at flirting over breakfast. But that might never happen now.

Elara shoved those thoughts into a corner at the back of her mind, instead doubling down on her efforts to seduce Caelan and somehow convince him to help her with her magic. He was clearly attracted to her. Despite his poor behavior, he'd promised to protect her family and saved her from embarrassment at the council meeting.

Now that he knew about her secret essence affinity, maybe he could teach her how to control her power. Manipulating him was her best shot at concealing her ability and finding her family—while she figured out a way to end their engagement with minimal political backlash.

The latest novel to find a home in her stack was one of Thalia's favorites. Her fingers skimmed its spine. For the dozenth time since the invasion, the weight of the last few days' worth of events washed over her. A surge of emotions threatened to consume her.

Tears streamed down her face as she sank to her knees, abandoning her pile of books and becoming a puddle on the floor. Alone, she wept for all that she was about to risk, to lose. If she failed, she would give up her own future, her own happiness, to save them.

Light crept through the windows as the sun rose, shooting gem-colored rays across the floor in front of her. Her tears fell onto the mosaic tile, shimmering like little diamonds themselves.

How could something born from such grief look so beautiful? she wondered.

"You look beautiful when you cry," a familiar voice murmured nearby.

Elara raised her head slowly to find Caelan leaning against one of the many large bookcases, arms folded, watching her.

What's he doing here?

She rose shakily to her feet, and he stepped toward her, offering his arm to steady her. She took it, and his eyebrows rose in surprise. Elara wasn't sure if she imagined it, but a tiny jolt of electricity buzzed up her arm where his skin brushed against hers.

Thump. The top book of her nearby precarious pile toppled to the ground. Both she and Caelan stooped to retrieve it at the same moment, resulting in their foreheads colliding.

"Ow!" She rubbed her hand against her head.

"Sorry," he mumbled, raking a hand through his hair and gathering up the books for her. "Doing some light reading?" he asked, gesturing to the stacks of books and her little table in the nearby alcove.

She nodded and headed over to the nook where she had been . . . researching. He followed her and acted the gentleman as he pulled her chair out for her before settling into the seat across from her. His eyes traced a couple of the titles, and though he smirked, he didn't comment on them.

Despite her better judgement, Elara didn't ask him to leave. Loud sniffles escaped from her, but she resisted the urge to wipe her nose with her forearm—a habit her mother loathed. She watched Caelan, the silence between them heavy. A shimmer at his hip caught her eye, the bronze stag on the ornate pommel of his sword winking at her.

"Admiring my sword? Or contemplating killing me with it?" he asked with a mischievous grin.

"Perhaps a little of both," she said. "Why do you even need a sword?"

"It's important for a captain to be well-rounded," he said, patting the hilt of his weapon.

Too bad Father didn't feel the same about his daughters, or I might actually know how to protect myself.

"What brings you to the library?" she asked. If she showed an interest in him, maybe he'd warm to her.

"I wanted to see you," he said simply. He stuffed his hands into his pockets. "My men told me you were in here." He pointed with his chin to the guard positioned in front of a nearby shelf.

Elara had grown so used to her new escorts that she had forgotten Silas was there.

"I didn't think that you might be having a, uh, private moment." Caelan cleared his throat before continuing. "So, you like to read?"

Why is he acting so interested in me? "Yes, I do. And you?" *No matter, I'll take it.*

"Absolutely," he replied. "History mostly. A little alchemy." He shrugged. "I like to learn." He smiled broadly, but when she said nothing, the brightness in his eyes dimmed. "I . . . I'm sorry," he said. "It's been a tiresome day, and I don't really know what to say to you."

Elara took a deep breath before responding. " 'I'm sorry' is a decent start."

Caelan nodded, eyes shining and lips dipping into a frown. "I am sorry about your family, Elara. Look, I want us to make the best of this situation. We're going to be married. We can at least get to know each other . . ."

There, she thought. *I can use that.*

"How can we make the best of this when I don't trust you? And what makes you think you can trust me?" she asked, keeping her tone light, while leaning back in her chair and folding her arms across her chest.

Caelan rolled his eyes. "How many noble couples in this court do you think actually trust each other?" He grinned at her, and his eyebrow arched. "Besides, the only thing that matters is how fantastic we look together."

Elara couldn't resist smiling at that. Still, she threw a ball of crumpled-up parchment at him. It found its mark, striking him square in the face before landing on the table in front of him. The look of surprise on his face, a mixture of disbelief and glee, was immensely satisfying.

"That's the spirit." He chuckled. "You should know," he began, serious once more, "I didn't know what my father had planned for your family. I was told that we were coming here to introduce me to the council and bargain for this . . . arrangement." He gestured to her and then to himself. "If I had known what he was really planning"—he shuddered ever so slightly—"I never would have agreed to come with him."

89

"Then why did you help him?" Elara asked.

Caelan's eyes flashed to Silas still lurking nearby.

What are you so afraid of? she thought. His father—likely using spies to monitor their behavior—scared him enough to make him cautious with his words.

"My father is a powerful man. We'll all be better off once he gets what he wants." His eyes grew darker.

"A royal wedding?" she asked.

"As a start. You and your family will be safer once we wed and my father has gained the political standing afforded him by this alliance," he said.

Elara nodded—she'd suspected as much. Violent men often got what they wanted in this court. "It would have been simpler for him to just kill us all."

Caelan balked at that, the blood draining from his face. He looked toward the ground, suddenly seeming to find the tile pattern more interesting than their current conversation.

"I'm glad he didn't," he whispered to the floor. He looked up at her from under his full lashes. Desire burned in that gaze, causing Elara's stomach to fill with butterflies. Butterflies with blades for wings.

"So . . . we get to know each other?" she asked, leaning forward a bit too far, ensuring her cleavage was on display.

He nodded.

Now is as good a time as any. Elara took a deep breath. "I need your help, Caelan."

"Anything." His eyes sparkled.

She glanced at Silas, who had busied himself with a book. "Teach me to hide my magic. We both know it's dangerous, and I feel so helpless," she admitted.

He leaned forward. "You are not as helpless as you think," he pointed out. "The way you fought back that night . . . And the council? I've never seen anyone look at your father—or mine—the way they looked at you."

She snorted. "Even after you had to drag me out of the meeting?"

His brow furrowed. "No one even noticed. All the courtiers were chattering about the heiress of Serendith coming into her own power. They adore you."

Only on the surface. "It won't take long for them to realize how misplaced their faith in me is, especially with the realm in your father's hands," she insisted. "I need you to help me with"—Elara ran her hand over the edge of a blank piece of parchment—"this." She felt the irritating sting of the paper slicing at the sensitive flesh between her thumb and index finger. Blood swelled to the surface. She held her hand out for Caelan to see the skin knit back together seamlessly.

Caelan's gaze flitted between her hand and face, his lips slightly parted.

"It's happening faster than before," she whispered. "I won't be able to hide it for much longer without your help. I need to learn more about it. Maybe how to control it? If your father finds out—"

Lord Stormrider's lust for power could drive him to turn the rest of the court against her family. *Liar,* Caelan had called her. The courtiers would kill for far less.

"He won't find out," Caelan said. "And if he does, I'll protect you. I swear it." He placed his hand over hers, intertwining their fingers and squeezing her palm gently. "You're my responsibility now, Elara. Mine. I'll help you."

Elara was speechless at his declaration. She didn't want to belong to any man, but . . .

His. Her heart raced. *Maybe it's a trick, to get me to let my guard down.*

After staring at her for another moment, he offered her a small smile. "Are you looking forward to the tournament?"

"What do you think?" she asked, grimacing.

He laughed, the sound rich and easy. "If nothing else, it'll give you a chance to see your handsome new tutor in action."

She couldn't help the smile that stretched across her face. *Maybe you'll get hit with a stray arrow.*

"Well," he said, "I shall leave you to your reading. We can start working on this"—he kissed her hand where she had sliced it—"after the tournament."

With that, he stood up, gave her a quick bow, and walked away, the sound of his footsteps echoing off the stone pillars holding up the library's ceiling.

Elara wiped her hand on her skirt. *If he can teach me how to harness my new ability, I can stay safe. I can get him to trust me. All I have to do is play along.*

CHAPTER 11

Elara

THE DAY OF THE tournament arrived. Elara had seen little of Caelan since their conversation in the library. The palace staff still seemed blissfully unaware of the truth as they continued on with the preparations for the tournament, and she'd had no word of her family in weeks. *Where are they? Are they being treated well?* She imagined Thalia behind iron bars, shivering and terrified. Her mind warred with the helplessness that clawed at the back of her mind, clinging instead to her plan to manipulate Caelan. *If I could actually spend any time with him.*

After Iris helped her dress and coiled her hair into an elaborate pattern atop her head, Elara was shuffled into a waiting carriage. Felix followed, taking a seat across from her. He glanced over at his gloomy companion, who filled the bench next to Elara. Before she could get a good look outside, Silas pulled the curtains shut. She frowned at him. Silas was the one who'd restrained her during the invasion, and he'd been aloof with Elara ever since. Recalling the way she kicked at his shins, she could hardly blame him.

One jostling ride later, Silas's tall frame and broad shoulders blocked her view as her guards deposited her into a tent—private, shaded, and silent. Sweat beaded on the nape of her neck and clung to the velvet of her gown. Based on the birds chirping and the equally chaotic chattering of nearby courtiers, she assumed she'd arrived at the outdoor arena that typically hosted tournaments.

A small table hosted a tray with an array of fruits and cheeses, along with a bottle of wine. Two comfortable chairs invited her to lounge, but nothing else furnished her fabric cave. Elara paced from one canvas wall to another, with her guards posted outside as her only company. She was alone again with her thoughts, a situation that was growing tiresome—her isolation felt strategic, a calculated move designed to wear her down.

At a loud trumpet that marked the top of the hour, Elara poked her head through the slit in the fabric that constituted a door. "Felix," she said.

"Yes, Your Highness?"

"Can we walk amongst the tents?" she asked.

Felix's gaze cut to Silas. The older guard shook his gray head from side to side.

Before Felix could answer for them, Elara tried again. "It is critical for those in attendance to see that I am present to support Caelan today."

At that, Felix nodded, eyes brightening. "Of course, Your Highness."

"Please, Felix," she said, "just call me Elara." She beamed at him and batted her lashes. Any way she could endear them to her might help. At least Felix tried to be cordial with her.

He shifted on his feet and cast his gaze to the dirt, saying nothing further, but a small smile played on his lips.

Elara emerged from the tent and began her promenade through the temporary city. Most of the other tents had their door flaps open and tied to the sides, creating rows of lovely canopies. She passed by several familiar faces, pausing occasionally to greet them and exchange pleasantries. If nothing else, she enjoyed the sun's warmth on her skin and the warmth her people offered her. With the equinox just around the corner, gone were the long days of summer. Soon the moon and sun would share the sky in equal measure.

Bidding farewell to a Molten City family, denoted by their amber cloaks and exquisite jewelry, Elara turned back to Felix.

"Where is Caelan's tent? I should wish him luck before the opening ceremony."

Felix nodded, then guided her to a tent with its door flaps tied shut, but she could see two shadowy figures deep in conversation within. Curiosity prickled at the back of her mind, guiding her steps closer. The silhouettes—oblivious to her presence—embraced, pressing their lips together. Elara blushed and turned away, but an invisible hand seemed to root her to the spot, drawing her close enough that she could spy through a narrow opening between the canvas flaps. She recognized those figures—the deep violet gown and the cobalt-blue tunic. One was the sorceress that had blinded her family—Lady Seraphine. And the other was Caelan.

The Nimireth's delicate fingers lingered over the buttons of Caelan's shirt, and he traced his hands across her lower back before pulling her hips against his. Elara held her breath, unable to tear her eyes away. Instead, she inched closer, her fingers gently brushing against the rough canvas to widen the gap and improve her view. Her heart pounded a frantic rhythm against her ribs as their breaths hitched in ragged gasps between kisses. Caelan's hands cupped Seraphine's face before his fingers tangled in her silvery-blond hair.

Felix cleared his throat behind Elara. Caelan whipped his head toward her.

Stars above, she thought, face heating. She backed away several paces, pretending to be enraptured by the pink petals falling to the ground from a nearby crape myrtle tree.

Caelan flung the tent doors open and stomped over to her. "Spying does not become you, Princess," he said harshly. He took in her flushed face and rapid breathing, and a smirk played across his lips.

If only you knew, she thought.

"That's only because I need more practice," she countered with a grin. Elara wasn't the only one who'd been caught—he was her betrothed, and he was the one acting shamefully, not her. She would not be embarrassed by him. "It seems you, however, have had plenty of practice seducing women. It's a shame that your charms don't work on me."

Whatever tentative truce they'd built shattered. Despite her words, Elara's chest ached. This man had called her his responsibility and had sworn to protect her. *I guess he doesn't think protecting my heart, or my honor, counts.* A steaming rage, like a pot about to boil over, bubbled inside her.

"Don't they though?" he asked. "Why else would you be watching?" He raised an eyebrow at her, one side of his mouth quirking up.

Now Elara was sweating—she didn't have a clever response to that. "Shouldn't you be getting ready for the duel?" she snapped.

"Archery first," he replied.

He hadn't flinched at the bite in her flirting back in the library—if anything, he'd looked intrigued—so she pressed her advantage. "I hope you get shot," she mumbled.

His eyes darkened, and he laughed huskily. He jerked his chin at Felix, who nodded and walked out of earshot. "Who knows? Maybe you will get to showcase your . . . talents in the next tournament." He had the audacity to wink at her.

The blood drained from Elara's face. "Have you told anyone?"

"No," Caelan said. "That's our little secret, for now. I was thinking—you could actually use some combat training. Healers don't really have much to showcase in the magical events, after all. I could teach you. Think about it," he said with a shrug before he sauntered back to his tent.

Lady Seraphine poked her head out and winked at Elara. "I hope you enjoy the show," she said, her smile sharp as a blade. She clutched Caelan's arm and dragged him back inside, out of Elara's sight.

AFTER ELARA'S ENCOUNTER WITH Caelan, Felix escorted her back to her tent. That was fine, considering her fiancé had given her more than enough to occupy her thoughts. She paced once more within the beige walls, trying to understand what she'd just witnessed. Of all the women at court, he had to fall into the arms of the sorceress who'd captured and tortured her family. The rumors, swirling like tea leaves in her mother's porcelain cups, had reached her ears before, but now they held a different weight.

When she saw Caelan with Seraphine, a flicker of betrayal, sharp and cold, had pierced her heart. *It doesn't matter. It's not real.* She just had to focus on surviving the next few months leading up to the wedding. *And maybe that sorceress of his means that he doesn't really want to marry me, anyway.*

Caelan seemed eager enough to help her learn how to control her power; he'd even offered to train her in combat. The idea left her tingling with excitement. He made for a powerful enemy, and she hoped to turn him into a powerful puppet. Hopefully training together would bring them closer, at least enough for him to care to truly help her.

The sound of trumpeting mercifully interrupted Elara's thoughts. The tournament was beginning. One side of her tent rose like a curtain, allowing her to view the arena. Rings of tents surrounded the central grounds. The grassy hills had been molded by the Tharven stonesmiths, creating a large bowl-like shape that allowed even the fourth and fifth rows of spectators a view of the action below.

A gentle fog flowed through the aisles between tents, forming swirling tendrils that crept into the arena. A reverent hush fell over the crowd as a smoky blanket settled over them. Flashing orbs of light danced through the smoke in a glistening waltz. The purple, pink, and scarlet lights morphed into distinct figures. First deer, then foxes, then naked human women. With joyous abandon, they pranced and swirled, their movements a blur in the thick swirling mist. The crowd cheered.

Elara swallowed hard, tensing as fear skittered down her spine. *Illusion magic.* The rest of the audience may have been enjoying the opening ceremony, but the surrounding energy made the hair on her arms and the back of her neck stand up. She balled her hands into fists at her sides. Even before Lady Seraphine had ensnared her parents and sister, Elara's parents had taught her to be cautious of the Nimireth. The fog was a prime example of how they manipulated the mind—it left her feeling damp even though she knew it wasn't real.

More figures shimmered into existence from within the fog, their forms solidifying into a circle of dancers. They grasped hands and danced together, flowing in and out, making their circle pulse like a heartbeat. A light flickered at its core, growing brighter with each beat. Music played in her mind, at once haunting and sensual, its notes weaving a spell. The flicker grew into a full-on blaze, the flames swirling around a womanly figure—Lady Seraphine.

She danced in the fire, her hair and dress tangling with the flames. They changed color, turning from orange to purple to green to gold. The fire's crackle morphed into a deep roar; the music swelled to a thrilling crescendo; and the dancers, spinning and leaping, moved faster and faster. Elara felt dizzy when Lady Seraphine exploded, transforming into a firebird with red-and-gold wings—a phoenix. A moment of stunned silence hung in the air before the audience erupted in a tumultuous wave of applause.

Numb, Elara forced her palms together, clapping in case anyone was watching her reaction and questioning the king's decision to allow this display. Illusionists were considered taboo, and to see their magic boldly displayed here, at a royal event . . .

Lord Stormrider sure knows how to stir the pot. Elara would play her part. Smile and nod. Keep herself and her family safe. Reputations be damned.

Besides, what would my subjects think if they found out I'm a Serathi? Would they praise me? Some arcanists—perhaps the Children of the Sky—might rejoice, but healing essence was unknown and therefore a threat. Elara thought about how Caelan had reacted. *Would they fear me? Despise me?* He'd slammed her into a wall, sneered at her, hurt her. But, she reasoned, he was more upset about the lie than her power itself. At least, that was what she could discern from her limited observation of him. She shook her head. It didn't matter right now.

The smoke evaporated, the performers bowed to conclude the opening ceremony, and the first round of competitions began.

Caelan was in the section nearest her tent—archery, as he'd mentioned earlier—and Elara allowed herself to be distracted by his prowess with a bow. His loose shirt revealed glimpses of tanned skin at his chest and forearms, pulled taut as a bowstring over corded muscle. She held her breath as he took each shot, his stance wide and confident as he breathed through his movements. He nocked his arrow, pulled back his bowstring until his knuckles met his jaw, and released. *Thwack.* Arrow after arrow found its target, obliterating the competition. When he finished, he handed Elara a rose, eliciting a flurry of eager cheers from the crowd.

Show-off. Despite herself, she couldn't help but be impressed. She'd known about his skill as a swordsman and as a Moiren, but she'd yet to find anything he wasn't irritatingly good at. Her mouth went dry. *What else can you teach me?*

CHAPTER 12

Caelan

S WEAT BEADED ON CAELAN'S brow, causing his messy hair
to cling to his forehead. He stood with his feet apart, his face
angled toward his target. He exhaled a smooth whoosh of breath
as his fingers released the arrow he had drawn back. A satisfying
whistle sounded, followed by an even more satisfying *thud* as the
arrow met its mark. Caelan relaxed his arms as his father nodded
toward him from his perch above—a subtle jerk of the chin to
signal his approval. Lord Stormrider eyed his son like a hawk from
his vantage point in the sea of tents surrounding the arena.

With a roll of his shoulders and neck, Caelan shook off his last
vestiges of anxiety. Though not quite pride, a deep satisfaction
filled him, and relief washed over him with the conclusion of the
archery competition. He was far more comfortable hunting game
than he was shooting under the judgmental gaze of his father—not
to mention the audience that was now assessing their future king.

Caelan was taking part in just three of the events
today—archery, dueling, and the Thal'Moira. *One down, two to go.*
He was eager to watch the Children of the Sky's closing ceremony.

Sera's opening performance had resulted in many raised eyebrows, and the rumored lightning display was sure to do the same. He shook his head. Damage control with the courtiers would occupy the rest of his week.

Hands forming a bowl, he summoned a pool of water into his palms and splashed it onto his face before running his fingers through his hair. He unlaced and removed the protective leather brace from his forearm and passed his longbow to a nearby squire. Another servant handed him a single long-stemmed red rose. *Here we go.* After bowing grandly to the audience, who responded with roaring applause, he tilted his head at the flower, which seemed to weigh as much as a gelding in his hand. His eyes searched the crowd for hers.

I'm sorry. His eyes glistened with those two unspoken words as he marched over to her seat. *I never meant to hurt you,* he wanted to say. Instead, he flashed all of his teeth and presented her the favor with a flourish.

"Your Highness," he said. "Please accept this rose as a reminder of our blooming love." It took all his willpower not to vomit at the ridiculous line.

"Well done, Captain Stormrider." Elara's answering glare burned with the fire of a thousand suns, but only for an instant. Her anger was gone in a flash, replaced with a rehearsed vague pleasantness as she took the stem into her grip.

The sharp heat of remorse prodded the back of his neck like a branding iron. He didn't want to feel guilty about kissing Sera, but he did. She'd been nervous about her performance in the opening ceremony, and he had tried to comfort her, until . . . things went too far. But the look of hurt on Elara's face had puzzled him, stifling his own indignity at being discovered. Why had she looked at him like that? And why had her pain struck his own heart like a stray arrow? Besides that, another feeling had flickered behind the betrayal in her eyes: curiosity.

Caelan's lips curved into a smile. He wasn't one to be embarrassed by such things, and the thrill of knowing that she was spying on him during such an intimate moment made him shiver with pleasure.

His task complete, Caelan returned to his designated tent to rest and quench his thirst before preparing for his next competition. Dusty earth crunched beneath his boots, and the sun beat down on his damp skin. Sera was promenading with his father in the distance, making the rounds and ensuring the events for the tournament ran smoothly. She looked in his direction and waved. He shook his head, unable to prevent his tiny smile. *I don't need any more trouble today, Sera.*

The two of them had weathered countless storms, their bond strengthened by shared hardships and laughter. Caelan had loved Sera for as long as he could remember. But, as they grew older, the breaks in their romantic relationship had extended. Both had made full use of their freedom to explore with others, engaging in countless ill-fated relationships. He was finally beginning to see Sera for what she truly was to him—family. But certainly not his future wife, even if they were free to wed.

Elara, however, differed from all the other women he had ever met. His charms did not draw her in—which made sense given the nature of their engagement. One moment she was batting her eyelashes, the next she was snapping at him, her emotions a whirlwind of flirtation and fury. The challenge was driving him crazy in the best way, serving up a delicious kind of torment.

The trumpet sounded again, pulling him back into the present moment. Caelan lifted a cup off the ornately carved wooden table, placing his hand over the empty goblet and using magic to fill it with cool, soothing water. After a refreshing drink, he began his stretching routine. Each pose brought a sense of peace as his mind emptied, replacing thoughts with physical sensations. The calm before yet another storm.

The sharp focus, the adrenaline-fueled clarity of combat, brought a stark contrast to the fog of his everyday life. That escape was a pleasure rivaled only by nights spent in the company of aether. Both offered him a way to silence his racing thoughts, to ground himself in the physical world, where the various aches seemed less intense than the pain that swirled in his mind. Caelan settled into his routine, but a voice in the farthest corner of his mind was persistent about Elara.

Don't let her get too close.

Caelan needed to be careful. He had an assignment from his father, a role to play in the grander scheme. The performance he was giving in the tournament paled in comparison to the acting he'd been doing his whole life—for his father, for himself. His engagement with Elara was the riskiest of them all; despite her allure, he couldn't afford to become attached. Lust would only be a distraction, and love would never be in the stars for him.

Shaking his head, he donned his armor, the metal scales clinking together in a rattling cacophony. He gripped his weapon with steady hands and returned to the arena.

A SKILLED SWORDSMAN, CAELAN was likely to be one of Serendith's finest by the time he reached his father's age. It wasn't surprising, considering his occupation as a guard captain, but he was uncommonly good for a Moiren. Most nobles with essence affinities only learned the basics of physical combat. Some of them didn't even bother mastering the basics of manners, relying instead on their bits of magic to cow people into doing their bidding. Caelan, however, had honed his skills until they were as sharp as the shining blade he now wielded.

After half a dozen matches, Caelan had landed in the final duel. His muscles strained as he wove around the ring, sweat dripping down his neck underneath his polished armor. Both combatants paused for a moment to catch their breath, the sound of steel scraping steel replaced with huffing. Then, with a predatory grace, he circled his opponent, observing and calculating his next strategic move.

"Having fun yet?" he asked. His adversary was a man nearly double his size, but also twice as slow. Caelan had already sliced into him—once on the back of his hand where the gauntlet had slipped off, and once on his cheekbone with a blow that had launched the man's helm a dozen paces away. While others might have labeled it cockiness, Caelan's signature swagger stemmed from his confidence in his abilities and experience.

The other man, a vibrant scarlet cape hanging behind him, sneered, his eyes flashing with contempt. Then he charged. Before Caelan could roll out of the way, his boot slipped in a shallow puddle of mud. His ankle twisted with a sickening pop, sending a jolt of pain up through his leg. The air rushed from his lungs, a grunt escaping his lips as his opponent's shoulder slammed into his torso, the impact jarring his bones.

The crowd gasped in unison, a sharp hissing sound that buzzed inside Caelan's skull. He lay on the ground, stunned, his back flat in the dirt as his opponent's blade pushed the scale mail collar up, exposing the tender flesh of his throat. The world slowed, and his head spun as he tried to catch his breath and regain his bearings. Cool steel tickled his neck, an almost sweet caress. Exhaustion settled over him like a thick blanket, weighing down his limbs and dulling his senses. With one fell swoop, this man could end it all.

No more training, no more lying, no more pain, no more . . . her.

Caelan strained his eyes to one side, searching for Elara again, finding her where she stood at the edge of her tent. Instead of a mask of nonchalance, a storm of emotions raged behind her eyes as her guards struggled to block her from bolting into the arena.

"No!" she cried. She was frantic, panic evident in every inch of her.

Why would she even care? he wondered. *Or is it just another act? Another lie?* He closed his eyes, the seconds ticking by in time with his heartbeat. Even if her fear was an act, he'd promised to protect her, to help her hone her essence affinity. He recalled her crying in the library, her eyes glistening, lips swollen. Hers seemed an isolating, heavy burden to bear, though he wasn't sure why the thought of her loneliness bothered him so much. At least, he couldn't stand the thought of leaving her here alone with his volatile father.

"Yield?" his opponent asked, his voice echoing across the arena and back.

Caelan's eyes narrowed. "Not a chance," he hissed. With a swift, brutal maneuver, he rammed the pommel of his sword into the back of the man's knee, sending him sprawling on top of Caelan. Grunting with effort, Caelan wrapped his arms around his waist and rolled. Not elegant. Not clean. But effective. His muscles strained as he dragged himself upright. Mercifully, adrenaline dulled the pain as his injured ankle bore his weight. A thunderous roar, a mixture of cheers and shouts, shook the tent poles as the crowd reacted. His heart hammered against his ribs, a frantic drumbeat that drowned out all other sounds as blood rushed to his head, blurring his vision with a crimson haze.

The rest of the duel was a blur of motion—a finish that left Caelan's adversary on the ground, just as Caelan had been moments before. Only this time, Caelan was on top. He slammed his boot onto the man's blade for good measure.

"I yield! I yield!" the man sputtered.

"Well done, sir," Caelan said, offering him an arm and pulling him upright. He readjusted the man's cloak—its dusty fabric threatening to fall from his filthy armor—and placed his hand on his fellow swordsman's shoulder. Caelan might be a warrior, but he was also a good sportsman, clinging to honor wherever he could.

"Thank you, Captain Stormrider." The loser hoisted Caelan's hand high above their heads, and another deafening roar erupted from the crowd.

Caelan had won.

As he limped back to his tent, arm draped over a squire's shoulder, his eyes searched the crowd for Elara's once more. She was gone. His chest tightened.

CHAPTER 13

Elara

E LARA SHIFTED HER WEIGHT in her seat, waiting for the final dueling match to begin. She folded her arms and narrowed her eyes when Lord Stormrider and Lady Seraphine sauntered past her tent. The cobalt-cloaked man only nodded at her, but the sorceress blew her a kiss. Out of that kiss, a tiny butterfly made of purple smoke flew into Elara's face, souring her mood even further.

Is she jealous? Elara wondered. *She shouldn't be.* Elara was engaged to Caelan, but a romance between them was impossible—given how much she despised him, of course, and that he was obviously unavailable. She shooed the butterfly, smacking at it with the back of her hand and waving away the smoke.

Lady Seraphine laughed—a delicate, tinkling sound—and Lord Stormrider smirked. He flexed his hand, drawing Elara's attention there. He flicked his wrist and wiggled his fingers in a rhythmic sequence. Something about the subtle movement tickled the back of her brain. The movement was similar to the one she'd witnessed during her fight with Caelan—when he'd used his magic to summon water. Her eyes scanned her surroundings, trying to discern what he could possibly be doing. Seeing nothing, she relaxed. His fidgeting was probably habitual.

After they had gone, Elara turned her attention back to where Caelan fought in the arena. He circled his opponent, both fighters pausing briefly, the sounds of their battle fading to a low hum. The midday sun beat down on his armor, the heat shimmering in waves as he moved with surprising grace around the arena. The swagger he affected, which Elara had initially perceived as arrogant, was instead a silent assertion of power, a quiet hum of competence that vibrated in the air around him.

As they danced around the ring, edging closer to the audience, Caelan gained the upper hand. Elara didn't know which was more attractive—his physique or his finesse. A blush warmed her cheeks, and she cast her eyes down at the delicate, colorful embroidery on her skirt, trying to distract herself.

The tournament was a strange experience for her. Growing up, she'd had little experience with magic. So few people had essence strong enough to worry about, let alone showcase in a pageant. Previous tournaments she'd attended focused on physical combat and skills, like archery and jousting. As a little girl, she'd always fancied watching the horses, while Thalia and their mother debated which knights were the most handsome.

Now the magical events took center stage for everyone in the audience. While the Tharven and Sylari hadn't put forth any champions, the Moiren and Embrathi would participate in the Thal'Moira and Thal'Embra, respectively. Elara didn't know what to expect from those ancient rites. The tournament had drawn the most powerful men and women from across Serendith together, offering a prime opportunity for her to evaluate threats to the crown.

Lord Stormrider is a genius for thinking it up, she thought. Elara would witness more magic in one day than she'd seen during her entire life.

The crowd gasped in unison, and Elara snapped her head up, returning her attention to the match below. Caelan was on the ground, his back flat in the dirt and his opponent's blade pressed to his throat.

"No!" Elara flew to her feet, only to have Felix and Silas bar her with their arms. Caelan had to win—or at least survive. He was her only hope for saving her family. *Get up! Get up!*

Caelan's golden eyes found hers. She shuddered as icy fear filled her veins. *Don't you dare die on me. I need you alive. Stars help me—I want you alive.*

"Yield?" The word hung in the air, waiting for a response. With a swift maneuver, Caelan bashed the back of his opponent's knee with the butt of his sword, forcing the man to fall on top of him. They rolled, armor clanking, until Caelan dragged himself to his feet.

A deafening roar erupted from the crowd, shaking the ground beneath her feet and rattling the tent poles surrounding the arena. Elara's heart hammered against her ribs.

Caelan ended the fight, mirroring the earlier hold from his opponent, roles now reversed. Caelan even stood on the man's blade, showing off for the wild crowd. A shimmer caught Elara's eye. An ill-placed puddle had appeared at the edge of the ring, right next to Caelan's muddy boot. Elara scrunched her eyebrows together, sure that it hadn't been there earlier.

It dawned on her that she'd been right—Lord Stormrider had summoned water.

Did he mean for it to fell his son, or was it meant for the other man?

Why would he want to see Caelan fail?

Once his opponent had yielded, Caelan offered him an arm and hoisted him up. The loser raised Caelan's hand into the air, and the crowd cheered wildly. A squire rushed to Caelan's side, taking his weight on his shoulder and helping him limp back to his tent.

Elara turned to her guards. "Take me to him," she ordered. This time, they didn't argue.

Upon their arrival, she pulled back the canvas of his tent to reveal Caelan sprawled out between two chairs—reclining in one with his injured leg propped up on the other.

"Are you all right?" she asked.

He jerked his head in her direction, startled. "I'll live," he said, wincing as he tugged at his boot.

"Here, let me help you." Elara kneeled next to his injured leg and gingerly removed the muddy boot.

"Ah!" he cried.

"Don't be a baby," she said. After searching for a moment in the tent, she found a clean towel and wrapped the cloth around his ankle. "Can you wet this?" she asked him. "It will help with the swelling." She watched in awe as he held his hand over it, his magic turning the dry fabric sopping wet.

"You get used to it," he said.

"The magic or the injuries?" she asked.

"Both."

They waited in silence, the air thick with tension, until Ursa, the royal physician, bustled into the cramped space.

"Oh, well, good to see you, Your Highness," she said to Elara. "You've done a wonderful job caring for our patient."

"Yes, she has. I'm very thankful that my foot is still attached, given our earlier . . . spat." Caelan winked at her.

"Ah, young love," Ursa said wistfully. "Full of fun and fury."

Elara fought a grimace but couldn't help but roll her eyes.

Ursa got to work quickly, setting her large leather satchel on a table and pulling various bottles out of it. Corked glass bottles containing different colored herbs filled the tiny space. She selected two, one with dried orange petals and another that looked like black ashes.

As the two substances mixed in Ursa's miniature copper cauldron, a bitter smell filled the air, causing Elara's nose to wrinkle. Ursa used a needle to prick her own finger and add three fat drops of blood to the concoction. As soon as the last drop hit, the cauldron glowed with a faint buttery light.

A flame from a portable enchanted burner danced under a kettle, and Ursa scooped the sooty substance into the boiling water. She poured Caelan a cup of the brew. When he sipped it, he gagged.

Ursa handed Caelan a pouch of the remedy. "Make this into a tea by adding two spoonfuls to a full cup of hot water. Twice a day for three days. It will help."

"Thank you," Caelan said, nodding, already rotating his ankle with a sigh of relief.

"And stay off that ankle too!" she added. "It'll heal faster the more you can rest."

With Ursa's quick departure, Caelan and Elara found themselves alone once more. The question of whether or not to tell him about the puddle gnawed at her, a silent battle waging within the confines of her mind. Telling him the truth might tempt him to her side, or it may reveal too much about her distaste for his father.

"Just spit it out," he said, breaking the silence. "I can tell you have something to say, so just say it. Otherwise, I'd rather watch the rest of the Thal'Moira."

Elara took a deep breath, deciding to accept the risk. "I think your father sabotaged you."

To her surprise, Caelan nodded. When she raised her brows in question, he sighed and said, "It wouldn't be the first time," his voice low and resigned.

"But why would he want you to lose?"

"We need to show strength, but my father always says that it's not wise to show your hand."

"He didn't want you to compete in the Thal'Moira," she said slowly. Lord Stormrider wanted to keep the full extent of their power hidden—to show just enough strength to garner favor from the court.

Caelan nodded.

"And he would gamble your life for that?"

"Have a little faith. I can handle myself." He winked, then winced as he adjusted his injured leg.

"Doesn't that bother you?" Elara almost felt sorry for him, to have a father so vicious that he would risk his son's life for political gain.

Caelan shrugged. "It's just the way he is."

Felix poked his head into the tent. "Princess Elara?" he asked sheepishly.

"What?" Elara snapped. She was finally getting somewhere.

"Apologies," he said. "You are meant to present the dueling champion with laurels. This way please." He held the fabric door open for her.

Caelan grinned. "See you out there."

Instead of arguing with Felix, she nodded and followed her guards down to the arena.

Once at the edge of the fighting ring, she was approached by a servant, who offered her a fragrant crown of laurels, its scent sharp and green against the smell of sweat and dust. Elara smoothed her skirt with her other hand, the rough brocade fabric irritating her fingertips.

The trumpet sounded. A magi's booming voice carried across the arena: "Please rise for Her Royal Highness, Princess Elara Evensong, and for the dueling champion, Captain Caelan

Stormrider!" She glided out to meet Caelan in the center of the arena. He walked from the opposite end of the bowl with only a slight limp.

"Well done," she said through the gritted teeth of her forced smile. "Kneel, please."

Caelan did as she asked. The sight of him in that position, a champion kneeling before her, covered in dirt and sweat, made her own knees a little wobbly. Her breath caught. This man who had been flirting with her was a true warrior, lethal.

She placed the laurels on his blond curls, and he grasped her hand, kissing each of her knuckles. Shivers raced down her spine with each delicate peck.

When he rose, the audience took up chanting.

"Kiss! Kiss! Kiss!"

Not in a million moons, she thought. But before she could turn and leave, Caelan wrapped an arm around her waist and pulled her into his chest.

"Shall we, Princess?" he asked.

She placed her hands on his chest and pushed, trying to put some space between them. "I'd rather not," she said, still smiling sweetly for the crowd.

"You really think we have a choice?" he asked, raising a brow.

"Fine," she huffed. She closed her eyes and leaned in, waiting for his lips to meet hers.

Caelan pressed his lips to hers softly, resulting in deafening applause from the audience. As soon as Elara tried to end the kiss and pull away, Caelan pulled her hips into his, their bodies molding together, leaving no space between them. The warmth of his skin radiated against hers. Her eyes flew open in shock, then fluttered shut of their own accord as he deepened the kiss. Someone in the crowd whistled, but it sounded so far away.

Caelan tasted salty, and a hint of whiskey swirled between their tongues. His shadow of a beard was rough against her skin.

Stars above, she thought. Her traitorous hands wove into his hair, gripping the damp curls lightly. Strong hands moved from her hips to her lower back, threatening to slide downward . . .

Elara snapped out of it, placing her hands on top of his and pulling them away. The audience laughed, and dozens of smiles flashed in the crowd. The couple had inadvertently shown the perfect display of affection—and restraint—to sell their story. Caelan beamed at her, offering her his arm to escort her out of the arena. Elara resisted the urge to scowl back at him.

Lightning flashed all around them in a spectacular display, courtesy of the Children of the Sky. The bolts split the blue sky, white-hot and bright despite the afternoon sun. As the electricity crackled around her, Elara followed Caelan's eyes as they cut to his father, then darkened.

Perhaps we have more in common than I thought. Like a common enemy.

CHAPTER 14

Elara

THE FIRST OF THE leaves had turned golden, red, and brown while they waited for Caelan's ankle to heal. Elara had endured weeks of maddening isolation. Aside from Iris—who prattled on about the tournament—Felix and Silas were her only company. She'd taken to meandering the familiar halls of the palace, noting the clever hiding places and entrances to her tunnels should she ever need them. On the rare occasions she saw Caelan, they uttered few words. He sulked, unable to do much of anything other than attend the council meetings with Lord Stormrider.

Elara shuddered, recalling the way Caelan looked at his father as they left the tournament arena. Maybe it wouldn't be too difficult to turn him against his father after all. While she couldn't yet forgive Caelan for his part in their engagement, nor his terrible behavior toward her, she was grateful to have access to a potential ally.

Today was the day Elara and Caelan would shove their differences aside and work together. She met Caelan in a shadowy, seldom-used room of the palace, a place she knew well but rarely visited. The worn mats and faded banners of the training hall whispered stories of her family's military legacy, making it more a symbol than a place of active practice. Many noble families had similar rooms in their manors or country houses, but few families used them for exercise anymore—at least not in Valoria. Caelan's training experience suggested Veilkeep operated differently. Curiosity about his home and his travels prickled at the back of her mind.

Focus, she told herself.

The faded walls hosted cracks that snaked their way out of several corners as the plaster started to give. Layers of dust covered the already-gritty stone floor. Piles of assorted weaponry and fitness gear—along with other miscellaneous objects sent here to disappear—leaned against tall windows. She and Caelan would train in a glorified storage closet, which suited her just fine. Caelan had pulled some strings to dismiss her guards, allowing the two of them to have complete privacy for the first time. Those savage butterflies were back to assaulting her stomach.

As she explored the room, pausing now and then to sweep away a cobweb with her arm, she watched Caelan digging through the equipment. He wore a loose shirt, the thin fabric clinging to his back, revealing the definition of his muscles beneath—along with some strange dark markings. His slim trousers, hugging his legs as he moved, stretched taut as he lifted and tossed various objects out of his way.

Heat crept up Elara's neck as she realized she was similarly attired. If Caelan made her mouth water dressed like that, what was he going to think of her? Although her skin was well concealed, her riding trousers clung to her legs and bottom. The blue silk shirt she wore over her most comfortable corset was almost translucent—and would become more so as she started to sweat. Hopefully it wouldn't stick to her chest *too* much.

Elara's father had always praised her appearance above her character, and over the years, Elara had watched the queen use her looks to her advantage, styling herself and transforming into whoever she needed to be to get what she wanted. Today, in her simple shirt and fitted pants, Elara would begin forging herself into a weapon, like the one Caelan now held.

Caelan had stopped plundering the piles, having found a wooden staff tipped with a blunted spearhead. He tossed it to her, a warm smile on his face as she caught it with a confident grip.

"Remember, this is simply a tool. As you well know, when you have no weapons, it is imperative that *you* become the weapon. Especially without an offensive magical talent . . ."

He trailed off, staring at her. His gaze traveled from the top of her head to her worn leather boots, then back up again before he finally returned to his riffling. Elara's neck and ears warmed under his scrutiny.

"You look . . . strong," he said after clearing his throat. Caelan's cheeks were a little flushed too. "I wasn't expecting you to be in such great shape," he admitted.

"Well, I may not be a fighter yet, but I like to stay active. Horseback riding, gardening, dancing—"

"Dancing?" he asked, tilting his head to one side, a smirk tugging at his lips.

Elara nodded, slamming the butt of the spear into the floor and placing her other hand on her hip. "Just you wait," she said. "You've never been to a royal ball before."

Caelan laughed at that, tilting his head back. "Anything else?"

She thought, pursing her lips. "This might sound absurd, but I think that my essence affinity isn't just healing me, but making me stronger than I was before, somehow."

"You didn't seem that tough when we first met," he teased. She scowled at him in warning.

"I didn't have my ability then," she quipped back. "After that night, I was exhausted. But by morning, my muscles had already recovered. And not only were they healed, but noticeably strengthened."

"That makes sense," he mused. "People think the way we train the body is in the breaking-it-down part. It's actually the rebuilding—the healing—that strengthens us, as you experienced. Though I'd wager that it happens faster for you."

"Does that mean I'll be able to learn to fight faster?" she asked, voice hopeful. Learning to fight meant that she could defend herself, that she'd never have to experience the humiliation of the invasion again.

"That has more to do with your mental discipline than anything else. But, with me as your instructor, maybe so." He winked at her. "Let's begin!"

Caelan reached out, his fingers brushing against Elara's as he took back the spear. He summoned water to his palm and shaped it into a whip. The ribbon of water snapped forward with a deafening crack, cleanly slicing the spearhead off of its handle. Dismissing the whip into a fine mist, he passed the staff back to her.

Elara blinked. *I don't think I'll ever get used to that.*

His hands on her shoulders, he guided her to the edge of the room before placing himself at its opposite end. "We will start with training your body how to move, balance, and block. Then we will try out different weapons until we find you a good fit. It doesn't hurt for you to have experience with a variety of them. Controlling your body is the first step to controlling your essence affinity."

Caelan stalked toward her—closer and closer, each movement smooth and lethal, but measured for her sake. Elara's heart raced, and adrenaline surged through her veins. She squared her shoulders, disinclined to let him see how much his presence impacted her body.

A confident smile played on his lips, and Elara licked her own, remembering the taste of their first kiss. She shook her head to rid herself of the unwelcome distraction.

"Ow!" she cried. Caelan's sword connected with her forearm as she failed to avoid his first strike. Thankfully, his weapon was made of wood and not steel. Her hand opened of its own volition, and her staff clattered to the ground.

Caelan lowered his wooden practice sword with infuriating calm. "You're supposed to block *before* it hits you, Princess."

She glared at him, rubbing her tender flesh. "I'll remember that next time you try to break my arm."

"That was me going easy on you. If I were trying, you'd be on your back." His eyes gleamed.

Elara shook her head, frowning. "Again," she said, falling into what she hoped would be a better defensive stance.

Caelan assessed her. "Legs wider. Good, now bend your knees a little. Firm grip—both hands. Ready?"

Elara nodded, her cheeks flaming.

"Go!"

The work proved painstaking for Elara. Though fit, her body ached with the unaccustomed exertion, muscles screaming in protest with each movement. Slow and stiff, she winced with each blow of Caelan's wooden practice sword, the impact jarring her bones.

"Come on, Princess! You can do better than that!" Caelan swatted her bottom with his sword as she failed to block his attack again. The sting paled in comparison to the burning of her ears. She clenched her jaw to keep a retort from slipping off her tongue. It appeared that, while he was making an effort to avoid hurting her, he was immensely enjoying mocking her every chance he got.

Their last match left Elara on the ground, tailbone smarting. Eyes brimming with hot tears of frustration, she watched him, waiting for another teasing comment. Instead, he crouched down in front of her. He ran a hand through his golden curls, already damp with sweat, and his gaze softened.

"We've got a lot of work to do. But your instincts aren't half bad. Here." Caelan held out a calloused hand.

Elara hesitated, then took it, allowing him to help her up.

"May I?" he asked, gesturing to her staff.

With a nod, she offered it to him. Instead of taking the weapon, his fingers wrapped around hers and pushed the staff in toward her chest.

"Follow me. When I move, you move."

With his hands warm and sure over hers, he pulled them through a flowing series of stances, her body mirroring his.

"Better." He grinned, releasing her.

His golden eyes met hers as he brushed her long braid off her shoulder, the unexpected caress sending a shiver down her spine. Each touch brought Elara closer to her goal—and chipped away at her resolve. *I need him to like me. To trust me. To help me.* She also needed to remember that he was the enemy. *A means to an end.*

A FTER A FEW HOURS, Elara collapsed gratefully against a stack of rough-hewn wooden crates, the splintery wood digging into her flesh beneath her clothes. As she reclined, catching her breath, the dust from the crates stuck to her sweaty garments and the bare skin of her forearms. Caelan slid into place next to her, an arm's length away. The musky scent of Caelan's sweat was stronger than her own odor, but not unpleasant, with its peppery cedar base. Her heart pounded against her ribs from exertion and his closeness.

"That welt on your arm." Caelan picked up her hand and examined her forearm. "It's already almost gone!"

Elara nodded. "It happens so fast. You've seen how cuts knit together almost instantly and now this. Is using magic always so exhausting?"

"Your power pulls from your essence. It's a limited reserve, but you can do more magic with less energy over time, with practice."

"I bet I'll sleep well tonight." She laughed half-heartedly, then frowned.

Nightmares had plagued her sleep for the last several nights. There were the ones about her family lying face down in a gutter somewhere or clawing their own eyes out as Lady Seraphine tortured them. Or the worst one: black tendrils of smoke snaking around her body, crawling up her neck and into her nose, her mouth, her eyes. Suffocating her. Blinding her.

Elara pulled her knees into her chest and wrapped her arms around her shins. Caelan scooted over to her until his hip was touching hers and placed a hand on her shoulder.

A crack had materialized in her armor against him. She would be a fool to let her guard down with him—for him—but after weeks of solitude, she couldn't help herself.

"This is so hard," she said. "I never asked for any of this. How can I feel so powerful and so helpless at the same time?" She curled further into herself, becoming a tight little ball.

126

"You can do this." He gave her a crooked smile, more genuine than all the fake ones and false flattery from before. "You're very brave, you know. For doing this for your family."

A faint flush colored his already-ruddy cheeks, but she couldn't tell if it was from exertion or not. They sat together like that until their breathing had slowed.

"Will I see you again before the festival?" She didn't want to delay her progress any further.

A smirk tugged at his lips. "Can't get enough of me already?"

She rolled her eyes, eliciting a deep chuckle.

"We'll meet here again tomorrow. I'll prioritize our training as best I can. I have other duties to attend to—now that Ursa isn't scolding me for walking. Until then, Princess." He rose and offered her a grand bow.

Elara stood too, fighting a grin. "Until then, watermage."

CHAPTER 15

Elara

T HE FRESH AIR WAS cool and thick with smells of cut flowers, roasting meats, and baked treats. Elara walked the carnival grounds, her shadows—as she now liked to think of her guards—on her heels. Cheerful music flowed from a band perched atop a wooden stage set up near the back of the affair. A stray jet-black dog—which looked unnervingly like it might be half wolf—nibbled at the remains of a discarded meal nearby. As she walked by, it stopped snuffling to look her in the eye, and the hair at her nape stood on end. Turning away from the strange creature, she passed wooden booths that looked like those one might find in a market at the center of any bustling mercantile town. The scent of various hot foods wafted by—heady spices and sugary treats that tugged on the edges of her childhood memories.

As she ambled on, biding her time while she waited to meet up with Caelan, she thought about what he'd been through to learn his skills. Despite his teasing, he'd been remarkably patient with her during their first lessons. His father had trained him well, but she suspected it had come at a steep cost to their relationship. A man who would risk his son's life in the tournament just to keep his strength a secret was not someone she was looking forward to crossing.

Although he'd been schooled in cruelty, Caelan's recent actions toward her spoke of an unexpected compassion. She'd gone from balking at the thought of touching him to sagging with relief every time he wrapped his hands around her waist or wrists. Guiding her movements, he'd helped her gain more confidence with each repetitive motion. What had started out as a tedious series of boring drills became a dance that made her heart race in anticipation of the chance to be near him again.

Elara hated it. Her body betrayed her mind, craving something that she knew could one day ruin her. Even now, she had to take several deep breaths to keep her head from spinning. They both needed to focus on their appearance together today—the lovely royal couple attending the local Mabine festival, celebrating the autumn equinox. For the city folk outside the noble courts, this would be their first glimpse of the future king and queen, a sight that promised excitement and apprehension.

One of the booths nearby caught her eye, distracting her from her nerves. It had a purple-and-gold-striped canvas roof and a long line of eager patrons. Elara approached the end of that line, but as folks began to recognize her, they urged her on ahead of them. Mumbling her thanks, she entered the booth, surprised to find that it had a homey feel to it. The furniture inside, the walls—none of it seemed temporary. Unlike the other vendors who popped up shop on these grounds a few times a year, this one appeared to live here year-round.

Elara had attended this festival almost every year since she was a child, but she had somehow never seen this cozy booth. On one side stood a solid birch table, its spotty white wood covered with books and bottles of various herbaceous tinctures. Additional herbs hung from drying lines on the ceiling, creating a fragrant makeshift forest canopy above. An iron stove on the opposite side formed a tiny glowing hearth. In the center of the room was a smaller round table and two worn, but plush, velvet chairs.

A gray-haired woman emerged from behind a dividing wall made from a thick tapestry. She gestured for Elara to sit without saying a word. Elara glanced at her shadows, who had already turned to exit and give her some privacy. Elara pulled off her hood and unfastened her woolen cloak, draping it across the back of one of the chairs. She sat and turned her attention to the woman.

Though her age showed in her stooped posture and weathered skin, a certain sweetness emanated from her—a lovely crone indeed. Silvery-white hair fell like a silk sheet down her back. The wrinkles on her pale face told stories of laughter and smiles. Her eyes were dark in color but bright with knowledge.

"My name is Narissa," she offered simply. "What can I do for Your Highness?"

Elara thought hard before answering. "I don't know," was all she could muster as she sagged back in her chair. She couldn't risk telling this stranger what was really happening within the palace walls.

"I am a seer, dearie," Narissa tried again. "Young women like yourself come to me seeking answers about their destiny."

When Elara didn't respond, Narissa let out a sigh and shook her ancient head. "Well, most people your age ask me about love, so why don't we start there?"

Despite her somber circumstances, Elara's ears perked up at that. *Is love something that I could even have one day? Perhaps after this nightmare is over.* A hopeful smile touched her lips as she nodded, clutching at the promise of a happier future. *Maybe even one with Caelan in it . . .*

Narissa held her hands out to each side, palms facing upward. She closed her eyes and tilted her head back before inhaling through her flared nostrils. Elara had expected cards, crystal balls, maybe even a palm reading. Fortune tellers were a common occurrence at festivals, though no one had ever seen evidence that any essence affinity allowed one to predict the future. Such things were the stuff of myths and fairy tales.

Before Elara could ask if she was all right, the woman's eyelids fluttered open, revealing fully onyx eyes. A small squeal escaped Elara as she jumped in her seat. Narissa's mouth fell open, and though her lips did not move, a deep, ominous voice spoke. The words swirled around Elara and the old woman like an encroaching mist.

The Druids danced away the night
The War, the ruinous delight
Man cracked the Well
Destroyed the spell

And cost the world the Light
One shall come with Death her boon
Born under the Cygnet Moon
One who hears the raven's call
By triple Stars to save us all

Elara's brow furrowed. *No one talks about the druids anymore.*

The old woman turned back into herself, rolling the tension out of her shoulders and smoothing her hair with her knobby hands. She looked deeply into Elara's eyes, a flicker of amusement in her own. "Well, Your Highness, what do you know of the Shattering?"

Elara thought back to her history lessons, wishing she had spent less time making paper flowers for Thalia's birthday under her desk and more time actually listening to that particular lecture.

"The Shattering," she recited, "happened over four hundred years ago. It was a war unlike any other. Humankind grew jealous of the powerful druids, who kept the ancient source of essence hidden."

Elara squirmed, eyes squinting as she pulled forth more details. "The human kingdoms' armies drove the druids to extinction. My great-grandfather claimed Serendith changed irrevocably. But no one really knows why."

Narissa nodded along, adding, "The druids are well-known as the ancient keepers of magic. Their ancestral home lies deep within the Verdant Forest, a place called Serelia."

"The Well?" Elara guessed. She'd heard legends of crumbling stone walls and moss-covered statues, remnants of a forgotten civilization that littered the Verdant Forest. *If the Shattering also destroyed Serelia* . . . "Is that why magic has been disappearing?"

The woman grinned, showing her gray teeth and gums. She tilted her head to the side in a birdlike gesture. "Clever girl."

"So," Elara started, heart pounding, "someone is coming . . . who can fix it?" Despite the thrill, the idea of puzzles and riddles left her with a familiar feeling of unease; an icy knot of apprehension settled in her stomach. "What is the Cygnet Moon?"

Narissa examined her long fingernails, playing coy now. Elara sighed and tugged at her waist. She placed her full coin pouch on the table, the gold pieces clinking together.

The seer snatched it up. "It is a rare and beautiful celestial alignment. The full moon aligns with the constellation Cygnea. But most people these days don't pay heed to its significance, instead favoring the stars alone as their guides. Another loss from the Shattering."

Elara nodded. Many courtiers and townsfolk—even Elara's own family, to a limited extent—relied on reading the stars' positions to guide their choices, navigating the crooked paths toward their destinies. Her father had thought the outdated practice of accounting for the moon's phases for anything more than harvests a silly superstition—fools worshiping an otherwise long-forgotten goddess.

"When?" Elara whispered, wiping her clammy hands on her sapphire skirt.

"The next Cygnet Moon is exactly three months from today, on the winter solstice." Narissa smiled, fingering the heavy gold coins.

Three months. *The wedding is on the winter solstice. Is that why Lord Stormrider invaded now? To have his son on the throne in time for essence to be restored by the savior? But that would mean . . .*

Elara swallowed the lump in her throat before asking, "Will my family survive the royal wedding?"

Narissa considered the question for a moment before reaching into her apron, revealing a handful of scrying stones. She whispered over them and rolled them out onto the table before Elara. The pale rocks stilled and revealed a series of cryptic symbols. Narissa tapped her crooked index finger against her chin as she pondered their meaning.

"That's up to you, dearie," she said.

Elara balled her hands into fists as heat crept up her neck. Finished playing games with this woman, she rose from her seat and gathered her empty coin purse.

"Will there be anything else?" Elara asked.

"Not today, Your Highness." The old woman flashed her a toothy smile again and went back to counting her gold.

Elara shook her head and shoved her annoyance to the back of her mind. Even as she stepped away from the fortune teller's booth, dread clung to her like a shroud, the cheerful sounds of the festival unable to dispel her fear.

"Come on," she said to her shadows. "Let's go find Caelan."

CHAPTER 16

Caelan

THE ROAD, HALF COBBLESTONE and half dirt, rushed toward Caelan's face. Throwing his hands out in front of him, he winced at the tiny sharp pebbles that lodged themselves in his palms. He had spent the morning meandering around the expansive fairgrounds, occasionally stumbling over his own feet. After rising and brushing off his knees, he reached into his doublet, secured his flask, and tilted his head back to drink the liquid within. Others jumped out of his path, not wanting to create more of a scene, especially not one involving the now-famous future king. The aether burned his tongue and coated his throat like honey laced with hot spices.

He'd never seen anything like this festival before. His home lacked sufficient flat land for such a festival. The islands were treacherous, covered in harsh rocky hills with many of the smaller isles completely uninhabitable because of the towering spikes.

Dozens of booths sprawled out in every direction, forming the marketplace. The sound of minstrels playing in the corners and a band playing on a stage flowed all around him. Fresh-baked sweets and hearty spices floated through the air to tease his nostrils. Even the muddy puddles glittered because of the aether in his drink.

He raised his hand to his forehead, shielding his sensitive eyes—another side effect of his drink of choice—as he gazed up at the clear blue sky. He would never grow tired of that. The Shadowed Isles were so named because they were blanketed by a near-constant cloud bank. Even with the slight chill in the air with the turning of the season, Caelan was warm from head to toe. The open sky reminded him of being at sea, where he used to spend as much time as possible—the only way to escape the darkness of his home.

His injured ankle still jolted a little with every step he took on the packed earth. He hated that his father would go to such lengths to prevent him from being in the Thal'Moira—though he wasn't entirely surprised, given that the man had gone to far greater lengths to get whatever he desired. A chill snaked its way down his spine as he remembered the reason they'd come to Valoria.

Elara made it all tolerable. Caelan admitted to himself that he hadn't expected to enjoy spending time with her, but their training sessions had proved more than amicable. She was an apt pupil, listening and learning far more quickly than he'd thought possible. Her essence affinity was incredible—he'd not seen its like. No one had in centuries. Still, Elara's ability to heal was only a small part of the equation. Her natural agility, stamina, and grace—combined with her sharp mind—made for a dangerous combination. That, and her dedication to making the best of their situation in order to protect her family.

I'm in trouble, he thought. *She'll be the death of me if I'm not careful.* He couldn't let Elara get in the way of his father's plans, or they'd both be doomed.

His stomach growled as he stopped at a booth selling various baked goods, intent on trying what looked like a latticework of crispy dough covered in a snowy white powder. Before he could place his order with the boy—who couldn't have been older than twelve—manning the booth, he heard a muffled cry containing his name.

"Caelan!" Elara called from a nearby sitting area filled with benches and a few mismatched chairs where couples and families sat or laid out blankets to enjoy their treats. The sound came out harshly, but garbled, as she was speaking around a mouthful of food. The disdain that flashed in her eyes made Caelan want to roll his own.

Instead, he walked over to her, intrigued by the pastry in her grasp. "What do we have here?" he asked, placing his hands on his hips. His mouth watered from his sugar craving—and from the sight of her. Her black satin hair cascaded to her waist, a few stray wisps curling around her flushed face. She was wearing a cobalt-blue gown—his family color. He hadn't anticipated how much the sight of her in that shade would affect him. *Must be the red stuff.*

Elara wiped some frosting from the corner of her mouth with a linen napkin. "Sit," she ordered. "Try this first," she said as she offered him a portion of her pastry. It was a light, doughy roll swirled with a dark brown filling and topped with a thick white glaze.

Caelan sat down on the wobbly bench next to her and took the food. He gave it a cursory sniff, teasing her a little, before he bit into it. He stifled a moan at the sweet-and-spicy flavor—a burst of cinnamon and lemon—as he enjoyed the fluffiness of the dough and the slight zest of the glaze.

"It's delicious!" he said around his mouthful, and Elara's eyes and shoulders softened at his delight. She laughed. Caelan savored that sound as much as the pastry.

"Felix, please go find us some coffee," she said, tone turning sour once more. When the guard wandered off in search of the bitter liquid, she turned to Caelan. "What do you think you're doing, strutting around here *drunk*?"

"I'm not drunk," he mumbled around another bite of dough.

Elara's mouth drew into a thin line as she leaned forward, inspecting his eyes. "Seriously, Caelan," she hissed. "Stardust?"

"Do you ever stop being such a prude?"

"Do you ever stop being such an ass?" she snapped.

"Oh, come now. It's not like you haven't heard the rumors about me. Besides, I saw you at a party once." He raised an eyebrow at her.

Elara shook her head. "That's . . . none of your business. Eat your food. We'll get some coffee in your system to sober you up."

"Do you have another one of those?" he asked, pointing to the other half of the pastry in her hand.

Scoffing, she passed it to him. "It's always been my favorite," she said, a touch of melancholy creeping behind her eyes.

"You've been here before?" he asked, startling himself with how much he longed to know more, to wipe that haunted look off her face and bring back the laughter.

Elara nodded. "My sister and I come here throughout the year to celebrate the shifting of the seasons. My mother usually brings us, but my father has made a few appearances over the years."

"You must miss them," Caelan said, a fist clenching around his heart. He opened his mouth to say more, then snapped it shut at her expression.

Elara turned to him, tears brimming at the edges of the eyes, threatening to spill over. She sniffed. "What about you? They don't celebrate the equinox in Veilkeep?"

He shook his head, licking the remnants of glaze from his lips. "Not like this. The weather isn't as pleasant as it is here, so we mainly keep indoors or out at sea this time of year."

"Do you at least have decent snacks?"

Caelan chuckled. "Yes, actually, but they tend to be more savory than sweet. Sera makes the best hand-pies for the winter solstice . . ." He trailed off, realizing that Elara probably didn't want to hear about Sera.

"How long have you two been together?" she asked, her tone neutral.

"We're not exactly together." He shrugged. "We've been friends since we were children, when her parents died and she came to live with my family. After my mother passed away, my father raised us

JENNIFER L ADAMS

both. Over the years, we became lovers, then friends, then lovers again."

"Go on," Elara encouraged him.

"I think we are both struggling to . . . adjust," he finally admitted. "I bet that sounds ridiculous to you, all things considered." It was regret, and maybe shame, that coated his throat, his words.

"I don't want your pity, Caelan," she whispered.

His heart hung heavy in his chest, beating rapidly from the aether, the sugar, or her. He lifted a hand as if to brush her cheek, then dropped it back down to his side, balling it into a fist in his lap. "What about a friendship?"

"Can captives be friends with their captors?" she retorted.

No, but we're both captives here, he thought.

They stayed silent for a while, processing the two unanswered questions hanging in the air between them. Caelan finished eating the roll.

"You didn't ask for any of this, did you?" Elara finally asked.

Caelan shook his head.

"I thought so. And neither did she. I'm sorry for her parents, and your mother, by the way."

The princess of Serendith was apologizing to him, after everything he'd put her through. Caelan stared at his boots. "That was all a long time ago."

"Still, this is a lot of change for all of us," Elara said. "Look, I know that you two have a history, but you know you can't keep seeing her, don't you?"

"I know."

"Does she?" Elara asked gently.

"Yes, she does." Caelan leaned forward, unable to resist brushing her hair from her cheek and tucking it behind her ear. "We haven't seen each other, in that way, since the tournament."

"Where does that leave us?" The hope glistening in her eyes was like a punch to his gut. He jerked his hand away, flexing his fingers to dispel the energy that pulsed between them.

"We should focus on your training. You aren't progressing as quickly as I'd like," he lied. "Your movements are slow, and you continue to hesitate during drills. Not surprising for a sheltered princess."

She sat back as if he'd slapped her. The confusion and hurt that clouded her features stung.

It's for the best. I can't do this with you, he thought. He didn't want to hurt her more than he already had. She didn't deserve that. And he didn't deserve her.

"Fine," she snapped, bristling at his accusation. "Let's just get today over with. Your father is expecting us at the main stage. Once you sober up, that is."

Caelan shrugged. "It's not like he'll care either way."

"Well, I care! I won't have my future husband—the future king—stumbling around in public like an idiot! Pull yourself together and come find me." She rose to her feet with a huff and stomped off.

As he watched her go, he couldn't help the small smile that played on his lips. *I am an idiot. An absolute fool, Elara. For you.*

With a sigh, he took the cap off his flask, tipped it, and watched the last of the shimmering red aether vanish into the dusty earth at his feet.

CHAPTER 17

Elara

E LARA PRICKED HER FINGER again with her goose-feather quill. A single drop of blood fell to the page of her open journal before the tiny wound closed itself. "Stars," she muttered. Despite her progress with combat training, her body's self-healing continued to betray her efforts to control her ability.

She had spent what felt like ages hunched over her journal and a stack of tomes. She rubbed her hand over the tense muscles in her neck. Dozens of pages in her journal were now filled with notes—and several drops of blood from practicing with her quill—but she found the studying futile.

Caelan had tasked her with researching the history of the various essence affinities. Elara needed to find answers soon or risk discovery. If her family's political allies knew she was a Serathi, it would put the Evensongs' tenuous hold on the throne in jeopardy.

She could almost hear the voices creep out of the woodwork, reacting to the news.

Liars.

Traitors.

The words hissed into her mind. Her healing essence was unknown and therefore dangerous to them.

Elara closed her ancient leather-bound book, sending a puff of dry gray dust motes dancing before her. She rubbed her eyes and rested her chin on her hand. The last story had detailed a heroine famed for performing miracles to save women who otherwise would have died in childbirth. Elara imagined the potential. If she could figure out how to harness her own power, in generations to come, it could be possible for a Serathi to use their affinity to heal others. The idea was both exciting and terrifying.

Elara ground her teeth. What she'd just spent the last several hours reading was impressive, but also akin to fairy tales. Stories of mystics, druids, and prophets. Old gods and goddesses, deities that few, if any, still worshiped. Each book she read, every new scroll she unfurled, provided no clues about mastering her powers, the source of essence, or the reason for its abrupt manifestation in her. She'd even looked for her birth records to identify the last Serathi in her family tree. Nothing. No mention of the Cygnet Moon anywhere either. Her current leading theory was that her power had something to do with the attack, shocking her system into waking the long-dormant ability within her.

Training, research, and occasionally promenading around the palace grounds with Caelan had left Elara exhausted. Still, she had plenty of time to think, but not enough pleasant thoughts to fill the open spaces within her mind. The fragile hope of a brighter tomorrow was all she had, but even that waned with each passing day, leaving her weary and heavyhearted. Despair over her family's absence gnawed at her, a persistent ache that grew ever stronger, threatening to consume her. She had to give her mind something fun to play with before it started playing with her. In a way, it already was. Between the nightmares and her tenuous alliance with Caelan, she was losing touch with reality.

Caelan. Their attraction was real enough. And his intentions toward helping her seemed genuine. Until he'd showed up intoxicated at the festival. Goose bumps prickled on her forearms as she recalled her conversation with the fortune teller at the festival a few days ago. It had taken every ounce of her self-control to pull herself together at the festival to hide the revelation from Caelan and other prying eyes.

Hot anger replaced the chill, and she snapped the fragile quill in half. She sighed as she opened her palm and watched the crushed feather float onto the marble-topped desk. *Not surprising for a sheltered princess.* Those words haunted her, hurting considerably, given that she had been so vulnerable in asking for his help. Thankfully, their training sessions had been productive since then, and he hadn't criticized her performance again, which protected her fragile ego.

What will happen when I free my family? Can I trust him then, when I don't even trust him now? Her thoughts were racing again. She pushed her notes aside and stood, deciding to wander the aisles between the bookshelves for a while. Moving her body helped her process. Frequent exercise was probably the only thing keeping her as sane as she was.

Elara questioned everyone and everything around her, but she was also building faith in her own abilities. She felt her body getting stronger. Her mind was sharper, and she felt more grounded when she was training. Her healing ability was growing too. She healed herself faster and with less energy, leaving her feeling less drained than before. But she still hadn't figured out how to prevent herself from healing unintentionally. She needed someone she could trust. A friend of her family who would do anything for them. Inspiration struck.

Elara abandoned her stacks of books and rushed out of the library, her shadows on her heel.

A FTER MAKING HER WAY down the stone stairs to the lowest level of the palace—and convincing Felix and Silas to wait outside—Elara knocked on the door to the infirmary. It swung open at her touch with an eerie creak, and she peered into the room. Cool, damp air flowed over her skin. Lanterns lit the room well despite the lack of windows. The exposed stone walls were lined with shelves holding jars and bottles, ingredients for medicines and poultices. At a wide maple table in the center of the room, Ursa worked a pestle into a mortar filled with bitter-smelling herbs.

The royal physician glanced up and smiled, creases fanning out from her eyes, when she beheld Elara lingering in the doorway. "Elara! It's so good to see you again!" She placed her work to the side and bustled over to envelop Elara in a warm embrace.

Elara wrapped her arms around Ursa, feeling the thick plait—made up of dozens of thinner braids—that fell to the woman's substantial waist. Ursa had been caring for the royal family for as long as Elara could remember—since before her own birth. She smiled as they parted. "It's good to see you too."

"It's been a while—not including the tournament," Ursa said. "What business does a princess have for calling on little old me? Take a seat, child, and tell me what's on your mind." Ursa gestured to a stool under the table and started a pot of tea in the corner.

"I . . . I want to tell you why I haven't had need of your talents lately." Elara watched Ursa fiddle with the teacups and saucers. She took a deep breath. "I've recently discovered that I have an essence affinity."

"You are a Serathi—you can heal," Ursa said, pouring boiling water into the porcelain to let the jasmine tea steep.

"Yes." Elara tensed, unnerved by Ursa's calm. "How did you know?"

A small smile tugged at Ursa's lips. "It wasn't hard to guess. I'm just thrilled that there is still some essence in the royal bloodline after all these years."

"Please don't tell anyone!" Elara's fingers curled into fists.

"Of course not, child! I was there when you were born, and I have cared for you all this time. I will keep your secret safe, for I know it is a dear one."

The room filled with the sweet floral scent of jasmine, which chased away the bitter smell of herbs, soothing Elara's troubled soul.

"Thank you, Ursa." Elara let out a deep sigh of relief. "I need your help."

Ursa sat on another low stool across from Elara, nodding fervently.

"What do you know about Lord Stormrider?" Elara asked.

Ursa sipped her tea, thinking for a beat before answering. "I know he is here, with his army and his son, and that his intentions toward you are ill."

"How?" Elara's heart raced. Ursa was the first person in the palace to acknowledge the truth. Everyone else—Iris, all the other servants, the courtiers—had been blissfully ignorant since Lord Stormrider's arrival. At least on the surface.

"I've worked in this palace for decades. You think I wouldn't notice that the king's guards have all been replaced, or, worse, don't remember who they are? I knew you would come to me when you were ready. What has he done to you?" Ursa asked.

Elara fought back tears as she told Ursa what had happened with her family, with Caelan, with her essence affinity. As she wove her sorrowful tale, Ursa went from leaning forward on the edge of her stool to draping a thick blanket over Elara, offering whatever comfort she could.

When Elara finished, she could no longer dam up her feelings of overwhelm and frustration. Hot tears streamed down her face as Ursa held her close, a comforting weight against her shaking body.

All the times she had cried before, she'd been utterly alone. Now she had an ally—a real and steadfast friend—that she could trust. The relief that washed over her raw soul was soothing, a balm to her wounded spirit, like a gentle hand on a fevered brow. Elara had come to Ursa to learn more about healing the human body, but she was getting more healing for herself than she had bargained for—the kind of healing not even her magic could achieve.

Elara composed herself after what felt like hours, wiping her runny nose on her sleeve and clearing her throat. "Ursa, will you train me as your apprentice? I want to learn about your healing methods so that I might understand my magic better, to control it, and maybe one day even put it to use healing others. Do you think that might be possible?"

"My dear, you have unlocked an essence affinity that has been dormant for generations. I believe that anything is possible."

T HE NEXT MORNING, CAELAN escorted Elara to the infirmary for her first healing lesson with Ursa.

"What did you tell my guards?" she asked.

Caelan shrugged. "The same thing I've been telling them when we're training."

"Which is?"

He smirked. "What do you think might occupy my time with a beautiful woman?"

Elara scoffed. "For that many hours?"

"You have no idea, Princess." He opened the door for her with a flourish. "Have fun."

Elara's neck and cheeks burned as she turned to watch him saunter away, and the heavy door creaked shut behind her.

Ursa cleared her throat, making Elara jump. "Ready?" Ursa asked, holding out a freshly pressed apron.

Elara took it and looped it over her head before tying the strings in a neat bow across her lower back. Her fingers were itching to begin grinding herbs and mixing potions. "I suppose we'll find out together, won't we?"

"Tell me what you've learned so far about your essence affinity," Ursa said. She busied herself by lining up several glass bottles, the one currently in her grip glowing a bright blue.

"Well, cuts and scrapes heal almost instantly. Deeper bruises take a little longer and leave me tired." Elara sidled up next to Ursa. "I just wish I could control it."

Ursa stilled. "How did you find out? Where did you get those injuries?"

"Caelan has been teaching me how to fight. To defend myself." Elara didn't know why, but she suddenly felt self-conscious under Ursa's discerning gaze.

"Good. What else?"

"I haven't been sick—"

"So, no infections? Did you clean your wounds before they healed?"

Elara shook her head. "It happens too fast."

Ursa pursed her lips. "My potions do the same—address and prevent any infection—for wounds. I would recommend removing any debris larger than a splinter though. Any broken bones?"

Elara's eyes widened. "Stars above, no! At least, not yet. Certainly not intentionally. I still feel pain as I did before."

The idea of testing that limit made her uneasy despite knowing it would be beneficial. An icy dread washed over her. She'd discuss it with Caelan later.

"If you do, make sure you set the bone properly before your essence heals the break. My grandmother once healed a boy's broken leg with a potion without a sure set—the poor thing hobbles on it to this day."

The blood drained from Elara's face. "How do your potions work?"

Ursa pulled an enormous leather-bound book from a nearby shelf. She placed it on the table with a loud thud. Elara leaned forward as Ursa's weathered fingers pried it open. "This grimoire has been in my family for hundreds of years. Most of these are natural remedies with herbs. But a few of them, like the one I made for Captain Stormrider at the tournament, rely on a special ingredient."

"Blood," Elara recalled, shivering. "Why?"

"Essence is in the blood. While most of us don't have enough of it to manifest as magic, every living being is blessed with it."

"I read a story about an ancient Serathi who could heal others with her essence affinity without a potion. How is that possible?"

"That I do not know. But mastering the art of potions is a good first step if healing others is your goal. Let's start with a simple one—a sleeping remedy." Ursa licked her finger and flipped through the thin pages of the grimoire until she found the recipe she was looking for.

Perfect, Elara thought, brushing her fingers over the dark shadows under her eyes. *I could use a good night's rest.*

CHAPTER 18

Elara

T HERE WAS A GRAVEYARD of arrows on one end of the long makeshift training room. Several lay on the floor, with a few sticking out of unfortunate pieces of furniture. Elara winced as another of her shots missed the mark, adding to the count when it skittered to the floor a few feet away. Her ears burned with embarrassment. The hay-and-canvas target was a mere fraction of a distance away from her compared to the shots Caelan had made in the tournament, yet she couldn't even get one of her arrows to the target twenty strides away. Her knuckles turned white around her bow.

"I don't think this one's for me," she finally conceded. The pair had been testing out different weapons each week, trying to find a suitable fit.

Caelan shook his golden head and strolled over to her. "Take your stance."

"Caelan, really, I don't—"

"Take your stance." His eyes bored into hers.

"Fine," she huffed, placing her feet hip distance apart and drawing an arrow back.

"Wider," he said, nudging her front foot forward. She held her tongue and glared at the target, which was also mocking her.

He inched closer behind her, placing a hand on her stomach. "Engage your core."

Heat bloomed under his palm, causing her already-warm cheeks to flare hotter.

"Good. Elbow down." His fingers brushed her arm, guiding her elbow down and sending a ripple of goose bumps across her flesh.

"Now use your mouth," he whispered, his breath hot on her neck, his cheek nearly touching hers.

"Excuse me?" She pulled away, but he held her firmly in place, one hand on her waist and the other on her shoulder. Her heart fluttered.

"Touch your cheek. Use your mouth as an anchor," he said, voice thick with amusement.

Elara rolled her eyes.

He wrapped his hand around her grip on the bow. "Relax, Princess. Now, inhale. Exhale. Release."

Thwack. The arrow hit the outermost ring of the target.

I did it!

Caelan stepped back, grinning at her. "How did that feel?"

"Incredible," she breathed, heart still racing from his closeness.

Caelan held out his hand, and Elara passed him the bow, their fingers brushing and sending a now-familiar jolt up her arm. She shook her head. "I still think we should keep trying other weapons." She sighed. The days were growing shorter and colder, the winter solstice—and their wedding—creeping closer. Her progress was agonizingly slow, and she was no closer to controlling her magic or securing her family.

"You did well enough with the short sword. We can continue to focus on that, along with hand-to-hand combat. That will give you enough to defend yourself in a pinch if needed." He leaned against the window, the leaded glass groaning.

"What does any of this have to do with controlling my essence affinity?" Elara asked.

"It's about discipline, Princess. A powerful body begets a powerful mind. Still, it wouldn't hurt for you to keep researching the Serathi, to see if you can dig up anything that might be useful."

Elara scoffed. "What do you think I do all day when we're not training? I'm sure Silas and Felix are tired of lurking in the library at this point."

Caelan grinned. "Keep looking. We'll keep practicing."

Elara folded her arms across her chest. "How old were you?" she asked.

Caelan raised his eyebrows in question.

She cleared her throat. "How old were you when you realized you were a Moiren?" She'd wondered about the origin of his power, never having seen its like—even at the tournament, since they'd missed the Thal'Moira and Thal'Embra.

"Ah," he said. "Just a lad, probably around six or seven. My mother was giving me a bath when I made miniature waves for my toy sailboat." His eyes warmed at the sweet memory, then he looked down at his hands, picking at his fingernails.

Elara's heart clenched, but she nodded, changing the subject back to her initial question "How long before you could control it?"

A line formed between his eyebrows. "A few years. My father was strict in my training, so I had to learn quickly." He rubbed his hands together absentmindedly.

"We don't have years," she said. She needed to control it—to conceal it from Lord Stormrider and the rest of the court.

"I know. But you're an adult, you're smart. You're catching on quickly."

"It doesn't feel that way." She sighed.

Caelan titled his head, considering her. "Give me your hand."

Elara held out her hand, palm up. He curled his fingers around her wrist and pulled her a step closer to him. Taking a small knife in his other fist, he made a deep cut on her palm. She hissed in pain but resisted the urge to tug her arm out of his grasp.

"Sorry," he murmured. "Now, essence is a natural part of your being. Close your eyes, picture it as something solid that you can hold on to."

"Like another arm?" she asked.

"No, like the physical manifestation of a memory. Something that represents who you are to your core. It's a part of your soul, as much as a part of your body."

Elara closed her eyes tight and took a deep breath, visualizing some of her happiest moments: gardening in springtime with

Thalia, the blooms bursting in their full color; baking with her mother, both of them covered in flour; reading her favorite book for the first time in her father's office, curled up at his feet under his desk.

Nothing stuck.

"It's not working," she grumbled.

"Give it time. It's not as easy as it sounds—"

"Wait! There," she breathed.

In her mind's eye, she was lying in a meadow, the sunshine soft on her skin, the grass tickling the backs of her arms and neck as she watched fluffy clouds roll by. A raven flew above her, casting a shadow across her eyes.

"I know you," she whispered.

As if responding to her presence, the raven landed with a soft thud, its head cocked, a low croak escaping its throat.

"Elara!" Caelan's hands were on her shoulders, shaking her roughly.

Her eyes flew open as the vision fell away. Caelan inspected her face, cupping her clammy cheek with his palm. Worry flickered in his eyes.

"What happened? Are you all right?" he asked.

Elara looked down at her hand. The flesh had already melded itself back together, staunching the blood, the only reminder of her injury a dull ache that soon faded to nothing.

"It didn't work," she whispered, deflated.

"What didn't work?"

"I found a memory—at least, I think it was a memory. Let's try again," she said.

"No, Elara," he said gently. "That's enough for today."

He said her name with such intimacy, it startled her into submission. It wasn't the first time she'd heard her name on his lips, but the way he said it—slow and deliberate—made her heart race.

Elara scowled and wiped her bloody palm on her trousers, ignoring her rapid pulse. "Ursa had an interesting idea," she said. "We should test the limits of my healing."

Caelan frowned. "What did you have in mind?"

"Well, what types of injuries are the most common in combat?"

He blanched. "No."

"But—" she protested.

"How about this: have dinner with me, and I'll consider it." He folded his arms across his chest, a smirk playing on his lips.

Dinner? Elara paused, considering his request. *Does this mean that he's falling for me?*

Caelan ran a hand through his hair, the confident gleam in his eyes fading.

"It's fine if you don't want—"

"No, I do," she said. "I'll have dinner with you. *If* you promise to really think about testing my limits."

"You've got a deal, Princess." He grinned.

CHAPTER 19

Elara

A FTER A FEW TOUGH days of training, Elara was itching for a reprieve from Caelan Stormrider—helping her, teaching her . . . driving her mad with his delicious flirtations. She might not have believed it if she hadn't been living it. Needing a distraction as well as rest, she changed into a simple outfit of a fine linen shirt and loose trousers, then threw her hair into a knot at the nape of her neck. She journeyed down to the kitchen—Silas a respectful distance behind her—and selected an apron and bonnet from a row of hooks. After covering her hair with the bonnet, she looped the top half of the apron over her head and tied the rest around her waist. Like this, she was invisible—not a princess, not a warrior or healer in training, and certainly not a doting fiancée.

The kitchen staff were used to seeing her here when she'd had a long or difficult day, so they gave her space and acted like she belonged. That was part of the appeal. She could silence her mind and wear herself out with simple, physical tasks much less intense than her workouts with Caelan. Down here, she could finally breathe, the scent of yeast and rosemary filling her lungs with each deep inhale.

She located an enormous pile of dough sitting on a flour-dusted table and began kneading. The dough was thick—definitely for her favorite coarse brown bread—and provided just enough resistance that beads of sweat quickly formed on her brow. She jabbed her fists into the dough several times, pretending that it was Caelan's handsome face. Satisfied with the way the punches landed, she continued palming the dough like normal.

Training that morning could have gone better. Cheeks warming, she recalled the look on Caelan's face as he'd leaned over her prone body on the ground. Her tailbone had already healed, but she resisted the urge to rub her backside to ease the ghost of the pain. Her pride had not yet recovered. She punched the dough again, imagining cracking the ever-present smirk on his face.

Elara was thankful for her mentors and their tutelage, but she was exhausted. She bounced back from the physical demands of her training, but her mind was bursting. Over the course of the last week with Caelan, she had learned dozens of new combat strategies. Adding in anatomy and potions sessions with Ursa filled an already-full cup that had Elara feeling like her mind was overflowing.

The lead baker tapped her on the shoulder to let her know it was time for the dough, and Elara, to rest. She found her next victim—a dirty soup pot that needed a good hard scrub.

Elara and Thalia had hidden out together in this kitchen all their lives. It gave the young princesses a way to escape the pressure of court life and the eyes that always watched them, even in Thalia's garden. Elara could almost see her little sister, with her brown hair lighter than Elara's own black strands, sitting on the countertop and swinging her gangly legs. They both had their mother's sapphire-blue eyes.

Elara scrubbed the pot harder, fingers protesting as her knuckles knocked against metal. When the queen had first found her daughters playing in the kitchen, the servants had scurried away as Elara prepared to defend Thalia from their scolding. Instead, their mother had tied a flour-coated apron over her shimmering ball gown and showed them how to make her favorite lemon tarts. The three of them had laughed and taken turns marking one another's faces with flour. A tear rolled over the tip of Elara's nose before falling into the pot with a soft plop.

A broom fell to the floor with a loud clatter, startling her and the others in the kitchen. Elara turned to discover a figure lurking in the corner near a cluster of mops. She wiped her soapy hands on her apron and investigated. As Elara got closer, she realized the intruder was a fluffy black cat. It emanated a calming aura, and as she approached, a sense of peace washed over her.

She chuckled as she stooped to pick it up. The cat rubbed its small head into her palm before melting into her cradled arms. Elara turned back to the kitchen staff, smiling, and a few of them let out embarrassed giggles, dissipating the tension.

"Does this little one belong to any of you?" she asked. They all shook their heads "no."

"Come with me, sweetheart," Elara cooed. "Let's get you some water and a tasty treat."

The cat tucked its head under her chin and purred, tickling her neck with its whiskers.

Happy to have claimed another friend, Elara watered and fed the little cat before taking it up to her room with her. Stoic Silas raised an eyebrow at her new furry companion. Elara grinned back at him. He shook his head, but the corner of his mouth quirked up as she passed through the threshold of her chambers. She placed the cat on her bed and changed into her nightgown. Then she tucked herself under the covers, humming to herself as the cat watched with its glowing green eyes shining in the lantern light. Once settled, Elara made *tsking* sounds to beckon it over. The cat—a female, Elara realized—melted into a puddle of black fuzz on her lap.

"What shall I call you, little one?" Elara wondered aloud.

My name is Lysandra, a soft voice said in Elara's mind.

Her hand stopped stroking the soft fur.

Great, Elara thought, *I've finally lost my mind. Thinking I can hear a cat's thoughts.* She shook her head to herself and scratched behind the cat's ears.

You're not mad, Elara. My name is Lysandra, and I am no ordinary cat.

Mouth falling open and heart dropping into her stomach, Elara asked tentatively, "Then what are you?" This had to be some sort of trick, maybe an illusion, courtesy of Lady Seraphine.

You've seen me before. With a stretch, the cat rose, and its form shifted, its fur turning into sleek black feathers as it became a raven. *I have been here since the Stormriders arrived at the palace, watching you.* Then, with a flash of dark feathers and a low growl, the raven transformed into a wolf-dog. The bed groaned under the animal's weight, and Elara was grateful it wasn't still in her lap.

Elara's heartbeat pounded in her ears, and she resisted the urge to bolt from the strange creature. Nothing in her books mentioned shape-shifting animals. Nothing in the fairy stories of her childhood mentioned them either. The raven was impossible to forget from the morning after the invasion—and her vision—and she remembered the canine eating scraps at the festival. Something in her gut told her that Lysandra was here to help her.

Come, the wolf commanded, leaping from the bed and turning back into the cat midair. Elara pulled on her robe and slid her feet into slippers before following the cat to the adjacent washroom. Lysandra pressed her tiny paw against a tile, and the wall behind the clawfoot tub creaked open. Elara's jaw fell open once more. She'd never seen this hidden door before. Her fingers brushed along the floral wallpaper, tracing the seams of the opening.

"How did you find this tunnel?" Elara asked.

You think you're the only talented spy in the palace? Lysandra replied.

Elara gulped, but followed her into the darkness.

The short tunnel let out in a familiar hallway. Elara straightened the frame of the portrait that concealed the exit. Her fingertips traced the canvas—it was a painting of her father. She shoved her longing down and turned back to Lysandra. The onyx creature trotted ahead, pausing occasionally to turn and check that Elara still followed. They headed to the library—Elara recognized the path since her own feet had worn a rut in the rug along the route. Lysandra waited for Elara to open the heavy oak door. Once they passed through the threshold, the odd pair climbed the gilded curved staircase to the mezzanine.

Lysandra morphed into a raven—the flapping of her wings echoing the fluttering of Elara's heart—and flew to a shelf that was at least twice Elara's height. She tapped her charcoal-gray beak against a spine. *Here.*

Elara found a rolling ladder and pulled it into place before scaling it to retrieve the tome. Tucking the book under her arm, she silently cursed herself—she'd yet to visit this part of the library and realized she might not have for several more weeks, according to her plan for dividing up the stacks and searching through them. She planted her feet back on the floor and cracked the book open, thumbing through the thin pages. The book contained messy scrawling handwriting, unlike the elegant looping letters of the palace scribes. She didn't recognize the language.

"What is this?"

Not here. The raven circled around another shelf, prompting Elara to jog to follow her once more. Lysandra landed on a desk in front of a tapestry, claws clacking. The sound echoed against the book stacks.

The tapestry looked familiar; the swirling patterns and rich jewel tones felt strangely nostalgic. This piece and the one depicting the woman and her daughters in the meadow that hid another tunnel entrance likely shared the same creator. Elara lifted a lamp from the desk to the art and ran her fingers over the fabric. Her fingertips came away black with dust.

"I don't think I've seen this one before." A wrinkle formed between her brows. She knew every inch of the palace—almost better than the king's guards. The tapestry stretched from the mahogany baseboards at her feet to the ceiling, thirty feet above her head. She stared, awestruck by its immense size. It wove a tale with the colored threads, the shapes and shifts in light depicting various tones to the story.

It began with a tree.

A tree with a thousand curling roots and lush branches against a midnight sky, dotted with constellations. Below the mighty trunk, the roots braided together to frame the world. The map spanned the entirety of the known world—the continent of Serendith, the seas, and even the mysterious unknown lands to the southwest.

Each city was marked and colored, with ornate depictions of key landmarks near each of them. To the north were the Stormspire Mountains, stitched in black, white, and silver—with a large watchtower being struck by a bolt of lightning representing the Celestial Summit. To the east were the Shadowed Isles and the grand citadel of Veilkeep, a deep cobalt blue. To the south, the palace of Valoria was stitched in emerald green and surrounded by pops of pink flowering trees. A glowing orange forge set into the side of a volcano oozing red lava represented their closest neighbor, Emberreach.

Elara's eyes widened as they drank in the scene to the west. The Verdant Forest spanned at least a third of the continent, far more than any map she'd ever studied showed. Trees dotted the landscape, forming a protective fortress around a palace similar to her own and a miniature version of the mystical tree above. Swirls of every color formed floating rings around the tree.

Essence, she thought.

The next panel below made her heart fall into the pit of her stomach. In that moment, Elara felt transported to a battlefield, the mud squelching beneath her boots, shoulder to shoulder with the other humans holding the line at the edge of the Verdant Forest. Arrows and swords, horses and wolves, druids and humans. All clashed. Bodies piled up on both sides.

Then another map. The land was now split by two mountain ranges that had doubled in size. The jade-green forests protecting the sacred tree were now black, scorched. The palace there was a pile of ruins, and the rings around the tree were gone.

The Shattering. Elara stepped back, clutching her chest. Never before had she understood the pain that war had caused her world. Now she understood how little she truly knew, that in many ways she was still a child, unlearned and raw.

Father was right, she thought. *I'm not ready to rule.*

You don't have a choice, Elara, Lysandra said into her mind. *Ready or not, Serendith needs healing. You must find a way to restore peace.*

Elara nodded slowly. "Starting with keeping Lord Stormrider away from my father's throne."

CHAPTER 20

Elara

L ADY SERAPHINE HUNCHED OVER a set of beakers, each filled with a different colored liquid. A tiny flame danced under the largest vessel, which bubbled and filled the room with a sour smell. She was humming a pretty tune as Elara stepped into the makeshift closet laboratory. Caelan had told her where to find Seraphine—holed up in her room, fiddling with her potions—and he'd been right. A bubble popped, and lilac smoke puffed out of the glass, turning into the shape of a butterfly before disappearing.

The last butterfly she'd seen like that from Seraphine had been a taunt. Elara swallowed her bitterness. "That's a beautiful song," she said.

Seraphine nearly dropped a beaker and peered up at Elara from behind gold-rimmed spectacles. "What do you want?" Her emerald-green eyes were hard, unyielding.

"I wanted to invite you to tea," Elara said, shrugging as if it wasn't a big deal—or the worst idea she'd ever had in her life. When she'd suggested it to Caelan, he'd encouraged her, claiming that his childhood friend was easily misunderstood. And Elara needed allies wherever she could get them.

"Why would I want to have tea with you?" Seraphine asked, running her hands down her blond braid before slinging it over her shoulder, smiling with feline delight.

"Look," Elara huffed, "we don't have to be friends, but Caelan cares about you. I thought it would be nice for us to set aside our differences and get to know each other."

Seraphine blinked, her face revealing nothing of her thoughts. "You could . . . do that?" she asked after several moments filled only with the sound of boiling. "After everything? After . . . what I did?"

For the first time, Elara saw the woman's carefully constructed facade crack, the tremor in her hands revealing her humanity.

"Was that you?" Elara challenged. "Or was it him?"

Seraphine cast her eyes down at her beakers, staying silent.

"I know that Lord Stormrider is . . . persuasive. I suspect he'd make things difficult for you if you defied his orders."

Seraphine nodded, a faraway look clouding her face.

"Besides, I trust Caelan's judgement. Any friend of his can be a friend of mine. I'm sure of it," Elara finished, hoping she sounded more confident than she felt. She wanted to trust Caelan, and if she could trust his friendship and ally with Seraphine, maybe she could tell them about the seer's prophecy.

"You're a better woman than I." She shook her head, a tiny smile threatening to soften her sharp features.

"Then let's start fresh, Seraphine," Elara said, offering her hand.

Seraphine grasped it and looked her in the eye. "You can call me Sera."

THE FOLLOWING AFTERNOON, ELARA fiddled with her teaspoon, foot tapping beneath her powdery-blue gown, as she waited for Sera's arrival. This was a bad idea. The tearoom was a hub for the ladies of the court, and dozens of them milled about, gliding between a sea of round tables in their formal outfits. Whispers bounced off the walls, dampened only a little by the dozens of oil paintings the queen had personally selected to decorate the space. A tiny sadness tapped at the back of Elara's mind—this was her first time in this room without the queen and Thalia present. She shoved the memories down.

Elara winced as one woman—Lady Isoldea—traipsed over to the royal table.

"I haven't seen you here in ages," she crooned. "Congratulations on your engagement." Lady Isoldea's half-hearted smile didn't reach her pretty brown eyes.

"Sorry I'm late," Sera mercifully interrupted.

Elara nodded at Lady Isoldea. "Thank you so much. We'll have to catch up some other time, I'm afraid. I have important wedding details to discuss with Lady Seraphine."

Lady Isoldea sniffed and turned on her heel, then headed back to her own table, where she joined half a dozen other women. The flurry of gossip that bloomed at that table quickly assuaged Elara's pity for her and her history with Caelan.

Elara turned her attention back to Sera. "Please, have a seat."

Sera shrugged and sat across from Elara in the chair a footman pulled out for her. The other conversations in the room faded to a low hum as the two women—the princess and the sorceress—sized each other up.

Elara cleared her throat. "I hope you don't mind, but I have a favor to ask of you. I have been researching more about Serendith's history and found something that could make an interesting gift for my sister Thalia. Her birthday is just after the winter solstice."

Sera glanced at Felix, who stood beside a nearby window well within earshot, then back at Elara. "At your service, Your Highness," she said, rolling her eyes.

Elara sagged with relief. *At least she knows how to play the game.* She thought back to the taunting, to the tears rolling down her mother's cheeks at Sera's hand. *Maybe she's been playing it well all along.*

"Here," Elara said, passing a piece of parchment across the table, then wrapping her hands around her warm teacup. "I found an old book in the library. It looks to be a children's book—fairy tales and nursery rhymes. I don't recognize the language and was wondering if you might help me translate it."

Sera picked up the parchment and laid it flat on the starched white tablecloth, smoothing it. Elara had copied down several lines of text from the journal Lysandra had helped her discover in the library, lines that she and Elara had already translated. Sera's brows knit together in concentration.

"Do you have a quill?" she asked.

Elara nodded, passing a quill and tiny pot of ink across the table. She sipped her tea and glanced around the rest of the room as Sera worked, thankful that the other tables were now fully preoccupied by their own conversations and appetizers.

"It's not a language I'm familiar with, but it's close enough to Iskren—my parents taught me when I was little. Here," she said, handing the parchment back to Elara and popping a dumpling into her mouth.

Elara read through Sera's translation. It was perfect—three simple lines of a poem from the journal:

In the hush of the hollow where moonflowers gleam,
The stones start to whisper and cradle a dream,
Tread soft, little sapling, the roots are awake . . .

"Thank you," Elara breathed. Sera had passed her test. Not only could she translate the language, but she'd been honest about it. A step in the right direction.

"I'm happy to help with your . . . translation," Sera said, eyes flashing to Felix once more, "whenever you'd like."

Elara nodded, gratitude for Sera's help—and secrecy—tugging her lips into a smile.

CHAPTER 21

Caelan

T HE STAFF SET THE table with the finest flatware in the palace, and bouquets of flowers filled the air with their sweet scent. A warm glow illuminated the dining room as candlelight flickered from the arms of gilded candelabras, casting long dancing shadows across the walls and ceiling. Caelan paced behind his chair, running his hands through his unruly blond hair. The thought of his first dinner here, a tense affair with his father where every glance between him and Elara had crackled with animosity, made him shudder.

Are we still enemies? He hoped not. Despite his best efforts—and hers, which were considerable—the two of them were drawn together. Their bond transcended the camaraderie of training partners or the formality of a politically motivated union.

Caelan stopped his pacing for long enough to pick out a tiny fruit tart and pop it into his mouth, savoring its sweetness.

He cared for Elara, trusted her. Together, they had overcome his arrogance and her ignorance. If someone had asked him when he first arrived in Valoria what his thoughts of the princess were, he would've told them she was a spoiled, naive girl—or worse, a liar. Now, after their weeks of training and joint pretending, she had proven him wrong. Not only did her beauty take his breath away, but the strength in her eyes showed a spirit that had endured much—just like he had. The selflessness with which she sacrificed for her family made his palms sweat.

Despite insurmountable odds, the pair found solace in each other. His feelings for her exceeded any he'd previously experienced, even those for Sera. Elara was now his reason to keep fighting, to escape his father's scheming once and for all. He straightened his coat, the velvet trim catching on his calluses, and picked at an imaginary fleck of dirt on the blue suede.

Elara appeared in the doorway, her emerald-green dress shimmering in the buttery light. The silver embroidery, a pattern of climbing vines swirling around her dress, highlighted the gray flecks in her bright blue eyes. Her dark hair fell in loose curls around her face and down her back, a circlet dripping diamonds onto her forehead. Her long skirts swished across the carpet as she glided over to him, smiling, her eyes sparkling and cheeks pink.

Caelan swallowed hard and strode over to her seat and pulled out the chair for her. She sat in it, expertly folding the fabric of her gown out of her way, and reached for her crystal wine goblet. The purple liquid deepened the flush on her cheeks as she drank.

She's nervous, he realized, placing his hand on top of hers.

"Thank you for agreeing to have dinner with me," Caelan said. He took his seat across from her and lifted his goblet toward her in a silent toast before they both took another long drink.

The camaraderie of their recent training couldn't quell the butterflies in his stomach—he felt more nervous than ever. From Elara's rapid breathing, he guessed she did too. This was their first proper date. He finally felt ready—the moment had arrived when he could tell her how much she meant to him, the words a weight on his chest. The wine he had in his goblet, and the few drinks he'd had prior to this dinner, gave him the courage he needed. But before he could speak, Elara cleared her throat.

"There's something I need to tell you," she said.

He nodded, encouraging her to continue.

"I met someone."

"Oh." His heart fell into his stomach.

"Not like that!" She shook her head, a small smile playing on her full lips. Her face became serious once more. "Her name is Lysandra. She's a new . . . friend. She showed me this incredible tapestry . . ." Elara trailed off, eyes flicking to the staff.

Caelan sat up straighter in his chair. He tapped his knife against his glass three times, and all the attendants in the room turned toward him.

"Excuse us. I'd like to have a private conversation with my future wife," he said. In moments, the room emptied save for the couple. "Please, go on."

Elara's shoulders relaxed, as if she'd been holding her breath awaiting privacy. "It's in the library. It tells the story of the Shattering. I never knew the war's effect on the landscape. Lysandra helped me find this journal too. It details the druids and their connection to the origin of essence. I have only made a little progress reading it, but it seems promising." Her words tumbled out of her mouth in a rush of excitement.

Caelan knew all about the war. He'd basically grown up on bedtime stories about it—ones that had given him nightmares as a boy. The way his father saw it, the Evensongs had betrayed the Stormriders, but the history books had recorded the reverse. Heroes in their own story, the Evensongs claimed to have defeated the druids and saved humanity despite the betrayal of their closest allies. The resulting exile left his family stranded in a strange, barren land filled with the dangerous Nimireth. Caelan's father had been plotting his return, and his revenge, ever since his great-grandfather had told him those same bedtime stories.

Caelan took a bite of steak, considering what she'd shared and shoving down his nerves about Elara's new ally. "The Shattering. The war that split our families apart in the first place. It can't be a coincidence that this friend of yours is leading us down this path. Tell me about her."

"Remember when I told you about the raven in my vision?"

"Of course."

"It's her." Elara winced, recognizing how ridiculous she sounded.

"Is she actually a bird?" he asked.

"Sometimes. I'm not sure exactly what she is. She's a shape-shifter and communicates with me telepathically. A protector, maybe?"

Caelan fought to keep a straight face. *Impossible. She has a familiar?* he thought. "Then a helpful ally, to be sure. I'd love to meet her," he said, unwilling to tell her what Lysandra really was, or what her sudden appearance might make Elara.

"So, you don't think I'm insane?" She beamed, her flirtatious self returning.

Caelan chuckled. "Not for that reason. Trust me, I've seen enough magic in my time that it'll take more than a strange animal companion to scare me off."

"Good, since I also wanted to talk with you about our wedding night," she said.

Caelan's eyebrows rose at the awkward change in the subject, but he said nothing, restraining himself so that she could continue.

"I assume your father expects us to consummate the marriage?" she asked boldly.

Caelan nodded, feeling his own cheeks redden and a rush of warmth at the thought of being intimate with her.

"And you? What do you expect?" She took another gulp of her wine and a bite of something cheesy from her plate.

She sounded calm, but shifted in her chair, clearly uncomfortable having this conversation. *That makes two of us. I'd rather keep talking about war*, he thought.

Caelan chose his next words carefully. It was imperative to him that she understood the true depth of his admiration for her—to show her the appropriate respect, his father's expectations be damned. "I . . . I want you to be comfortable," he said. "I don't care what my father wants. I want to be with you. And I want your—our—first time to be special. To be real. If that means we wait, then we wait until we are both ready." His words were raw, no trace of the infamously snarky rogue or arrogant warrior—just Caelan. His heart pounded as he awaited her response.

"Why do you even care?" she whispered, the soft sound like a dagger to his chest.

Sapphire-blue eyes met his as he reached over the table and took her hands, tiny compared to his broad calloused ones.

Caelan slowly, gently, lifted her hand to his mouth, kissing her palm, hoping she'd see the answer to her question in his eyes. *Because I love you.* Her face flushed, and she didn't pull away, so he lifted her other hand and repeated the gesture. He released her and drank deeply from his goblet.

Elara nodded, then pursed her lips. "It wouldn't be my first time . . ."

And then he was choking on his wine, caught in a fit of coughing. The fire of jealousy ran through his veins. He did his best to douse those thoughts and focus on her. He schooled his features into something resembling calm. "My apologies. That's, well, unexpected," he said. Elara opened her mouth to retort, but he cut her off. "But not unwelcome," he added quickly.

"Jealous?" she asked, raising an eyebrow at him.

"I'd be an idiot not to be. Who?" The image of another man touching her, holding her, flashed in his mind. He clenched his teeth.

Elara squirmed. "That's none of your business."

"Tell me. Who?" The question burned in him, envy tangled up with his own desire. "Please," he added, though it came out more as a growl.

"No."

He leaned back in his chair, crossing his arms. "I bet I could guess."

She rolled her eyes as he tapped his finger against his chin in mock consideration.

"Kaz? No, not him, the other one. Jalin," he said, recalling her former guards.

Her silent blush confirmed his suspicion, and he grinned. "I saw you two together at a party, the one where you saved that poor servant girl."

"Caelan, I—"

He held up a hand. "Please, there's no need to explain. You are your own woman, Elara. It would be unfair of me to judge you. Do you love him?" he dared ask, bracing himself against her answer.

"No, not in that way. Not anymore."

"Then it's of no concern to me." He sagged in relief.

Elara exhaled. "Thank you," she said.

"For what?"

"For being less of an ass than you usually are," she teased. "Really though, thank you. Not everyone is as . . . egalitarian with these things."

"I have a past too, as you well know."

"Don't remind me!" Elara laughed as she threw a small sausage at his face, which he expertly caught with a stream of water and redirected to his plate.

"I don't think I'll ever get used to that," she admitted.

"Good," he said. "That'll make it easier for me to keep impressing you." As much as he wished it weren't true, underneath his words of triumph lurked a trace of a deep, unending sort of shame and defeat.

"Do you think I could ever make you happy?" He thought about the countless hours they'd spent together—he'd been happy to train her, listen to her talk, or sit in comfortable silence.

"You already do," she replied, breath hitching—as if her own words caught her off guard.

Caelan shuddered and closed his eyes, every inch of his body going taut as her words washed over him.

"Will you tell me more about your family?" he asked, needing a reprieve to regain his composure. He immediately regretted the question, if only for the pain that flickered in her eyes.

"Caelan, will you help me free them?" she whispered.

"I can try to get a letter to them," he offered. "To let them know that you are safe—under my protection." It was all he could do to show her how much she meant to him.

"And then?"

His eyes stayed locked on hers. "We wed," he murmured.

She gulped. "And then?"

A muscle in Caelan's jaw twitched. "Then we get your family back." He held her gaze, brow furrowing before he spoke his next words carefully. "And get my father out of Valoria."

Elara's lips parted. "Are you sure?"

"He's dangerous. Not just to you"—Caelan grasped Elara's hand with his scarred one—"but for Serendith. I won't be his puppet. Not anymore."

Her eyes sparkled with tears. "Thank you," she said, her sad smile melting the ice wall around his heart. Not tonight, then, but when the time was right, he would tell her how he felt.

CHAPTER 22

Elara

THE PALACE WAS A whir of activity. Elara's long days had begun to blur together. The council meetings had ended—thankfully with little damage done by Lord Stormrider. The servants' thick wool skirts swished across the polished marble floors of the main ballroom as Elara directed them to complete their final tasks. She had offered to help plan the ball celebrating her engagement, to the great—and somewhat sickening—pleasure of Lord Stormrider.

Good, let him think I am still the docile princess. Elara was presented with two floral arrangements and selected the one on her left, which had blush and lilac blooms. Another checkmark on her never-ending list.

A private food tasting was next on her agenda for the day, and she had invited Sera to join her. Unfortunately, according to Caelan, Sera would not offer her a lot of input in the meal department. Her magical talents included being able to transform any food into tasting like her own favorite flavors. Elara didn't mind; she was just happy for the opportunity to have a meal with a new ally, which she sorely needed after weeks of training with Caelan and Ursa. And her cooperation had resulted in more freedom—her shadows wouldn't be present.

Elara settled at the little round tea table situated in one of the ballroom's many alcoves and waited for Sera to arrive. Before her lay a delicate spread of floral teas, light cheeses, a small selection of cured meats, fruit, and a tower of fluffy pastries. Several candelabras lit the room with their soft glow while the afternoon sun filtered in through the windows. A footman announced Sera's arrival, and she floated across the room to the table, clad in a tight lavender gown that highlighted her slender figure. Elara rose and embraced her roughly, causing Sera's emerald eyes to widen. After a heartbeat, Sera wrapped her arms around Elara's back, completing the embrace.

As both women sat, a deep rumbling growl from Elara's hungry stomach cut through the quiet. Sera let out a snort, causing Elara to stifle her own giggles before they eagerly filled their plates with the mouthwatering array of food before them. They ate in comfortable companionable silence.

Pressing her napkin to her lips in a graceful motion that would make any noblewoman envious, Sera asked, "So, what would you like to know?"

Elara leaned back in her chair, placing her hand on her now-full stomach. "Is my family safe?"

"No. Next question," Sera said. Her response wasn't unkind—Elara actually preferred the directness after weeks of platitudes and rumor-fueled half-truths from servants and courtiers. Elara's throat hitched. She'd yet to pen the letter to her family and thought about what she'd want it to say. *I just want them to know that I'm alive, engaged. That I will do anything to see them safely returned home.*

"I just want them home. Do you think Lord Stormrider will bring them back after the wedding?"

Sera's eyes widened, an almost imperceptible change in expression that years of court training allowed Elara to clock.

"He wants more than the wedding, doesn't he?" Elara asked.

"What do you think he wants, Elara?" She had her pointed chin casually propped on her fist, concern—and perhaps a bit of surprise at that concern—shining in her eyes.

"To use me to control my father? And to see his son on the throne one day, as king. But to what end?"

Sera shook her head. "You're thinking too small. I have lived with the Stormriders for as long as I can remember. I came to them as a girl, naive and trusting. He was never like a father to me, or if he was, he was a terrible one. He's not doing all of this for a legacy. Whatever he wants, he wants it for himself."

A pit opened up in Elara's stomach. *What if he doesn't want to wait for Caelan and me to ascend the throne? He could kill my father.* A chill snaked its way down her spine. She quelled it as best she could. *If he wanted the throne for himself, he would have killed us all already. No, he needs us for something . . .*

"You're close to him. What is he planning?"

"I'm not privy to the details. I'm simply a tool." Sera stabbed a morsel on her plate with such force that Elara feared she'd crack the porcelain with her fork.

A tool. And I'm a pawn. Both of us trapped, used, Elara thought.

"Sera, Caelan and I will wed. Once we get my family back, we will figure out a way to defeat him and free ourselves. Will you help us?" Caelan had made it clear during their dinner that the only way to save her family was to go through with the wedding. And Elara needed Sera on her side.

"Yes," Sera breathed, eyes shimmering with sincerity.

Elara released a breath she hadn't realized she'd been holding. "Thank you." A genuine smile tugged the corners of her lips upward.

Sera played with the end of her braid. "I'm sorry, by the way. About your family. About the part I played in their imprisonment. I know what you must be thinking—everyone thinks I'm a monster. A witch. A *sorceress.*"

Elara's heart lurched. She imagined the lost little girl that Sera had once been, orphaned and afraid. Like Elara, she'd had to forge herself into something formidable, at least on the exterior. Deep down, they weren't that different after all. Both were misunderstood by the world around them.

"I'm sorry about Jalin and Kaz too. He made me do it," Sera added.

"I thought so." Elara gulped. "What exactly did you do to them?"

Sera touched the pendant hanging from her neck. "I used my essence to conceal their memories after the coup—temporarily, of course."

A shiver ran dean Elara's spine. She was alone with the second-most dangerous being she'd ever encountered—after Lord Stormrider himself. The plaster walls of the room seemed to press in around her.

"You've grown up in the shadow of a monster, and yet here you are. A talented mage. A loyal friend to Caelan." Elara folded her hands in her lap. "I'm sorry that fate robbed you of a family like mine."

"It wasn't all bad. I had Caelan. And I remember bits and pieces of my parents. I catch my mother's eyes staring back at me in the mirror. Or hum the lullaby my father used to sing me to sleep."

Elara nodded, thinking about her own mother. Her striking blue eyes—which she'd shared with both her daughters—bright with laughter as the king bounced little Thalia on his knee while the queen brushed Elara's hair. She felt the echoes of her family's presence everywhere in the palace; around every corner she turned was a reminder of them. At least her memories didn't feel like ghosts just yet. With any luck, she'd make new ones. Perhaps even a few with Sera in them.

"Caelan really loves you, you know."

Elara's mouth fell open. *He loves me?* She'd suspected as much after their dinner, but to hear Sera say it so plainly . . .

"Do you love him?" Sera asked, raising a perfectly sculpted eyebrow.

"I care about him." Elara didn't hesitate, her voice sincere as she shared the truth out loud for the first time. "Do you still love him?" she asked nervously.

"Yes," Sera replied. "But not romantically. Not anymore. We were children, friends long before we were lovers. He is different with you. This whole thing has changed him. No more women, no more aether. He's growing into his own man, not just a shadow of his father. I am happy for you both, truly. To have found each other in the midst of this nightmare."

Elara swirled her goblet of sweet wine, staring into the liquid and wishing she could drown in it. A knot of guilt tightened in her stomach. Caelan desired her—was in love with her. Against all odds, her plan to win him over had somehow worked. And though she had no hope of escaping their wedding, she was no longer certain that was what she wanted.

CHAPTER 23

Elara

IN THE STAR-SPECKLED SKY, the full moon showed her face, casting the pond below in silver and shadow. Elara admired a family of swans—three gray fledglings trailing their mother—leaving peaceful ripples in their wake. It was unseasonably late for them to be present on the chilly lake, as autumn had ended and winter was creeping into the landscape. She leaned on the windowsill as she waited for Caelan to arrive to escort her to the ball. They would make another grand entrance, and she wasn't looking forward to it. The more that she was forced to pretend that she was in love with him, the harder it was to remember that it was supposed to be an act.

Fresh guilt bloomed in her stomach as she realized that, with all the planning for the ball going on, she hadn't thought about her training in a few days. Or the prophecy. The silliness of flowers, ribbons, music, and dresses had distracted her. Yet she understood it wasn't as silly as it seemed. Court life revolved around these things.

Elara, praised for her beauty from a young age, now wielded her appearance like a weapon, as she had watched her mother do so many times before. Tonight, a shimmering white gown draped over her shoulders and cascaded down her body. The many layers of tulle in her fluffy skirt made the dress difficult to walk in, but when she twirled on the dance floor, she looked like she was floating, each layer billowing and swirling around her. Iris had twisted her hair up into an elegant bun adorned with delicate white feathers. Elara wanted her audience to think her innocent—naive, even. The more Lord Stormrider, and any of his allies at court, underestimated her, the easier it would be for her and Caelan to rescue her family and defeat his father after the wedding.

The doors, which had been opening and closing with the entrances of other noble guests, finally opened for Elara. *Where is he? Is something wrong?* She raised a brow at Felix, but then schooled her features into a pleasant smile and entered without Caelan. With her first step into the hall, the voices quieted and all the guests turned from their conversations to gawk at her. Elara made eye contact with a few of her preferred nobles before offering the whole of the gathering a graceful nod as she glided down the curved staircase. Elara knew she had achieved her desired effect when she found Lord Stormrider in the crowd. His face was a mix of emotions—pride that his son would possess her, and envy that she would always have more admirers than him.

The bright singing of violins flowed through the ballroom, echoing off the ceiling and polished marble floor. The music filled the atmosphere with a cheerful energy, and hushed gossip intertwined with the notes. Dozens of silver trays held aloft by white-gloved footmen offered a selection of fine appetizers and drinks to the guests. While Elara wore white, all the other guests were clothed in shades of green and blue—a theme chosen by Lord Stormrider to celebrate his house joining with the Evensongs.

She reached the bottom of the grand staircase, and the echoing sounds of the crowd faded as Caelan appeared from the shadows, smoothing his doublet.

"You're late," she said. Elara's cheeks flushed, but she masked her surprise and annoyance as she took his outstretched hand.

"Fashionably so, Princess." Caelan pressed his lips to each of her knuckles, his smile lingering as he looked up at her. The burning in his gaze sent a pleasant shiver down her spine. "Shall we?"

He looped her arm through his and escorted her to the dance floor, his warm eyes never leaving hers. He gestured to the musicians to play their song. The other guests shuffled to clear the space and enjoy Elara and Caelan's first public dance together.

The couple arrived at the center of the dance floor, at the center of attention, where both of them seemed to thrive despite neither of them enjoying it.

"Ready for this, watermage?" Elara's face warmed, and her icy smile melted into a genuine one.

"I'd rather be impaled by a wild stag," he mumbled. "But since you're so lovely, I think I'll make do."

The song that started playing was sweet, the lilting notes light and twinkling. Nothing like the dark, hungry look in Caelan's eyes. He released her arm, offered her a bow, and turned away from her.

Elara mirrored his movements, offering a coy curtsy before giving him her back. They swayed, lifting opposite arms to the side before twirling to face each other.

"Not bad, for a swordsman," she teased.

"If only you moved like this in the training ring." He chuckled.

The beat quickened, becoming less innocent and more romantic. Elara's heart raced to match the new tempo. Their bodies now passed each other in a lively series of steps. Though they hadn't touched again, the air between them crackled with a tension so thick it was almost tangible.

Caelan moved with grace and agility. His flourishes matched hers in their elegance, but where he was the frame, Elara was the art. The audience watched, captivated by the mesmerizing movements and the power of her performance. Why this made her a worthy queen, Elara would never understand. With his controlled movements and unwavering focus, Caelan projected an aura of strength and discipline. They played the game well, even if the rules were suspect.

The last notes of the song rang out, breaking the spell. Caelan spun her around, catching her as she arched her back into a low dip that had the feathers in her hair tickling the floor. The moment she rose, a thunderous applause erupted, shaking the floor beneath her feet. Caelan held her hand while he bowed in triumph before the crowd. Instead of curtsying, Elara lifted her chin, her eyes flashing with defiance. Her cheeks were warm from the effort of the dance, but otherwise, she showed no sign that what she had done—what they had done together—was anything but ordinary for the future queen and king.

The couple emerged from the ballroom and onto a vast stone terrace, the scent of camellias and fresh air filling Elara's lungs. The moonlight cast a silvery sheen onto the pink blooms. The quick shift from crisp to cool air was a reminder that autumn had already crawled to an end. It was a wonder that Elara wasn't freezing in her sleeveless gown. Lanterns twinkled in the nearby garden, and the loud cloud of voices turned into the soft bubbling of fountains.

"You were incredible," Caelan said, his voice breathy. His fingers still held hers, a silent promise that hadn't been broken since that initial grasp. Caelan's gaze locked with hers as he kissed the back of her hand once more.

A sigh slipped from her lips as a buzzing sensation traveled up her arm and down her neck. She felt the weight of Caelan's undivided attention on her—on her every breath and movement. Her gaze warmed, just like her belly.

"Dance with me?" he asked.

"Really? Again?" Elara smiled.

"Just for us this time." Caelan cracked a lazy smile in return.

Elara wrapped her arms around his neck, and he pulled her in close, tugging her hips to meet his. They slowly turned around in a circle, nothing for music but the soothing fountains and their thundering heartbeats.

Caelan rested his chin on her shoulder, stroking the bare skin of her back, sending shivers up and down her spine.

"May I kiss you?" he whispered into her ear before pulling back to gaze at her lips.

Her thoughts raced, making her dizzy.

This wasn't supposed to happen, to be . . . real.

But her lips parted as she leaned in, nodding her consent.

Elara and Caelan's first real kiss was tender, nothing like the way they'd teased each other before. Hope swelled in her chest, a feeling as bright and expansive as the star-filled sky above. They parted, touching their foreheads together for a moment. Caelan wove his fingers into the hair at her nape and pulled her in for another one. This time, they kissed with a ferocious need, their bodies trembling, as if starving for the other's touch.

Elara caressed his chest as he kissed her reverently. She sighed with pleasure as he moaned against her mouth. It was bliss. Caelan trailed his hands down her back and onto her waist. She placed a hand on his cheek. After weeks of playing hunter and prey, each of them swapping roles at any given moment, the two now found each other equally vulnerable.

When they finally parted, Caelan leaned back, admiring her. Her cheeks heated, and he brushed a stray curl behind her ear.

"You're so beautiful, Elara." He said her name like a prayer.

"Thank you," she said.

Elara knew she was stupid to fall in love with her enemy—or rather, her enemy's son. But while she craved an ally, she also craved companionship. And not just any companionship. She wanted Caelan's. He'd trained her, kept her ability a secret from his father, and promised to free her family.

The spark between them—their chemistry evident in stolen glances and lingering touches—paved the way for a deeper connection. As she'd learned of his childhood—filled with such violence and sorrow—she wondered if perhaps his kindness, his generosity, was a rebellion to that.

They understood each other's pain. Just as she felt trapped in this horrid situation, he was a prisoner of sorts as well. No one could save them, and the only way out was through.

Caelan looked right into her eyes—into *her*.

"I don't want to be alone anymore," she whispered.

His breath hitched before he said, "You're not alone. I'm here—you'll never be alone again."

CHAPTER 24

Elara

LATER THAT NIGHT, AFTER the last drinks had been poured
and the musicians were ready to topple, Elara woke to a
soft knock on her chamber door. She rolled over, her knee gently
displacing Lysandra, who let out an irritated yelp before leaping
to the floor. Elara got out of the bed and slipped her top blanket
over her shoulders since the fire was down to embers and the chill
in the air was biting. Heart pounding as she guessed who might be
on the other side, she reached for the cold brass doorknob. Caelan
was the only one who could get past her guards. At least, he was
the only one who would have knocked with such courtesy after
passing them.

The heavy door swung inward with a groan, revealing a sight
that sent a shiver of excitement down her spine, confirming her
suspicions. Her heart pounded so hard in her chest that she
worried he might hear it beating. Caelan leaned on the doorframe
with one arm over his head. He looked casual but buzzed with
an unfamiliar energy. As he glimpsed her body beneath her
nightgown and makeshift cape, his eyes blazed with desire.

Without saying a word, he closed the short distance between them, tilting her chin up and crushing her lips with his. Elara flung her arms around his neck and pressed her chest against his. She melted into him as he drew her bottom lip deeper into his mouth, nipping her with his teeth.

"Wait," she breathed against his lips. "Not here." She looked into his eyes, and he frowned. "Your room?" she asked. She just didn't want their first time together to be in the same place they'd fought during the invasion.

Caelan nodded. He reached to the floor to pick up the blanket she had dropped and draped it back over her shoulders. He took her hand in his, a warm and reassuring touch. Elara's shadows stared straight ahead, ignoring the couple as they made their way past them and walked down the winding halls to Caelan's chamber. Elara squeezed his hand tighter.

Entering the room, Caelan faced her again, the silence broken only by the soft drizzle of rain hitting the windowsill. "Is this all right?" he asked.

A pair of abandoned boots sat on the floor near the freshly made bed, and several books—along with a worn leather journal—lay open on the mahogany desk. Elara nodded, beaming up at him. "This is perfect." She meant it. Not just about the room, but about him. About being together on their own terms instead of waiting for the wedding, when they would no doubt be performative and awkward.

This was real. And it belonged only to them.

Caelan brushed his hand across her cheek and tucked her hair behind her ear. Elara guided his face down to hers, fingers curling into the hair at the nape of his neck. Their lips met again, tongues dancing, searching.

Caelan held her close, the warmth of his body a welcome comfort against hers. Lost in the kiss, she tugged at him, a frantic energy in her movements, until she felt the cool, smooth edge of the bed against the backs of her knees. Elara's back hit the plush mattress, Caelan's weight settling on top of her as he moved over her.

Pulling his mouth from hers, he trailed kisses down her neck, leaving a trail of goose bumps in their wake. His lips, warm and insistent, lingered on the delicate skin of her collarbone, sending delicious shivers down her spine. She raked her hands down his back until she felt the hem of his shirt. She tugged it up, bunching the fabric around his neck and forcing him to halt so she could finish lifting it over his head. His growl at the interruption made her stomach flutter.

As she removed his shirt, he sat up enough for her to admire his bare chest. Her eyes lingered on the taut muscles of his broad shoulders, noting the way the dim light glinted off his sun-kissed skin, then trailed down to his chiseled stomach. His abdomen rose and fell quickly, his heartbeat echoing hers.

Calloused yet gentle hands wandered from her chest, over her stomach, and down her thighs, a slow, deliberate caress. He caught the hem of her nightgown and guided it up, revealing her legs. Elara wiggled under his featherlight touch as more goose bumps exploded across her skin. She arched her back so he could wrestle the rest of the fabric out from under her. He flung the garment away, the smell of wine and sweat and cedar lingering faintly in the air, and admired her for several slow, steadying breaths.

Caelan's eyes sparkled with sheer joy, an expression Elara was sure she mirrored. The world around them fell away as they continued to explore each other with hands, lips, tongues. Eventually, his trousers joined their other clothes on the floor, and the two of them became a frantic tangle.

Elara fell onto him, breathless and spent, and Caelan wrapped his arms around her, holding her tight against his chest. They stayed like that until the ragged gasps subsided, replaced by the quiet rhythm of normal breathing. He caressed her back and hips, his touch gentle and reassuring, while she ran her fingers through his soft hair, a sigh escaping her lips in perfect contentment.

Rolling off of him, she snuggled close to his side. Caelan gathered a thick, plush blanket from the heap of fabrics scattered on the floor and draped it over them. She felt utterly secure in his embrace, the silent understanding between them palpable and profoundly satisfying. That night, finally finding solace in his arms, Elara slept dreamlessly, a peace that had been a distant memory. The cedar-and-amber scent of his skin and the steady beat of his heart lulled her into a restful slumber.

A BEAM OF SUNLIGHT streamed through the window and across Elara's face. She blinked, trying to clear the sleep from her eyes and focus. She attempted to turn over, but Caelan's arm was heavy on her, pinning her to the bed. He was fast asleep, face serene, his breathing slow and even. Elara smiled and settled back into him, tugging the covers over her face to shield herself from the harsh daylight.

An hour passed, marked only by the shifting sunlight and the sound of birds chirping, before Caelan stirred beside her. He woke and embraced her before they stretched out their arms and legs, trying to coax blood into their extremities after being curled up all night. With a tender touch, Caelan brushed the hair from her forehead, the warmth of his fingers a comforting contrast to the cool morning air against her cheek.

"Good morning, Princess."

Elara wrinkled her nose at him, and he laughed. With a rustle of sheets, he scooted to the edge of the bed and, bending low, retrieved his clothes from the floor. For the first time, she saw his bare back, covered in markings from his neck to his waist—a series of dark swirls that evoked the idea of the ocean during a storm.

"What are those?" she asked, eyeing the patterns, only to notice several scratch marks of her own making. Her cheeks flushed with heat. "I've never noticed them before."

Caelan looked over his shoulder at her. "Ah," he said. "Those are my sigils." He shrugged. "Everyone with an essence affinity receives them during their Thal'Sira—it's an initiation ceremony."

Intrigued, she ran her fingers over the markings, tracing the waves down his spine. "Are they different for every essence affinity?"

"They're unique to each person—like a magical fingerprint, of sorts. But they tend to keep to certain themes. Waves or sea creatures for the Moiren, lightning for the Children of the Sky . . ." Having retrieved their clothing from the floor, he rose and placed her silken nightgown in her lap and shoved his arms into his own shirt.

"What was your Thal'Sira like?"

Caelan thought about it for a moment while he tugged his trousers on and fastened his belt. "I suppose, from the outside looking in, it would seem quite barbaric. After passing a series of tests, one of the magi from your order guides you through a Pyrael. It's a flame as tall as five men. As you pass through it, you're branded with your sigils. Rumor has it that the more markings you have, the more powerful you are."

Elara let the new information sink in. The sigils completely covered Caelan's back. *One of the most powerful mages.*

"Did it hurt?" she asked.

"I've had worse," he said, holding his hand out between them. Elara took it and stroked the burn scars. She'd noticed them many times before, but she still wasn't ready to hear the story behind them.

"I wonder what my sigils would be," she said. "I haven't seen any images depicting them in my research." *How would I even have a Thal'Sira? I have no other Serathi to guide me.* She shook the dark thoughts from her mind before she risked ruining their cozy morning.

"Breakfast?" she asked instead.

"I'd love to," Caelan replied. "Let me escort you back to your room so you can change first. And take care of this." He tried to run his hand through her hair, but it was instantly caught in the tendrils. Elara giggled, taking his hand and skillfully freeing his fingers from her tangled mess.

"Fair enough," she said. Caelan lifted their hands to his face, pressing his lips to her knuckles.

AFTER SHE HAD IRIS help her tame her wild hair and pick out a suitable dress, Elara made her way to the dining room. Her shadows were there, of course, grinning like idiots. They were probably happy for Caelan, and maybe even for her. The feeling that others cared about her happiness comforted her in her isolating world. She wished she could tell Thalia about last night. *I will get to tell her when this is over and we are all safe again*, she thought.

Clutching that small hope, she entered the dining room, her breath catching in her throat at the sight before her. A spectacular spread of her favorite flowers—yellow dahlias—and lemon cakes adorned the table. Dressed in fine formal attire, Caelan stood behind his chair, looking every inch a future king.

"What's all this? How did you know about the flowers?" Elara whispered.

"I asked Iris. Is it . . . too much?" he asked, lips dipping into a tiny frown.

Elara shook her head and took her seat, beaming. She didn't know what to say, instead reaching for a cup of piping hot coffee.

Caelan mirrored her—adding an obscene amount of milk to his beverage—before he cleared his throat. "What would you do if you weren't here? If you could do anything you wanted?"

Elara's brow furrowed as she considered the odd question. Not even Thalia had asked her that before. *What do I want?* "I don't know." She shrugged. "So much of my life has been planned out for me. I've only ever thought about being the best queen I can be. And now, all of this . . . it's hard to think about myself. About what I want." With her family's lives—and the fate of Serendith—in her hands, it seemed silly to think about her own happiness. "What about you? What would you have done if your father hadn't brought you here?"

Caelan's eyes warmed, his expression turning wistful. "I would've traveled the world. Explored the continent, maybe even sailed to the Unknown Lands."

Elara could see it. Caelan swinging from the rigging of a massive ship, skin coated with salt and sun, the wind dancing in his golden curls. *Free.* She frowned.

"But," he continued. "I'm glad that my father brought me here. To you." His eyes held hers as he rose.

Caelan took her hand, kneeled to the ground before her, and presented her with a stunning necklace—a silver setting surrounding a gemstone that perfectly matched the color of her eyes.

"This is why I was late to escort you to the ball—finding this necklace. It belonged to my mother. I thought it would be perfect for you."

Her heart squeezed. Caelan smiled, rubbing his thumb over her knuckles.

"Elara, I know we are already engaged. But I needed this to be for us, not for anyone else. My love for you . . . it is real. I cannot imagine my life without you. I love you with all of my soul. So I ask you, Will you be my wife?"

Fear sent her heart hammering in her chest. One part of her wanted to run, to decline his offer, to listen to the small voice in her head that told her not to trust that this was real. She searched his golden eyes, and her fear melted as she gave in to her desire.

Tears welled in her eyes, and she nodded, unable to speak. He rose and fastened the chain around her neck. Their lips met in a fiery kiss that left her breathless, before she buried her face in his chest, her heart pounding.

"I love you too, Caelan," she whispered.

CHAPTER 25

Elara

THE LAVISH, THICK DOOR panels to the binding marquee opened, and Caelan led Elara to their opulent wedding reception, the scent of perfume and expensive liquor heavy in the air. His eyes sparkled with pride. Elara smiled, mirroring the joy in his eyes. Snowflakes danced around them before melting on the path beneath their feet. Several landed on her face, and she laughed, savoring the coolness of the melted snow on her flushed skin.

"As much as I like you wet, Princess, we best get you inside before I melt," Caelan said with a wink.

Elara blushed further at that statement. He was right though. A frost-kissed princess wouldn't suit their wedding reception. So they abandoned the privacy of the fresh air and joined the fray inside the tent, ducking through the threshold.

Caelan swept her into another dance, this one faster than their previous ones, and she begged for a reprieve. Sera took her place for the following song, and much to her surprise, Elara grinned, happy to watch the two old friends twirl around the dance floor. Her growing confidence eased her concerns about Sera and Caelan's past. She focused on the future now, one that included Caelan as her husband and Sera as a friend.

Elara was swaying a little from side to side, humming along to one of her favorite songs and watching the throng of guests, when she saw her. There, in a sky-blue gown that made her look oddly like the cake being served, being spun around on the dance floor by their father.

Thalia.

Disbelief washed over Elara; she couldn't process what she was seeing. Her sister and father were here. Dancing. *Safe.* Nearby, her mother clapped to the lively beat of the music, her face glowing with joy.

With a sharp shove, Elara bypassed a richly dressed noble couple, their startled expressions barely registering as she strode toward her family. The tent became a suffocating crush of people, each an obstacle in Elara's path to what she desired most. Keeping to the perimeter of the tent, she used a serving table to steady herself. Her heart hammered against her ribs, a deafening sound that matched the queasy churning in her stomach.

My family . . . is . . . here? How? Why?

The long train of her gown caught underneath her shoe and sent her tumbling. She stopped her fall, but the delicate white silk ripped beneath her heel. As she bent to gather the fabric in her arms, a shadow loomed over her, setting her teeth on edge.

"I see you've noticed our *special* guests," Lord Stormrider said.

The chill in his voice sent a shiver up Elara's spine.

Something's not right, Elara. Lysandra's voice sounded a distant warning in her mind.

She shook her head, trying to focus.

"Indeed," Elara said. "A most welcome surprise on this happiest occasion." She shoved down her instincts to recoil from him, instead focusing on playing along.

Lord Stormrider ran a hand through his gray hair—a gesture she'd seen from Caelan a dozen times—causing his cobalt cape to shift and reveal a decorative sword at his hip. A gaudy gold ring flashed on his finger as he stroked the hilt. "Enjoy them while you still can, little princess," he said, sneering at her.

His expression rarely matched his words, something that annoyed Elara, though she had grown used to it. But the venom he was spitting made little sense—he had what he wanted. She'd held up her end of their bargain by agreeing to marry Caelan. Now it was his turn. Her family was here, and she was going to speak with them.

With a sharp turn, she fled Lord Stormrider. The familiar tingle of magic—a warmth like sun on skin—spread through her fingertips. The sound of the celebration around her was deafening, her ears ringing as she inched closer to her goal. With a deep breath, she took another step forward, reaching out to touch her mother's shoulder.

Elara's fingers brushed velvet, and the queen turned to face her. "Hello, darling!" she said.

"Mother," Elara breathed, clarity returning and the fist around her heart loosening slightly. "Are you all right?"

"Wonderful! You look so beautiful, my dear. I am thrilled for you and Captain Stormrider. It is such a smart match. I'm proud of you, Elara."

Elara forced a smile. "Thank you. I must say, I was genuinely surprised by how much I liked him."

The queen nodded and patted Elara's arm fondly.

"Where have you been?" Elara asked, brow furrowed. There was no telling what her family would remember, what Lord Stormrider had done to them—or rather, forced Sera and others to do to them.

"At the country house. Remember, dear, I wasn't feeling well. And poor Thalia had it much worse than I did!" her mother said, brushing off Elara's concern.

Elara nodded. "But you're feeling better now?" Elara hoped that her mother would give some sign that she knew something was amiss. Perhaps not now, with an audience, but later, in private, they could discuss what had really happened.

"Indeed," was all the queen said before Elara's father pulled her away for a dance.

"Father!" Elara called as he moved them away. He winked, saying nothing. Before Elara could pursue her parents, they faded into the mass of dancing people.

He never winks at me like that.

Arms wrapped around Elara in a warm embrace. "Hello, sister. Congratulations!"

Elara inhaled Thalia's scent . . . and it was completely wrong. The tingling of magic migrated from her fingertips up her forearms, burning in its intensity. Elara grasped her sister's shoulders, holding Thalia out at arm's length, her eyes scanning her face with concern.

Her eyes . . . Instead of their usual blue—like Elara's—Thalia's eyes were hazel. *Her eyes are the wrong color.*

Elara backed away from Thalia.

"What's wrong?" Her sister's voice held no trace of real concern, her face doll-like and strange.

"You're not real," Elara whispered. Tears pooled in her eyes, threatening to spill over onto her cheeks.

Elara turned away from her, desperately searching the crowd for Caelan and Sera. Instead, she collided with Felix, who was flirting with one of the servant girls.

"What's wrong?" he asked, now on high alert and scanning the room for threats. "You look like you've seen a ghost . . ." He trailed off as his eyes fell on Thalia, then the king and queen. "Impossible," he murmured.

"Help me find Caelan, please," she said. "Something is terribly wrong."

Felix nodded and moved to search the room for the missing pair. Meanwhile, Elara scanned the room for Lord Stormrider. Before she could find him, Felix cleared a path in the bodies, Caelan on his heel.

"Elara," Caelan breathed. "What is it? What's wrong?" He reached out and took her hands in his. The room was spinning, threatening to knock Elara off her feet.

When she didn't answer him right away, he turned to Felix, who nodded toward her parents on the dance floor.

"No," Caelan hissed. "Where did Sera go?" he barked at Felix.

Felix shrugged. "I searched for her too. She's gone."

Caelan shook his head, accidentally squeezing Elara's hands in his frustration. "Find her," he bit out.

Elara focused on their hands. The pressure, the slight pain, helped her focus. It helped anchor her to reality.

"Here now," Caelan said gently. "Let's get you something to drink."

Elara tried to nod, but she couldn't move.

You're in shock, Lysandra said to her. Elara didn't even know where Lysandra was, but she feared she was right.

"Elara?" Caelan took her face in his hands and looked into her eyes. "Stars," he muttered. "Come on." He pulled her away from the party and into a quieter alcove of the tent.

He sat her down on a chair and helped her take a few sips of water. He rubbed her back, soothing her, coaxing her back into her body.

"What did Felix mean?" she finally asked.

"Felix?" Caelan asked, confused. "About what?"

"He said it was impossible," she said, her lips the only things that moved. "Why would it be impossible for my family to be here?"

"Shh, Elara, my love," Caelan said, kneeling in front of her. "Don't worry about that right now. You are in shock from seeing your family here tonight."

"No," she snapped. "Those *things* are not my family. They're illusions."

Caelan said nothing as a look of pure pain flashed across his features.

"They're Sera's illusions. I could sense it. I've felt it before in her presence. Why would she do this to me?"

Caelan took a deep breath. "If they are Sera's," he said, "then there has to be an explanation. It's my father's doing, Elara, not Sera's. I'm sure of it."

"Where is my real family?" Elara was all but whimpering now. Hot tears cascaded down her face.

"I don't know," he said. "But we will figure this out together."

"I trusted her," she said. "She's supposed to be my friend." *I should've known better.*

"I know, love," he said, voice fading as darkness closed in around his face.

E LARA BOLTED UPRIGHT IN her bed, waking from her vision. Sweat coated her, causing her nightgown to stick to her clammy skin. Caelan breathed softly beside her, moonlight shining on his golden curls. Lysandra sat in her lap, fur black as night, pointed ears upright and alert.

Good, you're back.

Back? Elara thought. *You saw that too?*

The feline nodded.

It . . . That wasn't just a nightmare, was it? Elara asked.

No, Elara. That was a vision. Of your future.

Elara trembled from the adrenaline still coursing through her veins. Her palms burned with phantom pain from touching the illusions in her vision.

The wedding is in a couple of weeks. I have to find my family before Caelan and I wed. I can't trust Lord Stormrider . . . or Sera.

Lysandra's glowing gaze zeroed in on Caelan's sleeping figure. *Can you trust him?*

Tears fell onto the blanket. *I don't know. I don't think I have a choice.*

CHAPTER 26

Caelan

THE MORNING SUNLIGHT SHONE through the narrow slit in the curtains, blinding Caelan even with his eyelids squeezed shut. Groaning, he rolled over in his bed, hands searching for Elara's sleeping figure. His fingers brushed across the empty sheets, their coolness telling him she had been awake for a while. The two of them had spent the last several nights tangled up together, whispering and laughing as they explored each other's bodies and minds.

"I thought royals got to sleep in," he said, sitting up and rubbing his hand over his stubbled chin. Elara sat in a high-backed chair at the fireplace, her wild hair and sheer nightgown reminding him of the night of the invasion. The dying flames cast a glow around her like a halo, while ominous shadows loomed around the rest of the room.

"Elara? What is it?" he asked when she didn't respond, taking his blanket and draping it over her shoulders. Her bare skin was like ice where his palms grazed it.

JENNIFER L ADAMS

"I had another vision last night," she said. Her voice was hoarse, as though she had coughed up a gallon of salt water. Caelan steadied his breathing as his eyes widened at the news.

"Tell me." He pressed a kiss to her cheek, the vanilla scent of her hair filling his nose. With soothing circular motions, he used his thumbs to massage the knots out of her shoulders.

"I saw . . . the future. Our wedding. It's impossible, but Lysandra told me . . . and I believe her, Caelan."

Elara's familiar—though he hadn't yet told her what Lysandra was—was dangerously close to becoming a drowned cat. She lounged on the floor near Elara's feet, licking her paws clean. Caelan shook his head. Between Elara's healing essence affinity, Lysandra, and this vision, he worried his father was right about her destiny. The thought made his skin crawl.

"Slow down," he said, kneeling before her and placing his palms on either side of her pale face. "I've learned to expect the unexpected when it comes to your magic." He offered her a tiny smile. "I'm here. Just breathe. Start from the beginning."

"You were dancing with Sera, then I saw them. Thalia. And my mother and father." Elara could barely form the words, as if they burned her throat as she spoke them aloud.

Caelan stiffened. *No.*

The room shrunk around him. The soft crackling of the fire was a roar in his ears. The drawn curtains threatened to fly open at any moment and expose him to the world.

Elara was his world now, and he focused on her face, keeping his breathing steady.

"But it wasn't really them. They didn't act like themselves. And Thalia's eyes . . ." Elara shuddered, her own eyes glossy and haunted. "They were illusions, Caelan." Her faraway gaze came back into focus, staring into his eyes, searching. "They were Sera's illusions." She started sobbing, curling in on herself as her cries jolted her slender shoulders.

Caelan's heart ached for her, and icy dread pulsed through his veins. *I should tell her.* He'd known this day would come—the day his shameful secret would be revealed, the weight of his cowardice crushing him. He stroked her hair, trying to soothe them both.

"Sera wouldn't do that unless my father ordered her to," he said, choosing each word with intention.

"He was there too, Caelan. Threatening me, threatening *them* again. He told me to 'enjoy them while I still could.' "

Caelan shook his head, his hair falling over his eyes, and brushed his thumbs over her damp cheeks. "Elara, darling, I know you are hurting right now. But I need you to listen to me. If Lysandra is right and this is really a vision of the future, I think it means that my father plans on killing your parents after we wed."

"I know it's real. And I'm not surprised that your father would do such a thing." She paused, searching his eyes once again. Then she exhaled, her shoulders sagging. "There's something else I need to tell you. I've experienced a glimpse of the future—or maybe the past—before. From a seer."

"What seer?" Caelan's brows drew together.

"At the Mabine festival. She told me of a prophecy about someone who would restore essence to the world."

Stars, another prophecy? Caelan thought. A prophecy had brought him across the sea to this palace. "My father believes in seers too . . ."

"How is this possible? I've never heard of any essence affinity that allows someone to see the future."

"Just look at Lysandra, or the artifices they're building in the North. There is magic in this world that we don't understand, Elara. Knowledge lost to the ages and new discoveries that we can't even imagine."

Caelan thought about Sera's amulet, the one that allowed her to use her illusion magic to conceal memories. *What could Elara do with the right tools? The right spells?* Time was running out—he had to tell her the truth or figure out how to prevent her from discovering it.

"Do you remember the prophecy the seer gave you? The exact words?" he asked.

Elara nodded. "They were impossible to forget." She took a deep breath, then recited:

The Druids danced away the night
The War, the ruinous delight
Man cracked the Well
Destroyed the spell
And cost the world the Light
One shall come with Death her boon
Born under the Cygnet Moon
One who hears the raven's call
By triple Stars to save us all

Caelan's head spun. *The Druids, the War, the Well . . .*

"A raven's call? Do you think that means . . . ?"

"Lysandra. But it can't be . . . It can't be about me. The seer said the Cygnet Moon is rare, and the next one is in a month. Our wedding night."

Caelan nodded his agreement. It couldn't be about Elara, but it wasn't a coincidence that his father planned for their wedding to be the night of the Cygnet Moon. The prophecy made little sense to him, and it didn't match what his father was expecting—the reason they'd come to Serendith.

"What about your father? What prophecies does he believe in?" Elara asked, rubbing under her nose with the blanket.

Caelan moved to sit across from her in a matching chair and leaned back. "He knew about my mother's death before it happened and tried to prevent it. He knew that you and I would wed and made sure it happened. As for what else . . . I'm not sure. I don't know what he's really after or why he would want to kill your family after the wedding," he lied.

"I can guess. He wants you on the throne as king, and he doesn't want to wait. If he can make Sera create those illusions, he can use my family as puppets for as long as he likes before he'll claim they perished in some accident."

"He'll thank the stars that you were here, safe, and that our marriage ensures the royal line." His hands balled into fists in his lap.

"But why? Why does he want you to be king? Trade deals? I know he was angry with my father for backing out of some arrangement. I thought it was the engagement, but what if it was something else entirely?"

Caelan scrambled to pull together a half-truth that would satisfy her. "Vengeance. Remember the tapestry and the journal you found? Your family exiled mine generations ago, after the Shattering."

"After they betrayed us," she added.

"That's not how my family told the story. I grew up on it, and so did my father and grandfather. This is more than a coup . . . It's a blood feud that started centuries ago." He placed his forehead in his hand. "I've been so blind. He wants me on the throne and a long line of Stormriders to rule Serendith."

"But you'll only be king consort. Does that mean he'll kill me?"

"No. At least, not right away. He'll only force you to transfer your power to me and take my surname. I promise I won't let him hurt you, Elara." His stomach turned in on itself at the thought of losing her.

"And my family?" Fresh tears pooled at the edges of Elara's eyes.

"We'll find a way to get them somewhere safe before the wedding. I'll reach out to some trusted soldiers under my command." Caelan raked a hand through his tangled hair.

"Good. I'll go talk to Sera."

He grimaced. "Be careful. As much as I want to trust her, I don't think you should tell her about your healing essence affinity yet. Or the prophecy. See what she knows of my father's plan, and we can come up with a counter."

Elara nodded. "I'll be careful. But we need her on our side, Caelan. Keep my family safe, for now. We'll need more allies at court, regardless of your father's plan for us. I'll see what I can do."

CHAPTER 27

Elara

E LARA DRAGGED HER ARM across her brow, leaving a trail of flour on her forehead. The clanking of pots and pans and the chatter of the kitchen staff flowed all around her. Lysandra, in her feline form, was curled up in the corner, belly full from the treats Meg—the servant girl Elara had rescued in the red parlor—had slipped her.

"I almost didn't recognize you." Sera's voice drew Elara's attention away from the pie crust she was rolling out on the counter.

"Thank you for meeting me here," Elara said, wiping her hands on her apron. "Any more progress on the journal?"

Elara—with Lysandra's help—and Sera had taken turns painstakingly translating the mysterious journal from the library. They'd made out a few poems and a brief first-person account detailing the last battle of the Shattering.

Sera, to Elara's surprise, grabbed an apron from the wall and donned it, covering up her glistening silver dress. "I've been working on some sort of recipe. I think it is for a potion, but I can't tell what for yet."

Elara nodded as a wave of nausea washed over her. "Thank you for your help." Aside from her vision, Elara had no reason to mistrust Sera, but worry prickled at the back of her mind.

Sera smiled and pointed at the dough. "What are we making?"

"Beef and onion hand pies."

"My favorite," Sera whispered. "What's really going on, Elara?"

Elara froze, her gaze sweeping over the bustling, noisy kitchen. She pressed her fingertip into the pie crust, tracing out the letters: "F-I-N-D-T-H-E-M."

Sera's emerald eyes widened with realization, and she nodded. She smoothed the message out of the dough with her own flour-coated hands.

"Why?" she mouthed.

"Can you help me?" Elara asked, gesturing to the pot of meat and vegetables simmering behind Sera.

"I'll do my best," Sera said, ladling the pie filling into a bowl and placing it on the counter for Elara.

Elara smiled. "Meg," she called over to the servant, who quickly hid a piece of chicken—surely destined for Lysandra's belly—behind her back. "I have a job for you too."

I N THE MONTHS THAT Elara and Caelan had been training and scheming, winter had finally come. The last fortnight had passed in a blur, the cold days spent training and the insufferable evenings spent waiting for Sera and Meg to report back on her family's location. Elara hoped Caelan was faring better with his soldiers.

She woke early, the stars still shining in the breaking dawn, to a powerful cramping in her lower belly. After tossing and turning, unable to get comfortable in her too-soft bed, she finally swung her legs over the side of her bed and stood. As she rose, the thin fabric of her nightgown brushed her thighs, coated with sticky crimson blood.

I wish my healing essence affinity could save me from my monthly cycles. She riffled through one of her nightstand drawers for cloths and stumbled over to the adjacent washroom, still half asleep. As she cleaned herself, she noticed that her bleeding was much heavier than usual. Clumps of bloody tissue came away from her body, and a sickening wave of nausea washed over her, the metallic scent of blood filling her nostrils. Returning to the bed, she peeled back the top blanket, and an enormous stain glared up at her from the sheets, a shocking splash of crimson against the once-pristine white.

Elara sensed what was happening, but she needed to speak with Ursa to be sure. At the ringing of a bell, Iris hurried in with Elara's breakfast. The sturdy woman gasped, almost dropping her tray as she entered the room and beheld the scene before her. Her eyes darted between the blood and Elara's drained face before she placed the food on the table and wrapped her arms around her trembling charge.

"Can you please send for Ursa?" Elara asked, fighting back her tears.

"Of course, dear. Stay put. I'll be right back." Iris bustled off, wiping a stray tear from her own cheek with the hem of her apron. The small motion was almost enough to crack Elara's thin facade of composure.

When Ursa arrived a short time later, Elara had changed out of her soiled nightgown. Iris had insisted on leaving the sheets undisturbed so Ursa could inspect them. Ursa, her wrinkled face mirroring Iris's somber expression, embraced Elara, her grip conveying unspoken understanding and support. A strange coldness enveloped Elara as she hugged the woman back, her arms feeling numb around Ursa's torso.

I never even knew I wanted a child. The realization of her loss hit like a blow, a desperate longing for something she couldn't begin to grasp. A wave of need washed over her—more than anything, she wished for her mother's comforting presence, safe and sturdy, able to guide her. Her thoughts warred, leaving her speechless and uncertain. But words proved unnecessary. The other women cleaned up her room until all evidence of tragedy had been removed. Iris procured fresh blueberry pastries for them to eat, and Ursa handed Elara a steaming mug of jasmine tea to drink.

"Why?" Elara whispered.

Iris shook her head. "It's not your fault, dear. I've seen this many times. There's rarely an explanation other than the stars' will." A hand flew absentmindedly to her own belly, and Elara wondered if Iris had not only seen it, but experienced a loss herself.

Ursa placed a hand on Elara's arm. "Your miscarriage was early enough that you don't require medical treatment. Your magic will allow your body to heal without my intervention," she said softly.

Why didn't my essence prevent this from happening in the first place? Elara thought.

After months of breaking herself down in training and reveling in her body's ability to rebuild itself with her healing power, she was shocked that this loss was even a possibility.

Will it happen again when we are trying?

Is something wrong with me?

What if I can't have children at all?

Elara's thoughts raced to the worst-case scenarios. Tears finally fell down her cheeks, and she curled into a ball in her fluffiest chair, holding on to her warm cup of tea so tight she could almost hear it groaning. Ursa stroked her hair, her featherlight touch a welcome distraction, and Iris squeezed her arm.

"I'm so sorry, Elara. We can leave—give you some privacy," Ursa said, standing.

Elara grabbed her wrist, stopping her. "Please stay," Elara muttered between sobs. "I don't want to be alone right now."

KNOCK, KNOCK. THE FIRM familiar taps drew Elara's attention to the door.

"You're late, Princess," Caelan called out from the hall. "Training started an hour ago." The playfulness in his voice was laced with a hint of concern.

Iris, obeying Elara's pointed look, opened the door and hurried him inside. He beheld Elara in her chair, a small, shivering ball of misery—her eyes were puffy, her nose running. Sheer exhaustion washed over her for the first time since they'd met. He rushed to her side and kneeled down by the arm of the chair, taking one of her frigid hands and wrapping it in the warmth of his.

"What happened?" Caelan looked from Elara to the two women attending her, eyes wide with fear.

Elara only shook her head as fresh tears spilled down her cheeks. Caelan turned to Ursa, who was sitting on the edge of the bed, and gave her a questioning look. She gestured for him to step back outside the room. Elara overheard Ursa's hushed, urgent voice through the door, followed by Caelan's sharp intake of breath. He entered the room alone, his footsteps echoing on the hardwood floor.

Brushing away the tears that blurred her vision, Elara met his gaze, searching his eyes. She worried she would see pity there but was relieved to see only grief. *Someone to share the loss with.* Caelan's devastation mirrored her own, which gave her an odd sense of comfort.

"I'm here, my love." His voice hitched on the endearment, but the sincerity in his statement rang true.

"You're not relieved? With everything going on, it's not exactly an ideal time to start our family." She sniffled.

"I would never think that. We would be stars-blessed to have a child." He stroked her back, soothing them both. Elara leaned into his touch, savoring the roughness of his calluses as his palms moved from her mid-back to her bare shoulders. She placed her hand on top of his, where burn scars bubbled and smoothed the flesh. *I'll never gain another scar in my lifetime. Not any visible ones, at least,* she realized.

"What if this means we can't have children? What if my essence affinity is the reason?"

Will you still love me? Will my kingdom survive without an heir? Elara's eyes pooled with tears, offering a silent prayer that he would understand.

"Think about it, Elara. Your ancestors passed this power down to you through the generations. How would that be possible if this loss was caused by your magic?"

Hope, both sweet and terrifying, crept its way into her fragile heart.

"And we will have children someday. I'm sure of it."

"What if we can't?" she whispered. The despair was a crushing weight, threatening to suffocate her.

"I love you no matter what," he said, offering her a lifeline in a sea of doubt and uncertainty.

Elara sagged in relief at his declaration, clinging to his words. "I will love you no matter what," she whispered back.

Caelan scooped her into his arms, cradling her, and carried her back to the bed. He climbed in next to her, the solidness of his body a comfort against her shaking form, and they lay there until her tremors subsided and his tears dried.

CHAPTER 28

Caelan

C AELAN PUNCHED THE STUFFED dummy, savoring the crunch of his knuckles against the stiff canvas. The force of the impact launched the dummy backward, the energy traveling up his arm and into his shoulder. He let out a huff and shook out his well-battered hands. He'd been at it for hours, training in the room his father had set aside for the purpose.

Sweat poured off him, drenching his shirt. With a frustrated grunt, he tugged at the cloying fabric, ripping part of the hem as he yanked it over his head. He wadded it up into a ball and flung it across the room with all his might. But the shirt, light as a feather, unfurled and drifted to the floor just a short distance away, mocking him.

Losing the baby had overwhelmed him with grief for himself, but especially for Elara. He didn't know how to help her—how to fix the problem. *There's nothing there to fix.* His inability to help her gnawed at him; once more, he felt the bitter sting of powerlessness.

Caelan had intended to tell Elara the truth, but the image of her fragile form, the fear in her usually bright eyes, had stopped him cold—he couldn't risk losing her. The impact of his words, the potential for shattering her world, had silenced him. Eventually, the weight of loss and grief would become too much for her to bear. She'd lost her home and her freedom—and her kingdom was slipping away. She was resilient, yet he knew if she found out what he'd been keeping from her, she—and their relationship—might never recover.

The door creaked open, and one of his father's men entered the room, his armor clanking. "Excuse me, Captain Stormrider," he said, casting his gaze to the tile upon noticing Caelan's bare back. It was uncommon for sigils to be on display, and the size and intricacy of Caelan's were intimidating.

"What news?" Caelan asked.

"Your father has requested your presence in the throne room. Along with the princess," the man said.

Caelan's eyes bored into the man's. "Why?" he asked through gritted teeth.

"Uh, I . . . I don't know, sir."

Caelan gave the man a once-over, noting the slight trembling in his knees. "He's in a sour mood today, then?" A chuckle rumbled in his chest, a low, warm sound intended to lighten the mood.

The man nodded fervently. "Indeed, sir. Forgive me. He said you are to attend to him urgently."

"Then I better get cleaned up. I don't want to offend him. Or my lovely bride." He winked.

The man smiled, relieved, and scurried off.

A deep frown creased Caelan's face. *Father knows about the baby,* he thought.

With a swift movement, he grabbed his scabbard, the cold steel a stark contrast to his sweating palms, and hurried from the room.

P RIMPED AND POLISHED LIKE a prized stallion at auction, Caelan paced just outside the throne room. Elara arrived, a vision in a flowing midnight-black gown. The color—and the shadows under her eyes—spoke of mourning, but the shimmering gossamer fabric and stylish cut of her dress made it appropriate attire for beguiling a warlord. The sapphire necklace he'd given her glittered on her neck.

"Brace yourself," he whispered. He took her hands in his, pressing a light kiss to the knuckle of her ring finger.

"What does he want?" she asked, voice hoarse from another day of crying.

"I'm not sure," he lied. "But whatever it is, he's angry."

Elara's eyes widened, but she nodded and squared her shoulders. "There's nothing else he can take from me."

If only that were true, my love. Caelan pulled her hand, positioning her at his left as he wrapped her arm around his. He placed his right hand on the cool bronze of his sword pommel as a footman announced their arrival, and they walked into the throne room.

Lord Stormrider sat on the king's throne, his eyes blazing with fury. A deep scowl was set into his face, and his hands gripped the gilded chair so tightly that his knuckles were white.

A primal fear washed over Caelan, making the hair on his neck stand up straight as his body tensed, ready to react to the threat. The doors swung shut behind them with an ominous thud, leaving them alone with his father.

"Well, well, if it isn't the happy couple." Lord Stormrider sneered at them. The sharp, warning edge in his father's voice roused his protective instincts. Caelan released Elara's arm, and he edged in front of her.

"Indeed, we are happy, Father. I thought you would be thrilled. You are getting what you wanted, after all. We are willingly uniting our houses, and our family is gaining both power and influence through this union." Caelan spoke formally and with a false sense of calm, his voice steady and even while his pulse quickened.

"You stupid, insolent boy!" Lord Stormrider rose from his perch. "And you," he hissed, pointing at Elara with a crooked finger. "You useless whore."

Now Caelan was fuming, his face hot and his fists clenched as he stepped between his father and his fiancée. "You have nothing to be concerned about," he said through gritted teeth, trying to keep his temper. "We will do our duty and produce an heir when the time is right." He ignored the tiny gasp that escaped Elara's lips.

But his father, consumed by rage, was beyond the reach of reason. In a flash, Lord Stormrider summoned icy shackles, their chilling grip freezing Caelan's boots to the stone floor, trapping him. Lord Stormrider turned his attention to Elara. Caelan watched in horror as a torrent of water, roaring and churning, headed straight for her. The gush hit Elara in the chest and covered her mouth and nose.

Caelan's own throat and lungs burned as he watched her drown. He couldn't move, couldn't melt the ice—he hadn't even known his father was capable of ice magic. He clutched at his chest, unable to breathe. Dark spots clouded his vision as he struggled to maintain consciousness. The weight of his inadequacy crushed him, a leaden silence settling over his soul as she slipped further away. He barely heard Lord Stormrider continuing to berate Elara as her head smacked the floor with a sickening crack.

The sound was enough to snap him out of his episode. With the force of a typhoon, Caelan became a blur as he pulled his feet from his trapped boots and raced to save her. He redirected his father's water toward the sky, causing a misting rain to fill the room. It mirrored the storm now brewing inside him.

Elara sputtered, coughing up gushes of water. She remained on the floor, her ragged breathing filling the quiet room, as Caelan locked on to his father. The fire in his veins was matched only by the ferocity of his assault; Caelan's blasts grew faster, more violent, each one a destructive wave. Elara watched, face pale and eyes wide with shock, and a small corner of his mind noted her expression. He didn't blame her. Every other time she had seen his power, it had taken on his signature cocky, playful sort of energy. This was different. This was pure hatred, a lifetime in the making.

Lord Stormrider held his own against his son, and Caelan would soon lose, as he always did. Another torrent of water struck him in the chest, and he felt a popping sensation. *Cracked sternum*, he thought. His adrenaline kept the pain at bay, but his breaths became shallow and labored. He tried to maintain his balance, but the force of his father's blasts had him reaching to shield Elara, then stumbling backward. He barely regained his footing without his boots on.

"Please," he rasped. "Leave her be." Caelan raised both hands, summoning a wall of water, a tidal wave of a shield to keep Elara safe from his father's wrath. His arms and shoulders strained with effort, sweat mingling with the salt water dripping from his hair.

He watched in horror as his wave crystalized into ice, then shattered.

Caelan crumpled to his knees, exhausted and emotionally drained. While he was younger and faster, his father had more power and experience. The apprentice could not surpass his master. The angry son could not beat his abuser.

Elara dragged herself to him and draped her body over his. His father would be insane to push them any further—to risk his ultimate plan failing. Instead, Lord Stormrider walked past them, his face eerily calm once more.

"I take it I've made myself clear, boy?" He didn't turn to Caelan, or wait for his son's response. As if nothing at all had happened, Lord Stormrider sauntered out of the throne room.

He's lost his mind . . . again. Caelan had lived his whole life alongside his father, a man perceived by others as a formidable figure with an exceptional intellect. Little did those people realize that the father, just like the son, was broken inside. They'd never been the same after Caelan's mother passed.

Lord Stormrider's anger had recklessly jeopardized Elara's life. Caelan knew now, beyond any doubt, that Elara was the key to his father's prophecy. The loss of her pregnancy must have cracked something deep within the man's careful facade. While his father had remained composed thus far, Caelan suspected that the pressure was building as the wedding approached. His father's desires were finally within reach after decades of careful planning, only to be sabotaged by his son's careless behavior.

Caelan hoped that this would be the last time he'd lose a battle with his father. He heard his father's voice echo in his mind, a phrase he'd heard all his life. *You are powerless. Do not displease me again.*

Caelan felt the weight of Elara's body crushing his, shielding him from his own father. Of its own accord, his hand found its way to her neck, brushing away her drenched locks, his thumb caressing her jawline. Her skin was a sickly gray, a color he had seen many times on waterlogged sailors recovering from near-death experiences at sea. From the looks of what she'd coughed up, Elara had inhaled the equivalent of half the narrow sea herself, courtesy of his father's magic.

He reached around to the back of her head, his fingers brushing against something warm and sticky; when he pulled them away, he was surprised to see glistening red. The smell of iron and salt water tinged the air. *Well done, my love.*

Clearly, Elara had made the connection that she needed to control her essence affinity. Her ability to sustain her injuries—instead of her magic automatically healing them—had allowed them the luxury of their secret. His father may have known about the baby, but he didn't know about her power. He didn't realize *why* Elara was the key to the prophecy—the key to his plan. *At least we still have that advantage*, Caelan thought. Between Elara's combat training and her ability to heal, they might stand a chance if it ever came to a battle.

Elara breathed heavily, still shaking. Caelan's gut twisted with guilt—he should have stopped this long ago. He knew her pain would only worsen and that soon he would be revealed as the cause of it all. But loving her felt like sailing a small sailboat on a stormy sea—a beautiful, terrifying, and exhilarating sensation. She was the breeze on his face, allowing him to feel the world fall away to sweet freedom. He imagined that loving her was the closest thing in the world to flying. *But I wasn't flying at all*, he thought. *All this time I've been falling. And dragging her down with me.*

Defying his father was impossible, like trying to capture smoke in his bare hands—every time he drew close to grasping victory, it slipped through his fingers. The room closed in around him as shadows clouded the edges of his vision, creating a bloodred halo around Elara's heartbreakingly beautiful face. He saw the familiar crinkle between her brows, a deep furrow of worry etched across her forehead, before his world went dark.

CHAPTER 29

Elara

I HAVE TO GET him out of here. Elara would heal with her essence, but Caelan needed immediate medical attention. She assessed his injuries—leaning on Ursa's lessons—and determined that he had a cracked sternum, at least one broken rib, and likely a concussion.

She dragged his heavy limp body to the door. Elara's shadows were just outside the throne room, their faces bleak. They each took one of Caelan's arms and helped tow his unconscious form down the hall.

"Take him to Ursa! Hurry!" Elara said, needing to change out of her dripping, freezing clothes.

"We'll see you in the infirmary, Your Highness," said Silas, nodding. The guards glanced at each other, a pained look passing between them.

They love him too, she realized, her chest a little lighter, knowing that she could trust them to get him to safety.

When she got to her room, Lysandra was on her bed, staring at her with wide green eyes and meowing with concern. The feline bounced onto the floor and bolted out of the room, nearly tripping Elara.

"Hey! Wait!"

It was no use. The creature was long gone, and Elara had more pressing matters to attend to. As she came back to her full faculties—her body already healed from Lord Stormrider's attack—she was struck by the idea that Caelan's anger toward his father wasn't only about her.

If he did all of this to me, she thought, *what on earth has he done to you?* She remembered the scars on his hand and his father's sabotage during the tournament. *All of this to his own son.* Shivering, she hastily changed into a dry set of training clothes—since they were the easiest to put on alone—then slipped into the tunnels and rushed to Ursa's infirmary.

The familiar smell of herbs and rubbing alcohol filled her nose, and she relished the warmth pumping from the hearth. The comfort was short-lived, however. Elara swallowed, wrapping her arms around herself. Caelan was lying prone on the large center table, shirtless, as Ursa ladled steaming liquid into his mouth. He gagged a little, but swallowed all of the foul-smelling potion. Felix and Silas hovered in the corner.

"I'll watch Lord Stormrider," Silas said, face pale and sickly, like he was moments away from vomiting.

"And I'll tell Lady Seraphine what happened, if that's all right, Princess Elara?" Felix asked. She nodded.

Her shadows gone, Elara flew to Caelan's side, grasping his hand and pressing it to her heart.

"What can I do to help?" she asked Ursa, gaze fixed on his closed eyes.

"His chest took a hefty blow," Ursa said, shaking her head at the floor and wiping her hands on her apron. "And he has two broken ribs. Grab the bandages from the lowest cabinet."

Elara obeyed, riffling through the cupboard for the strips of linen, then handing them to her mentor.

"Help me lift him up," the physician said. The two women pulled the dead weight of his form into a seated position, eliciting a moan from him. As Ursa wrapped the bandages around his torso, she asked, "What happened to him?"

"His father," Elara whispered, brushing blond curls off of his forehead.

Ursa's eyebrows shot up. "What?"

"He found out about the baby. I don't understand why he was so livid about it. There has to be something else going on here, Ursa. I can feel it. Lord Stormrider wants more than an alliance. Maybe even more than a line of Stormriders on the throne."

"Stormriders? But that would mean . . ."

"Yes, abdicating my throne and passing the rule of Serendith to Caelan as king. It's that, or Lord Stormrider would kill me anyway, especially if he thinks I won't be able to have children. I've been so focused on my family, I didn't realize how much danger I was in myself."

"Finished. Lay him back down," Ursa said. "Have a seat. I imagine you've been through quite the ordeal. I'll make you some tea."

Elara shook her head. "I'm fine. Is there anything else he needs?" She all but fell into her chair, heavy with overwhelm.

"All he needs now is rest. Stay with him, and wake him in an hour. Give him more of this." Ursa handed her a vial filled with silvery liquid.

Elara's brow furrowed as she pressed the back of her hand to Caelan's cheek.

"I'll leave you to it, then," Ursa said, slipping out of the room.

Stars, please don't take him from me, she prayed. "Please don't leave me," she whispered.

"Wouldn't dream of it, Princess," he croaked, squeezing her hand before losing consciousness once more.

E LARA WOKE TO LOUD meowing. She sat upright in her chair, neck stiff and chest aching—an empathetic echo of Caelan's pain. He still lay on the table in Ursa's infirmary.

"How long was I asleep?" she asked Lysandra.

The feline was curled up on Elara's lap. *Not long. I heard your guard telling the Nimireth what happened. Are you all right?*

"Better than Caelan." Elara shrugged, then brushed the back of her hand across his forehead, checking for fever.

You have blood in your hair.

Elara scowled. "I was attacked. And he's hurt. You think I care about my hair?"

Lysandra shook her head. *It is a lot of blood, Elara. Your wound did not heal itself.*

Elara reached up to the matted spot on the back of her head, fingertips probing the area. "It worked. I kept myself from healing." She'd kept her power hidden from Lord Stormrider—a small mercy. A tiny spark of pride flickered in her battered heart as she watched Caelan's chest rise and fall.

CHAPTER 30

Caelan

C AELAN STIRRED. EVERY INCH of him felt like lead. His limbs were heavy, and his chest ached—at Elara's words and the soreness of his injuries. He tried to sit up, but her steady hands gently guided him back to lying down.

"Let me get Ursa first. To make sure it's safe for you to move." She leaned down, kissing him on the forehead. As she left, Caelan swiveled his head from one side of the strange room to the other, surveying his surroundings. An infirmary. Not a place he was unfamiliar with. While he had yet to visit this particular one, the dead herbs and odorous medicines were a minor comfort.

He'd spent half his adolescence in rooms like this, tended to by physicians at Veilkeep or medics in the training field. He tucked his chin to his bare chest, trying to get a better look at the bandage that was squeezing his rib cage. He gingerly touched his aching side, flinching at the sudden sharp pain. *Broken*. He sighed.

Not for the first time, he wished he had Elara's ability to heal himself. It certainly would have spared him trips to these suffocating rooms for the rest of his life. He wished she could heal him. Maybe one day, with practice and the right tools, she could learn to do just that—heal others as well as herself. For now, he tapped his fingers on the table and tried to ignore a sliver of wood poking his back.

Elara burst through the door, Ursa on her heels. "See, I told you he was awake already!"

"I can see that, child." Ursa grinned at her pupil, weathered eyes crinkling at the corners. Caelan saw then that Elara had been fortunate enough to grow up with two doting mother hens—maybe three, if he considered Iris. He shoved down the slight bitterness of envy he felt, having lost his own mother so young. He wouldn't wish that fate on anyone, least of all Elara. Another pang, this time one of sadness, pierced his heart.

"Follow my finger, dear," Ursa commanded, holding up her index finger and moving it in front of his face.

He obliged, but not before saying, "I can stick my tongue out for you too, if you'd like."

Elara laughed, a light tinkling sound that made him melt.

"Very amusing," Ursa said. "Now, sit up. Slowly, that's it. Pressure here."

He pressed his palm into his side to stabilize his broken ribs and sat upright.

"How's your head?" Ursa asked.

"Fine," he said. "I've had worse."

Ursa looked into his eyes, searching. A quick glance at his scarred hand held the answer to her unasked question. "You have a bruised sternum and two broken ribs. Does anything else hurt?"

"Only my pride. Are you all right?" he asked, reaching out to take Elara's hand.

"I'm fine. Already healed with my magic," Elara said.

"I'm so proud of you." He flashed her a crooked grin.

"For what?" A puzzled look flashed across her features.

"You controlled it. Concealed your power from him. After everything he did to you, Elara. It might not feel like it, but that was a small victory."

"I couldn't have done it without you. I doubt my power could bring me back from drowning to death. You saved me."

You saved me first, he thought. *The moment we met.*

Caelan's head pounded like a hangover after a night of partying with aether. Fortunately, he wasn't too proud to ask Ursa, "Do you have anything for the pain? Or to help me sleep it off?"

"Of course. Elara, help me mix up a tincture."

Caelan watched as the two women bustled around the small space, collecting herbs and colorful liquids. Elara pressed a pestle into a mortar with such determination that he thought it might crack.

After drinking the bitter tincture, his eyelids fluttered closed, and he fell into a deep sleep, one more peaceful than he deserved.

S ERA SAT UNDER THE stained glass window of Caelan's chamber, innocently reading what he could only imagine was a torrid romance novel. He smirked as he recalled the stack of similar titles Elara had toted around the library in the days following the coup. When Sera's eyes widened and her cheeks turned a deeper shade of pink, Caelan cleared his throat.

She yelped, nearly jumping out of her seat and onto his bed.

"Enjoying a little light reading, are we?" he asked, restraining a laugh and raising a brow at her.

The four posts of the canopy bed were wrapped with delicate painted vines that climbed the ash pillars. The tiny flowers that dotted the vines were no match for Sera. She slammed her book shut, and the vines turned into vicious snakes, their forked tongues lashing out toward Caelan.

"Glad to see someone's feeling better," Sera said, her own eyes as beady as her serpents'. At his grin, her sour mood vanished, and Caelan relaxed back against his headboard as the creatures disappeared in puffs of purple smoke and all returned to normal.

"You and me both," he said, rubbing a hand over the back of his head and stretching his stiff arms upward. He winced as his side smarted, but the sharpness of the pain had already dulled significantly. "How long have I been out?"

"A few hours. I gave Elara a break so she could get some rest too. I've had to rouse you every so often to make sure your brain hasn't gotten too big for your skull—though, to be fair, I think you've always had that problem."

"I didn't notice." He laughed, but the vibration hurt his chest and ribs.

"She'll be back in a little while. You should go back to sleep. The palace physician gave me some more of her sleeping potion for you if you want it."

He nodded. "Can we talk first? About Elara?"

"Caelan, you can talk to me about anything. Always. You're my oldest friend," Sera said, sitting on the edge of the bed and placing her hand on his shoulder.

"I don't know what to do. I can't protect her from him. I was a fool for thinking I'd ever be able to." He picked at the edge of the comforter, a habit he'd had since boyhood, his fingers tracing the vibrant damask pattern.

"I know. But none of this is your fault."

"That's not true. I've made choices. They seemed impossible at the time, but they were still mine to make. And I made some wrong ones."

"If you truly believe that, then you should tell her the truth—all of it," Sera said, folding her arms across her chest.

Panic washed over him. "It will break her."

"No, it won't. She's stronger than you think. And she loves you, Caelan. Trust me, I should know." Sera's lips tugged into a small sad smile.

"If I tell her the truth, then I won't deserve her."

"If you don't tell her, you definitely don't deserve her."

Caelan considered that for a moment, weighing his decision. *If I tell her, I'll lose her. I can't lose her.* "We can at least tell her about my father's prophecy."

"And the rest?" Sera narrowed her eyes at him.

"I'm not ready."

"You're running out of time."

"I know." He ran a hand over his stubbled face and prayed to the stars that it would be long enough.

CHAPTER 31

Elara

SERA WAS READING BY the fireplace in Caelan's chamber when Elara came in to take over. She looked up from her book, and Caelan stirred, sitting up in the lavish bed.

"Thank the stars you're awake. How are you feeling?" Elara sat on the edge of his bed, caressing his cheek. The heat of his skin was an inferno against her hand. She procured more of Ursa's potion and forced him to drink it.

"Like I want a rematch." He smiled half-heartedly, sputtering from the bitter-smelling liquid.

Elara's nose wrinkled. "Not funny. What *was* that?" she asked. "Why was he so enraged? And how did he find out about the baby?"

"Should I . . . ?" Sera got up from her chair and gestured to the door.

"No, please stay," Elara said. Though the vision of the wedding night left Elara wary, a rapport had blossomed between them over the last few weeks, and Elara sensed Sera possessed valuable information, despite her lingering doubts. Sera nodded but cast a quick nervous glance at Caelan. If they were to become genuine friends, Elara supposed it was time for them to be open with each other, even if that meant her making the first move to earn Sera's trust.

Caelan cleared his throat. "Elara," he began. "I don't know how he found out. My father was upset that you and I had consummated our relationship prior to the wedding night. And that we lost the child . . . He is likely worried that you won't be able to conceive an heir." His words were simple, logical, but they cut at her like knives.

"Who does he think he is?" she hissed. "I am the future queen of Serendith—not some pawn in his schemes and certainly not some broodmare!" She marched over to the stained glass window, the panes of red mimicking the haze that covered her vision. Leaning against the windowsill, she turned to face them. "He has no right to take my life from me—nor my throne. Certainly not my future children."

Sera stood and placed a supportive hand on her shoulder. "No. He doesn't."

"We have to stop him," Caelan agreed. He and Sera shared another look, and the raw fear in their eyes transformed into grim determination.

"How?" Elara asked. "He may not have the right, but he certainly has the power. My family is gone, my father's forces are scattered, my home is a prison." Her gaze fell upon Caelan. He already knew this, but it felt different voicing it, especially to the one she loved. To the ones whose efforts had made her pain possible.

Caelan, a deep sadness clouding his eyes, replied, "Yes, but he is a madman. The move he made on the throne wasn't based on sound political strategy."

Sera nodded. "Lord Stormrider spoke to his inner circle about a prophecy. It suggested that your firstborn child would be a Serathi. That power has been absent for generations, and he desperately wants it for his bloodline." Another look at Caelan, who nodded solemnly.

Elara's eyes narrowed. *What aren't they telling me?*

Caelan shifted in his bed, fidgeting with the velvet blanket, clearly uncomfortable with what he was about to say next. "Elara, my father is planning on killing you after our firstborn child is weaned."

With a sharp inhale, Elara squeezed the nearby starched curtain so hard that the metal rod above rattled. A searing pain shot through her tongue as she bit it, the metallic tang of blood filling her mouth. She'd anticipated something like this, but hearing the truth weighed on her.

Elara blinked, gathering herself. "What exactly did the prophecy say about the child?"

Sera thought a moment, then said, "The child would be conceived under the Cygnet Moon. That's why he's waited so long for the wedding."

Elara nodded, sitting on the edge of the bed. "I, too, have received a prophecy. A seer at the festival told me about one who would be 'born under the Cygnet Moon.' Could they be about the same child?" She placed her hand on Caelan's. "Our child? But 'born' and 'conceived' aren't the same . . . and why does your father care so much about having a Serathi in his bloodline? Don't you have enough power as Moiren?" The questions flowed out of her as her mind processed the overwhelming information.

Realization dawned on Caelan's features. "What if the prophecies aren't about a child? What if they're about you?"

"How? I wasn't born—or conceived—under the Cygnet Moon."

"How can you be certain?" Caelan asked.

Elara's brows rose. Since the Cygnet Moon hadn't been celebrated or documented in decades—she and Lysandra had scoured the library to be sure—there was no way to be sure that she wasn't the child of the prophecy.

"But Elara isn't a Serathi," Sera said.

Caelan looked at Elara, a question in his eyes. She nodded. *Tell her.*

"Yes, she is," he corrected.

Elara expected Sera to be shocked, or even hurt. Instead, a broad smile crossed her face.

"That," Sera said, beaming, "we can work with."

"WE HAVE TO PUT a team together," Sera said. She took a sip of her steaming beverage, much darker than common teas, from a gilded porcelain cup. Caelan sat across from her at the little round table under the window. Elara paced the length of her room, as anxious as Sera was calm. Caelan nodded and continued scribbling notes in his journal. It was worn, the pages yellowed, and wrapped in musty leather. Elara had seen him making notes of their training plans and progress before. She had also caught him doodling in it once or twice. This time, strategy filled their minds and those weathered pages.

"We need more allies in the palace. Not the courtiers or the magi. Is there anyone who knows the truth?" Elara asked.

Sera glanced at Caelan. "I might be able to refresh some memories."

"Iris? Kaz? Jalin?" Elara asked.

Sera nodded. "I can start with them, if you'd like."

Elara pinched the bridge of her nose, then nodded. "Caelan, what about your men? How many are loyal to you and not your father?"

He tapped his pen to his lips. "I have half a dozen men who will stand by me. The rest are too afraid of him."

"And there's still no chance of recovering my father's forces?" Elara asked, her voice thick with hope.

"No, they were sent to the Stormspire Mountains on false orders. By now they are snowed in and stranded up there. Besides, it would take too long to get missives to them *and* have them travel back in time for the wedding."

The wedding, Elara thought. "That's it! The wedding. Do you think we could attack then? With such a small force, we need a public scene to distract him. What better than the wedding?"

Sera rose, determination blazing in her eyes. "It has to be me. I'm the only one who can get close enough to him. I can trap him, blind him like I did with your family, long enough for Caelan and his men to capture him."

"Let's beat him at his own game. Once and for all," Caelan said.

Elara beamed at him. At Sera. Her life was now ruled by prophecy—perhaps it always had been—but she'd been freed in another way. Now that her heart belonged to Caelan—along with her family and her kingdom—love like she'd never known before filled her with hope.

CHAPTER 32

Caelan

"C AREFUL NOW, PRINCESS," CAELAN teased. "We wouldn't want you to get hurt." For the dozenth time that morning, he had his steel pressed against her slender neck. Elara lay on the floor at his feet, glaring up at him.

"Again," she said.

He pulled his blade away from her throat, leaving a thin line of red behind, and reached down to help her up. She shoved his arm away and stood, dusting herself off before trying to tame the loose strands of black hair that fell in her face, having freed themselves from her braid. Her movements were stiff, distracted.

"Sorry about that," he said, shrugging. "You know we can take a break."

"Do you need a break?" she huffed, falling back into a starting stance, ready to pounce.

Caelan smiled and shook his head. This morning, she was a determined little thing, her eyes bright with purpose, a slight set to her jaw. They had been training for hours, and she was doing quite well. Her strength and stamina had improved over the months, her magic enabling her to recover and rebuild her muscle faster than anyone else he'd worked with.

Her true talent, though, lay in the sharpness of her intellect. He'd drilled into her the dozens of fighting stances and strategies that had taken him years to master. Her grace in the face of certain death didn't hurt either. While he tried to be gentle, her growing pain tolerance only left her afraid of the most deadly strikes, giving her an advantage over her potential adversaries.

Caelan had to admit that she impressed him, even if she couldn't appreciate the significant progress she'd made in such a short time.

But a silent dread hung between them, a shared fear that their efforts would ultimately be in vain, despite their progress.

Elara lunged at him, a vicious attempt to hit the weak spot in his side with her elbow, which he appreciated. He grunted as he allowed her to land the blow, doubling over. "Good," he gasped. "You're finally learning the number one rule of swordplay."

"And what's that, exactly?" she asked.

He grinned wickedly. "That there are no rules." He swept his leg under her leather boots, causing both of them to topple to the ground. Her short sword, the weapon that they had chosen for her after trying a bow and a staff, clanked to the floor, rolling just out of her reach.

Caelan tossed his own sword to the side, catching her arms and pinning them to her sides as he mounted her. She wriggled beneath him, distracting him from the fight at hand. A surge of adrenaline left him aching, consumed by need. When she caught his eyes, her own darkened, and she stilled.

"Sorry, love," he said, brushing his lips against the spot where he'd nicked her earlier, the skin already smooth, fully healed by her magic. "I just don't think today is your day." He nuzzled her neck, enjoying the vanilla scent of her hair mixing with the salt from her sweat.

"Maybe not," she purred. Her lips brushed against his ear, sending delicious shivers through his body. Until her teeth clenched down on his earlobe and the sharp pain jolted him.

"Hey! No biting, Princess."

Elara took advantage of his surprise, wrapping her legs around him and using her now-free arms to flip them both over. She pulled a dagger from her boot and pressed the cold metal to his throat.

"You said there were no rules, watermage." A grin brighter than the stars spread across her face.

"Fine, I surrender." He held his palms up. "When did you start carrying that in your boot?" he asked, gesturing to the dagger.

"Wouldn't you like to know? It's my little secret." She resheathed the weapon and grasped his wrists, wrapping his arms around her waist.

Caelan longed to rip the leather armor from her torso. *Stars above. If we could just stay like this forever*, he thought as he looked up at the woman he loved, victory and pride twinkling in her blue eyes. Every brush of her body against his made it harder not to lean into her entirely, to smell her, taste her. Not to mention the fact that she was straddling him, her weight on him a captivating distraction. But not distracting enough.

My little secret. The words echoed against his skull. His jaw stiffened, and he gave her hips a tender squeeze, gently lifting her off of him.

"What's wrong?" she asked, the joy in her eyes replaced with concern. "Did I hurt you?" She examined his ear and prodded lightly at his torso.

"No, you didn't hurt me," he said. "But we should be done for the day. I have work to do." He stood, offering her his hand once more. This time, she took it.

"You're leaving? Caelan, no. I need more practice."

"You've done exceptionally well, Elara. But the reality is that no further amount of training is going to make much difference. At this point, we need to rely on my men and Sera and hope that you never have to use this." He picked up her short sword and held out the hilt for her. She gripped it, knuckles turning white. "Or that," he added, nodding toward the dagger concealed in her boot.

"You think we'll lose, don't you?" A haunted, glassy-eyed look overtook her lovely features.

I think I'll lose. Lose everything. No matter what happens with my father.

"It's . . . not that simple," Caelan said, the words catching in his throat as he swallowed his pride. "I've lost to that man my entire life."

"I don't accept that. You must have faith. At the very least, you need to have hope."

Perhaps he'd never won before because he lacked her conviction. Maybe fighting for his own survival wasn't enough. He looked at

Elara, her silk shirt and trousers drenched in sweat beneath her armor, hair escaping her braid. A flicker of hope, bright as a firefly, danced in her eyes. Faith in their plan. *Faith in me.* His heart pounded against his tender ribs.

Caelan had witnessed her struggles firsthand. She'd fought for survival from the moment he and his men had captured her the night of the invasion to the hours she'd spent learning to conceal her healing gift. Now she fought for freedom—the freedom of her people from a tyrant like his father. Most importantly, she fought for love—the love for her family, for *him.* His stomach turned to pure acid.

"Do you really think me that incapable?" she whispered, her eyes sliding down over the blade in her hands. He swore he glimpsed a tear in her reflection.

"No! Of course it's not that. I just . . ." He held his hands out in front of him, glancing through the window to the bare-branched trees outside, wishing he could flee into the peaceful snow.

"Then prove it. Fight me," she commanded, backing away from him and lifting her blade.

"Elara, no. I don't want . . ." He floundered, not knowing what to say. The room shrunk around him, adrenaline running through his veins once more and clouding his judgement. *Please don't make me do this, my love.*

"Fight me!" she roared, face turning crimson.

Caelan's shoulders sagged. She was so stubborn. To protect her, he'd have to break her spirit—to show her the brutality she would face in a real battle.

"As you wish, Princess."

In a flash, he was on her, the sound of steel scraping steel and grunts of exertion echoing around the dusty room. He backed her into a wall of wooden crates, her weight sending a few of the top ones tumbling to the ground as her back hit it. Elara's eyes closed, beads of sweat dripping down her forehead. He sensed she was using all her strength, from her powerful legs and core to the thin muscles wrapped around her forearms. She was strong. But not strong enough.

His face was a breath away from hers, the tips of their noses almost touching.

"Yield," he whispered. He barely recognized his own voice. The sound that came out was a menacing rasp, a low, gravelly sound that set his teeth on edge.

"No," she grunted.

"Isn't this what you wanted, *Princess*?" he hissed. "For me to 'prove it'? I don't think you're weak, Elara. Just naive. You don't know the way the world works the way that I do. You don't know the way *he* works the way that I do."

Elara's eyes widened at his sharp, accusing tone. For the first time since they'd met, a look of utter defeat filled her eyes as she stared at him. Caelan's heart sank like a stone, regret washing over him. He released her, backing away slowly.

"I'm sorry," he said, sword clattering to the floor. He dropped to his knees, his lungs burning, the air heavy in his chest.

"Don't be," Elara said, wrapping her arms around herself. "I shouldn't have pushed you."

"No, you shouldn't have. You should have listened when I said we were done." His hands balled into fists.

"You were right," she said, and his head snapped up in surprise. "We can't rely solely on brute strength. Certainly not on my combat skills." A half-hearted smirk tugged at one corner of her rosy lips. "We need to approach this from a variety of angles."

Kneeling before him, she cupped his face in her hands, her touch featherlight. "Go, talk to your men, and to Sera if you want. I'll see you later." She pressed a kiss to his cheek, her soft lips warm against his clammy skin.

As she walked toward the door, he called out to her back, "Where are you going?"

She didn't face him as she answered, "To speak with your father."

Caelan was on his feet in a flash, reaching for her. "No! Elara, don't . . . not without me. Please, wait!"

"Please," she whispered. "Let me do this on my own."

He dropped his arm, and the door closed behind her with a sickening click.

CHAPTER 33

Elara

E LARA WAITED, TAPPING HER fingers on her thigh to soothe herself. She sat in her father's study, a familiar room she had spent countless hours in. As a toddler, she'd played in the corner with the wooden horses he had carved for her while he pored over paperwork from behind his giant oak desk, humming to himself.

Her heart ached at the sight of his desk chair, a tall wingback with curling brown arms and claws for feet. It was wrapped with well-worn crushed green velvet. Elara's mother had nagged him to replace it for months, but he'd simply smiled and nodded, never making a move to obey her wishes. The queen didn't mind. Her parents had a loving relationship and let little things go easily. Elara only hoped that she and Caelan could be the same one day.

The door swung open, interrupting her thoughts, and a footman announced Lord Stormrider. He waltzed into the room, haughty as ever, before plopping himself into her father's chair. It groaned under his weight, and Elara worried it might crack. She frowned at him. He smirked at her. They faced each other, finally alone.

Caelan had all but begged Elara to let him accompany her, to be a buffer between her and his father. But Elara had insisted that this conversation happen in private. She wanted Caelan in the dark. Even though he and Sera had disclosed Lord Stormrider's plot to kill her and exploit her child, she still had a lingering feeling that things were not as they seemed.

She hoped that Caelan and Sera were simply not privy to Lord Stormrider's ultimate plan and weren't intentionally keeping more secrets from her. Her goal was to see if she could get Lord Stormrider to slip—to give her any more information than she and her allies already had in order to defeat him.

"Thank you for accepting my invitation to meet," she said.

"It was the least I could do, considering our last . . . unfortunate encounter," he mused, plastering a tight smile onto his face. His eyes weren't warm though—they were an icy gaze as sharp as a raptor's. "I assure you, this was never how I wanted this to go. My intention was an amicable alliance between our prestigious families, but your father made that impossible." He looked down at his nails, as if they were more interesting than whatever Elara had to say to him.

I need to be careful, Elara thought.

"Indeed," she said, keeping her tone light. "I believe that we have a misunderstanding of the expectations of our current . . . arrangement." She almost choked out that last word. Lord Stormrider's eyebrows rose. *Good, I've got his attention.*

"Indeed," he echoed. "I can clarify anything you wish." He leaned in, his hands clasped and his elbows on the desk, fingers interlocked under his chin.

"Your original stated desire was that I agree to marry your son in exchange for my family's safety. Since then, it has become clear that you have other desires, including our abstinence until our wedding night. Is that correct?"

Lord Stormrider's face was burning red—not from anger, but from embarrassment. He seemed uncomfortable being spoken to openly about such intimate matters.

"Correct," he said. "Though I didn't realize that I would have to spell that part out for you." He frowned.

Elara nodded, unfazed by the implied insult to her character. "Very well. Is there anything else I should be made aware of?"

"You are very simple, aren't you?" Lord Stormrider said, as he realized he may in fact need to spell things out for her.

"I simply want to ensure that you are satisfied. To keep my family safe."

He laughed, a cruel, cutting sound. "Your family? You think you are in a position to negotiate with me now? Do you think I need *you* that sorely?"

"I believe you do, Lord Stormrider. Without me, you have no access to my future children."

Take the bait, she thought.

His frown flipped into a genuine grin, pleased that he was no longer in a position to be embarrassed and could instead educate a stupid young woman on the way of things.

"Your child? Your naivety betrays you, *child*. Look at you, little princess. Heir to the Serendithian throne? Pathetic, just like your coward of a father. Your family has no power—doesn't even know the meaning of the word. I could find a dozen girls for my son to marry in your stead. You're just another pretty face." He leaned forward, brushing the back of his hand down her cheek and setting her teeth on edge.

"Well, your son and I make such a handsome couple, do we not?" Her stomach churned at his touch.

"Indeed, you do. And based on his attempt at protecting you the other day, he's grown quite fond of you."

"And I of him," she whispered.

"You love him, don't you? Poor things. Love blinds the best of us. Drives us to do things we never imagined we could do, often to those we claim to love most."

Power blinds you, not love. Certainly not for your son, she thought.

"What is it that you want from us?" she asked. *What else haven't you told me?*

He sat back in the chair with a creak, gazing behind her at the bookshelves filled with tomes and scrolls. "What do you know about prophecies?" he asked.

"Prophecies?" She glanced behind her. The sun's last beams of light spotlighted dancing dust motes. "I thought they were just for children, or townsfolk silly enough to fall prey to swindlers."

"You're mistaken. Few possess the talent—it isn't linked to any essence affinity. But the magic exists, if one knows where to look."

Yes. Here we go. Elara leaned forward in her seat, willing him to continue.

"Your father and I could have been true friends, you know. If it weren't for the war. Our families have been rivals ever since. Such a waste. You Evensongs were raised here." He waved a hand at the ornate painted ceiling, which depicted a serene forest scene. "My family started over with nothing." His eyes went distant before he focused on Elara once more. "How's your geography?"

"Fine."

"Then you know what borders my home?"

Elara nodded. "The mists to the north of Veilkeep."

"Very good. Now, some believe that all arcane knowledge lives in those mists—that, before the Shattering, the Nimireth maintained a hidden library with all manner of ancient tomes and relics. It has since been lost to the ages."

A lost library? She imagined the information she could find about her own magic if such a place existed.

"When I was a young man—a new father, in fact—I found a curious object that had washed up on shore. A stunning bangle cast in solid platinum. Naturally, I gifted it to my wife. The infernal thing drove her mad. She started having these . . . visions. Nonsense at first, but once translated, they held information about the future." Lord Stormrider's eyes darkened, one of them twitching in the corner. "Before she passed, she told me of a child, to be conceived under the Cygnet Moon, who would be the key to restoring the Well."

"The spring of all essence," Elara whispered.

Conceived under the Cygnet Moon? She gulped down her dread. With control of that child—perhaps her child—Lord Stormrider could play a hero to the entire continent. He would control which families had access to the Well—the source of all magic in Serendith. *Ultimate power*, she thought, fighting to keep her expression neutral and hide her natural reaction. The few bits of information he'd revealed lay before her like priceless gems. *One of our prophecies is wrong.*

"Imagine all the good I could do in the world, Princess. Being able to choose who is blessed with the gift of an essence affinity instead of hoping that a child is born with it? I could guarantee that noble families stay in power and that peasants need not carry the burden of magic at all."

"I see," she said. *You really are a monster.* Worse than her own father's secrets and schemes—the games Lord Stormrider played, with people's lives as pieces on the board of Serendith, made her stomach sour.

"Oh, do you?" he asked, smirking at her. Elara balled her hands into tight fists in her lap, the gesture hidden from Lord Stormrider's view. "Well, then we shall have no other unpleasantness. After all, you are going to be my daughter-in-law. And your offspring will be *my* grandchildren."

Unable to look him in his golden eyes—Caelan's eyes—Elara rose. "Thank you for your consideration. I believe that I have a much better grasp on the situation now."

CAELAN WAS PACING IN a nearby corridor when she finally exited her father's office. He stopped in his tracks when he saw her, eyes narrowed. "How did it go?" he asked, breathless and eager to debrief the conversation.

Elara shrugged, acting nonchalant. "He said nothing we don't already know. He clearly underestimates us though. We can use that to our advantage." Elara knew in her bones that it was best to keep her newfound knowledge of Lord Stormrider's endgame close to her chest. Caelan and Sera had waited to tell her about Lord Stormrider's plan to kill her—and she still didn't know why.

"I'm glad the meeting was uneventful, though I'm sorry to hear that it was unproductive too."

"Well, we know what he wants, after all." She placed her hand on her lower belly. "Now all we have to do is defeat him before he gets it."

Caelan exhaled in relief and placed his hand over hers. "We will. He fights for power. We fight for love. And love always wins." He flashed her a crooked smile.

"Caelan, he mentioned your mother . . ."

He stiffened, his mouth drawing into a thin line.

"You rarely talk about her. Why?" she asked softly.

"She died when I was a boy. It was a long time ago. I don't remember much of her."

Elara nodded. "I'm sorry that you lost her so young." *And that you had to watch her descend into madness.*

"It was a long time ago," he said again.

When Caelan wrapped his arms around her, Elara wondered again if she might not be the only one still keeping secrets.

CHAPTER 34

Elara

A LONE WHITE ROSE reached for the sunlight, stretching out its stem and leaves. The poor thing looked like it would topple over, trying to soak up the rays that seldom passed through the sliver of a window near the ceiling of Ursa's infirmary.

Elara watered the pitiful desdemona cutting, its leaves withered and peachy-white petals browning at the edges. Lysandra tittered nearby in her raven form. Explaining the unusual creature to Ursa had been a hoot. The first time Lysandra had shifted from a cat to a raven, Ursa had dropped a beaker, its contents staining the floor bright blue. Now the woman was quite fond of her, bringing her little lemon cakes as treats during Elara's healing lessons.

"Come now, beauty," Ursa cooed at the bird, coaxing her over to the table where, just weeks ago, Elara was worried Caelan would take his last breaths. With three jilted hops and a flutter of onyx wings, Lysandra landed on the table with a soft thud and began pecking at the crumbs in Ursa's hand.

I like this one, she said in Elara's mind, causing her to grin at the older woman.

Me too, Elara sent back.

"Now, what do you get when you combine hawthorn and olive leaf extract?" Ursa asked.

Elara tapped her chin dramatically. "A tea for chronic headaches, or, in stronger doses, a remedy for high blood pressure."

"Excellent! Your potions knowledge is coming along nicely. And so is your anatomy."

Elara nodded absentmindedly, offering Lysandra a scratch on the top of her feathered head.

"I know that look, child." Ursa rested one hand on her hip and the other in the wide pocket on the front of her apron. "You're not happy with your progress. Whyever not?"

"You've been testing me on tinctures and proper bandaging technique for weeks. Don't get me wrong, I'm grateful for our lessons. But I feel like I'm missing something."

Ursa nodded and pursed her wrinkled lips. "And you've been training with Captain Stormrider. Long days make for weary hearts, my dear. You're being too hard on yourself. Here, give me your hand." She held out her palm, and Elara placed her hand on top of it.

Ursa pulled a scalpel from a nearby drawer—Elara feared that she'd never learn where the woman kept everything, her memory already bursting. In a flash of movement, Ursa ran its chilly edge from Elara's wrist to the base of her index finger. Fat red droplets joined the blue stain on the floor, and Lysandra cawed her dissent at Elara being harmed.

"There now, you see?" Ursa nodded to Elara's bloody palm.

"See what?" Elara asked, brow furrowing as she willed her skin to knit itself back together.

"You didn't even flinch! A mere month ago, you would have jumped out of your skin at a wound like this. And now, you could let it bleed as long as you like or heal it. That's progress."

Elara nodded slowly. *Progress.* When she'd first discovered her magic, she hadn't been able to control it, to protect herself by keeping her power hidden. Progress wasn't something often afforded to a princess, who was expected to be picture-perfect at all times. Appearing flawless didn't leave room for the growing pains and failures required for real learning.

Between her training with Caelan and lessons with Ursa, she'd forgotten to be proud of herself. For a moment, Elara reveled in the feeling—the freedom—that accompanied her willingness and ability to be a beginner, for once. The feeling was foreign, out of place beneath her skin. But she smiled graciously at Ursa. "Thank you."

Ursa looked her over again and sighed. "I know when we started this journey you were hoping to learn more about the potential of your power to heal others."

Elara nodded. "Something just isn't right. I can't grasp it though. The journal from the library that Lysandra found outlined all the known uses for natural magics—for those born with essence affinities. Obviously, the Stormriders and other Moiren have kept the most power, followed by the rest of the elementalists. Why were the Serathi the first to disappear? And why would they—we—return now?" She didn't expect Ursa to answer and was musing aloud for her own benefit. She thought back to the journal—she and Sera had spent countless hours translating the infuriating tome but had only managed to crack the first half. It made her long for Thalia's keen eye, as she had a knack for languages, history, and all things arcane.

Why am I so different? Elara thought, saddened by the idea that she might be the only one like her in the world.

You are no different. You are just like the others.

Elara jumped, almost knocking over a rack of glass tubes. Lysandra wasn't supposed to hear that thought, let alone answer the question.

What others? she asked.

The raven shook out her feathers again, blinking her beady eyes. *Not ready yet.*

What do you mean, I'm not ready? Lysandra sounded like her father, and Elara's hackles rose.

No. The others are not ready yet.

"Well, you could waste your time pondering the past, or you could focus on the task at hand," Ursa chided.

"Lysandra says there are others. Others like me?" Elara asked. The bird tilted her head at an angle only natural to a predator.

Yes. Like us. Don't you know?

Elara's patience was wearing thin, the urge to tear out her own hair battling with her desire to keep Lysandra's soft feathers unharmed.

"She said that there are others like 'us' and that they aren't ready yet." Confusion, thick like fog, settled over her.

Ursa froze, the rag she was using to wipe down her work surface drifting to the floor. "Of course," she whispered. "I don't know why I didn't think of it before. Elara, did that journal you found mention anything about druids?"

"Druids? Yes, the book mentioned the druids were the protectors of the source of all magic. But they were just limericks. I thought those were fairy tales for children."

Of course they're real, she thought. *I've seen enough magic in the last few months to last me a lifetime. Why should I disregard those legends? Especially after learning about the Well . . .*

Ursa wrung her wrinkled hands together. "They aren't just protectors; they *are* the source of magic. My grandmother used to tell me it was born of their blood."

Narissa's prophecy floated into her mind once more. "Ursa, what really happened during the Shattering?" Elara asked.

"Well, my grandmother was a young girl. Your great-great-grandfather was king. He joined forces with the Stormriders and wanted to use the threat of that alliance to broker peace with the druids and end the war. But he betrayed both the druids and the Stormriders—destroying the first and exiling the other. Essence had already been declining before that, but after the druids were gone . . ."

Elara balked. Caelan had been right—it was the Evensongs who'd betrayed the Stormriders.

The older woman's eyes narrowed. "Ask Lysandra what she is to you."

Elara turned to the raven and raised an eyebrow. *Go on, then.*

The bird puffed out her feathers with pride. *I am your familiar.*

"She says she's my 'familiar.' Do you know what that means?" Elara asked.

"Elara, a familiar is a *druid's* companion. Their protector and guide," Ursa said, giving her a pointed look.

Elara's heart pounded, and she turned back to the rose. "Impossible. I can't be a druid. My parents aren't. My sister . . . No one in my family has even had an essence affinity, not for hundreds of years."

It is not impossible. You have druid blood in your veins. It was just hidden before.

"How? Why?"

I do not know.

"But . . . my family," Elara protested again. *What if my parents were keeping this from me?*

Ursa placed a hand on Elara's shoulder. "I miss them too."

A tremor ran through Elara as she stared at the rose, its thorns seeming to prick her soul, and silent sobs racked her body. Her hot tears pelted the dark soil in its clay pot. The familiar weight of the world settled onto her shoulders. *Princess. Prisoner. Healer. Savior. Druid. It's too much.*

"Don't worry, child. I know you'll bring them back to us. And then we'll get your answers. With a familiar—and a Stormrider—at your side, anything is possible. Look." Ursa gestured to the rose. The flower's petals were pure pearls in the moonlight, its leaves restored to their vibrant emerald green. "You healed it."

CHAPTER 35

Elara

T HE GRANDEST PARLOR IN the palace was empty save for
Elara and Sera. A fire roared in the hearth, crackling and
popping. The air hung heavy with unspoken tension as the two
women faced off. Elara slammed her hands—which were holding
a fan of playing cards—onto the table. The force of the motion
threatened to knock their crystal wine goblets onto the ornate
carpet.

"Come on! You're cheating. You have to be." Elara pouted.

Sera offered her a knowing smile. "I've been playing this game
since I learned to talk. It's not my fault no one can keep up."

"And I've been hustling drunken, bluffing courtiers since I
could sneak my way into the gambling parlors!" Elara shook her
head, reveling in both the wine and the company. Both offered
her a much-needed reprieve. The two women had spent the entire
morning eating, drinking, and playing strategy games.

With a laugh, Sera tossed back her blond hair and refilled her
goblet with wine. She pulled out a delicate silver case the size of
a playing card. With a soft click, she opened the ornate box and

offered it to Elara, who eyed its contents with suspicion, a slight frown furrowing her brow.

Out flew a series of cards, much like the set they used to play their game. These cards floated in front of Elara, each one illuminated by the signature purple glow of Sera's illusion magic. The figures on each card danced, cried, or kissed, animated by magic. More than any other, the Moon card held Elara's attention. It featured a woman draped in flowing white robes lounging in the crook of the crescent moon, stars woven into her long hair. Elara snatched the card out of the air and inspected it.

"If I wanted to cheat, I'd be using these instead," Sera teased. With the snap of her fingers, the card in Elara's grasp shifted from the Moon to the High Priestess, who winked at her before changing back.

"Beautiful," Elara whispered in awe. "Where did you get these?"

Sera ran a slender finger over the silver case, tracing the whirls etched into its surface. "I've had them since I was a child. I believe they belonged to my mother."

"My mother gave me and my sister enchanted music boxes. I never realized how many magical devices there are in the world. The possibilities are so exciting."

Sera clutched the pendant hanging against her chest. "Not all of them are beautiful. Or harmless."

Elara resisted the urge to press her friend, admiring the woman depicted on the Moon card instead.

Sera leaned closer to examine the card in Elara's grip. "She looks like you," she mused.

"You think so? Something about her seems so familiar." Like Elara, she had long dark hair, a detail the artist had captured along with the spirited glint in her eyes and the resolute set of her jaw.

"Well, we've been playing for hours, so you've seen the Moon's face at least a dozen times today."

Elara laughed, passing Sera the card with a quivering hand. "That must be it."

"Don't feel bad, you're a quick study. You actually make it hard for me to beat you, which is more than I can say for Caelan."

Elara frowned, recalling how tense their last training session had been. She still couldn't shake the feeling that he was keeping something more from her. Maybe Sera was too.

"I'm worried about him, Sera."

Sera stiffened, clenching her jaw. "Me too," she whispered behind the sound of her card shuffle. She tapped the edge of the deck on the table.

Elara weighed her next words, not wanting to reveal what she'd learned about Lord Stormrider's intentions. Or what she and Ursa had learned about Lysandra's true nature. Neither fact was critical to their current objective, and she didn't want the information to fall into the wrong hands. "Do you think our plan will work?"

"With enough allies to support us and the element of surprise? Yes." Sera didn't lift her gaze from the cards in her grip.

"And . . . without them?" Elara asked, biting the inside of her cheek.

"Caelan has been quietly preparing his men for days. You've had Meg and Iris rallying the palace staff, yes?" Sera asked. When Elara nodded, Sera continued, "And I've been keeping my eyes and ears open, ensuring that Lord Stormrider suspects nothing."

"I don't think we're ready," Elara said, mind wandering back to her frustrating conversation with Caelan.

"Is anyone ever truly ready for war?" Sera rose a sculpted brow.

"It's more than that. Caelan was harsh on me in our last training session, and he's right—there's not much I can do if it comes down to a battle."

A haunted look crossed Sera's face. Her usually sharp features softened, revealing the young girl behind the stoic woman.

"What is it? You don't have to protect me from the truth," Elara said.

"There won't be much any of us can do if it comes to battle. No one has ever beaten Lord Stormrider. Certainly not Caelan. And we are relying on Caelan's men to be more loyal to him— and you—than they are afraid of his father."

"But once you blind him, Caelan should be able to capture him?"

Sera sighed deeply. "Lord Stormrider has known my magic for a long time. He has built up certain protections against me." She touched her necklace again. "I won't be able to hold him for long, but I will do my best to give Caelan enough time."

"Can Caelan really do it? Imprison his own father?"

"I hope so. And I hope that capturing Lord Stormrider is enough to put an end to this nightmare."

Elara nodded. "He has many supporters. It's delicate work. Rebellion has been brewing for a while, and I'm sorry to say that

Lord Stormrider wasn't the one who started it. The nobles will take sides if the capture doesn't go smoothly."

"It's a good thing you two like each other, then. A wedding with the new head of the Stormrider family and a renewed alliance between your two houses will strengthen your family's position." Sera appraised Elara with a look and sighed. "I have to be honest with you. I've seen Caelan falter when facing his father."

Elara shuddered, recalling Lord Stormrider's assault on her in the throne room after her miscarriage. Caelan had frozen before he saved her. "I've seen it."

"We might want to land on a backup plan, in case he needs rescuing. How far do your healing capabilities stretch?"

Elara sat back in her chair, folding her hands in her lap. She loved Caelan and would fight for him however she could, even if that meant betraying his trust. "What did you have in mind?"

With a frustrated sigh, Sera shook her head, her shoulders slumping. "It's important to understand the bounds of your magic. But your situation is so unique. No proper mentor—no offense to your physician friend. We can't simply cut off your finger to see if it grows back. It's not worth the risk."

"I'm glad you think so." Elara chuckled darkly. "I heal well now from most injuries that could occur in the course of battle. Deep cuts, broken bones, burns."

"Caelan actually let you break a bone?" Sera shuddered. "I didn't realize how . . . intense your training was." To Elara's surprise, she sounded impressed.

"And my pain tolerance has increased immensely," Elara said, her voice barely above a whisper, the vulnerability of the moment making her feel exposed.

"I'm sorry for that," Sera said, almost to herself.

Elara could only imagine the torment that Sera had experienced at Lord Stormrider's hand. If it resembled Caelan's so-called upbringing, it must have been arduous. The familiar sting of being judged for another's actions struck Elara, giving her a newfound appreciation for what her friend had endured.

"It's the price we pay for power," Elara said, placing her hand over Sera's across the table. "Power and greedy men."

A mischievous grin spread across Sera's face, her eyes sparkling with a sudden idea. "Remember your vision? The one with your family at the wedding?"

Elara nodded, a slight smile playing on her own lips.

"I have an idea. How do you feel about being bait?"

CHAPTER 36

Elara

E LARA GLIDED THROUGH THE muddy slush formed from melted snow, the mud clinging to the bottom of her navy blue embroidered skirt. Caelan trudged along behind her, his boots squelching with every step. Wedding plans were the couple's focus for the day. The last time she had planned an event of this scale, it was for the grand ball held early in her captivity. Then, she'd faced a dozen seemingly insignificant decisions alone, each potentially impacting her standing in her own court. Now she had Caelan.

How far we've come.

"Do we really have to do this today?" Caelan grumbled, fussing with her heavy wool coat and securing it around her shoulders. "You might not freeze to death, but I'm not an Embrathi, and it's cold out here."

"Afraid of a little snow, watermage?" Elara tilted her head back and opened her mouth wide to catch a snowflake. With a flick of Caelan's wrist, a tiny flurry floated to her tongue, and they both grinned at each other.

"I didn't know you could make snow." She beamed at him.

He laughed, the sound like bells. "I didn't either."

She planted a kiss on his chilly red cheek. "Today, I get to train you." Her breath appeared as swirls of mist between them.

Caelan crinkled his nose. "As you wish, Princess." Ever the gentleman, he extended his arm and pulled her in close to the warmth of his side.

The pair scrutinized the tent city that had blossomed on the festival grounds over the last few days. Seven concentric circles formed around the massive wedding pavilion in the center. These tents were more lavish than the ones the nobles had brought for the tournament. Intricate gold detailing shimmered in the sunlight, and the air smelled of expensive perfumes and polished wood. The canvas was thick, and the ropes and beams fastened tightly, each one fortified for the soon-to-arrive harsh weather.

The dozens of nobles and merchants who'd made the journey to witness the wedding of the century had set up their temporary homes, the wealthiest in the circle closest to the center. Workers had already shoveled the grounds, and fires in lightweight metal stoves lined the pathways, providing light and warmth. Elara assumed that Lord Stormrider had hired flamewards to keep the fires lit, either with their essence or with enchantments.

Elara and Caelan walked down the path until the heaters' comforting glow engulfed them, the warmth blissful against Elara's numb cheeks. Despite the fires, she shivered as they neared the wedding pavilion. Braided silver tassels hung from the flaps of the entryway, dancing in the breeze.

"This was my parents' binding marquee," Elara said as she ran her fingers over the tassels.

Caelan's eyes softened, and he placed a gloved hand over hers. Snowflakes stuck to her lashes like frozen tears.

"Come," Caelan said. "I have a feeling I have a lot to learn. And I'm a terrible student. Do your worst."

Elara sniffled, but she smiled and let him lead her under the threshold.

Pure-white silks cascaded from the top of the king pole to the earth, where workers covered the ground in plush sapphire-blue rugs. Everywhere, vibrant red peonies and fluffy pink astilbes created a breathtaking display, their sweet fragrance reminiscent of spring, at odds with the frigid air outside. Ornate brass lanterns hung from the ceiling and queen poles, combating the chill with their own magical flames.

An attendant escorted them to a table with half a dozen place settings, each with its own combination of their house colors and crests.

"What do you think of this one?" Elara asked, gesturing to a place setting.

"They all look the same to me." Caelan shrugged nonchalantly, but he squinted at the silverware with distaste.

She shook her head. "This one will do nicely." Elara selected a setting with a cobalt-blue charger and a white plate accented with emerald-green vines curling around the edges. The attendant noted her choice and scampered off to complete the next task on his to-do list.

Elara turned to Caelan. "Obviously, the color palette is the same for all of them, but why do you suppose I chose this one?"

"Because you like being on top?" For all the finesse and skill Caelan had with his magic and his sword, he lacked the taste for this kind of battle. Where most men, and a few lucky women, could flaunt their power in shows of force, she was forced to protect hers through the complex and often ridiculous details of court fashions.

Elara punched him in the arm. "You're not entirely wrong," she said. A smirk touched his lips as one eyebrow rose in amusement. "Not like that! It's important to balance representation for both of our houses, while maintaining the authority of the crown," she clarified.

"All that from a plate?" Caelan placed his hands on his hips.

"Imagine what goes into selecting the menu that fills it," Elara said, rolling her eyes at him. He snuck a few extra bites of the cake samples while Elara made her selections. The right tablecloth—made from Valorian silk and embroidered with swans and sea serpents—sent a powerful message of wealth and unity. The right sculpture—two swans bowing their heads together to form an elegant heart—celebrated young love's innocence.

"Stars, Elara." Caelan ran a hand through his blond curls. "We're going to be here all day, aren't we?"

"Don't worry, I've been working on this for weeks. We just have to make a show of putting our stamp of approval on everything as a couple. Besides," she whispered, "it gives you a chance to survey the grounds, find any weak points."

Caelan nodded, a proud grin spreading across his face. "Dangerous little princess."

If only you knew, she thought.

Between decision-making, Elara conducted her own surveillance, creating an exit strategy should she and Sera need to implement their backup plan. Elara watched the man she loved, a calculating look on his face as he scanned the pavilion and noted key locations for his own plan. *Should I tell him?* she thought. *No. I don't want him to think I've lost my faith in him.*

Several leafless birch trees lined an aisle that led up to the dais where Elara and Caelan would exchange vows in just a few days. The pale branches were decorated with more flowers, along with glittering crystal garlands. Rows of cushioned benches sat upon either side of the aisle, but most of the witnesses would stand, so that the benches could be moved after the ceremony without forcing guests out into the cold. After the binding ceremony, the marquee would transform for dancing. Servants would pass food and drink about on platters. Music would fill the space, encouraging revelry in celebration of the couple and Serendith's future.

Elara's people needed something to celebrate. She placed a hand on her belly—the heirs of this union could ignite a resurgence of magic and the longstanding peace that accompanied powerful rulers. She took a deep breath. The wedding would be her only chance to defeat Lord Stormrider, save her family, and secure the kingdom. Elara prayed to the stars she wouldn't fail.

CHAPTER 37

Caelan

Aᴛᴛᴇʀ Sᴇʀᴀ ꜱᴛᴏʟᴇ Eʟᴀʀᴀ away to look at wedding dresses, Caelan made his way back inside the glorious warmth of the palace. Taking off his cloak, he shook the snow from his damp hair. He ran a hand over his stubbled chin. *So much work to be done.* He undid the top buttons of his shirt and tugged the scratchy collar away from his neck.

Court life, with its suffocating etiquette and endless obligations, didn't suit him. Not like it suited Elara. This was her birthright, a skill set nurtured in her from the start. Caelan had been raised to fight with swords, not wit—and certainly not with fancy silver butter knives. Sure, he knew he had his own charms, but he was thankful that he and Elara seemed a well-matched pair for ruling.

He ignored the chill that ran down his spine at the thought of becoming king and continued his journey through the winding alabaster halls until he reached his destination. As he descended the dank stone staircase that led beneath the palace, a musty smell filled his nostrils.

"Sir," Silas said, standing at attention at the bottom of the stairs.

Caelan offered him a quick nod. "Report?"

"Your men have been briefed on their positions. Patrols begin tonight. Any gaps will be identified and addressed," he said.

"Good. Thank you, my friend." Caelan placed a hand on the man's shining pauldron. "Any other news?"

Silas stretched his arms overhead and rolled out his neck, relaxing. "Lorian is complaining about her post."

"Why? Where did you station her?" Caelan asked.

"Undercover in the laundry room." A crooked smile spread across Silas's bearded face.

Caelan chuckled, picturing the capable swordswoman, who was twice his age, wearing a bonnet and scrubbing sheets. While she might not enjoy it, Caelan had to admit it was a genius assignment for her. He'd give her a nice gift after all of this was over to make amends. "You know she's going to make you pay for that later, right?"

"I'm counting on it, sir." Silas waggled his eyebrows. Elara's second guard had been flirting, unsuccessfully, with Lorian for years, though Caelan was certain the two of them were enamored with each other.

Scanning the dungeons, now empty thanks to Sera's previous brainwashing efforts, Caelan asked. "So, why did you want to meet down here?"

"I needed to show you this." Silas gestured for Caelan to follow him, grabbing a glowing torch from its sconce in the stone wall.

With every step and every empty cell they passed, his heartbeat quickened, matching the infuriating *drip, drip, drip* against ancient stone. The hair on the back of his neck and arms stood on end. Every cell in his body screamed at him. *Trap.* But Silas was one of the few people in the world that Caelan trusted with his life. The grizzled guard had helped patch Caelan up countless times and had even helped him avoid the worst of his father's wrath as a boy. Which was why he'd entrusted Elara's life to Silas.

"Here," Silas said, stopping. In the flickering torchlight, Caelan peered into an open cell. His heart sank. The bars between this cell and its neighbor had been removed, doubling its size. If a prison cell could be considered comfortable, this one came close, with an ornate bed, a small table with two plush chairs, and a copper washtub. Even a cast-iron stove provided a makeshift hearth, its faint scent of woodsmoke hanging in the air.

It was a cage fit for a princess.

"It can't be. You think it's for her?" Caelan's voice was gravel.

Silas nodded solemnly. "Yes. It's for Elara. It seems your father wishes to confine her after the wedding."

"Why? Why would he need to keep her down here?" Caelan's ears and neck burned red-hot with the rage bubbling up inside him. "She's enough of a prisoner as it stands. And people will start asking questions if she suddenly disappears."

"Why does your father do anything, if not for power?" Silas asked.

A wave of understanding washed over him. "He's afraid of her." All the blood drained from Caelan's face. "He knows that I've grown too attached, that she is too difficult to control."

"And the council has concluded its meetings. With winter setting in, most of the magi at court will retire to their own manors after the wedding. The remaining visitors will journey back home before it's too dangerous for travel. As for the rest . . ."

"Sera," Caelan finished. "She can create an illusion of Elara whenever my father needs it. If he decides not to let her out of the cage to play."

The wedding was truly their only chance to put a stop to his father—he'd thought they'd have more time to recover in case things went wrong. But with Elara imprisoned after . . . *Failure is not an option.* His hands shook.

"Come on, let's get out of this horrid place." As the two men marched down the hall and started climbing up the stairs, Caelan cleared his throat. "How is she?"

"She likes Felix better than me," Silas said.

Caelan nudged him with his shoulder. "Of course she does. From what I've seen, you never talk to her."

"I'm not there to talk, remember?" He gave Caelan a pointed look.

Caelan sighed. "And I suppose I should thank you for that too, my friend." He rubbed at the tension plaguing the back of his neck. "Does she suspect anything?"

"She's smart. Observant. And the shifter that follows her around is a little spy. But no, I don't have any reason to believe that she knows the truth," Silas said.

"Good." Caelan breathed a sigh of relief, and the heavy burden on his shoulders felt slightly lighter.

"When are you going to tell her?" Silas asked.

"I don't know." The lies gnawed at him. He'd struggled for months under their oppressive weight, each day a heavier burden than the last.

"Sir, it's the right thing to do," Silas said, narrowing his eyes.

"I know. Just not right now." *I'm not ready.*

Silas stared at him, his expression a mixture of disbelief and suspicion. "Caelan, you need to tell her. You should have told her ages ago."

"How do you honestly think she'll react to the news that her family has been dead since the night of the invasion?" Caelan snapped.

"I don't know," Silas whispered, deflating.

"It would destroy her. Let's earn our freedom first, then figure out how to pick up the pieces after. If she doesn't trust me, then our entire plan falls apart." Caelan's heart hammered against his ribs with such force that he stopped walking, sinking to a seat on the stairs, back scraping against the cold stone.

Trust wasn't the only issue. It was about the bittersweet ache of love lost. "I can't lose her, Silas," he whispered. A hole had formed in his heart the day his mother died, and it had just begun to fill, thanks to Elara. He felt the ghost of his mother's expectations, a constant reminder of his failings, a shadow made darker by his current circumstances. But perhaps with Elara, there'd be an opportunity for redemption, a glimmer of hope in the darkness.

I can't lose her too, he thought, listening to the soft echo of rustling feathers in the eaves of the corridor.

Exhausted from the day of silly politics and his father's scheming, Caelan flung open the heavy oak door to his chambers, the sound echoing in the stillness, and kicked off his mud-caked boots.

"Long day?" Elara's voice floated to him from the bed. Propped up by a mountain of pillows, she paused her reading, slipping a worn bookmark between the pages as she gazed at him. Her silky black hair was loose, cascading over her shoulders. Mischief danced in her sparkling blue eyes as a playful smile lifted the corners of her lips, a single dimple appearing on her left cheek.

"Indeed. My wedding planning 'training' was particularly brutal." He melted as she yawned, stretching her arms overhead with languid grace.

He shed his shirt and trousers, the smooth coolness of the sheets a welcome contrast to his warm skin as he collapsed into bed. With a sigh of contentment, Elara nestled against him, her vanilla scent captivating his senses as his arm enveloped her. *If only we could stay like this forever*, he thought.

"You seem to have emerged unscathed," she said as she traced her fingertips over the smooth skin of his bare chest, tickling him.

"I had a brave defender to guide me through the fray." He pressed his lips to her forehead before burying his nose in her hair.

"Caelan . . ." She said his name like a caress, and her hot breath tickled his neck. Her back arched slightly. He wanted the softness of her body against his—her mouth and tongue and teeth on his bare skin.

"Have all the other preparations been made?" she asked, and he knew she was no longer talking about the wedding decorations.

"You've coordinated a beautiful battleground for us." He scoffed. At the concern that flashed across her features, he added, "Don't fret, Princess. It won't come to that."

I can't let it come to that.

"We've done all we can at this point. Now there's nothing left but to wait and pray that the stars are on our side," she said.

Caelan envisioned her beautiful face, tear-streaked and etched with worry, locked away behind the rusty iron bars of the cage he'd visited. A fist clenched around his heart. *Silas was right. She deserves to know the truth.* His fingers traced the silken strands of her hair, the caress a balm to his troubled mind, as he gently touched her cheek. She looked so serene that he couldn't stand to rob her of her temporary peace.

One more night, he promised himself. *Then I'll tell her everything.*

CHAPTER 38

Elara

"IF HE'S NOT CAREFUL, Silas is going to squander any chance he has with Lorian," Sera said, shaking her head and sipping her coffee.

Caelan chuckled. "Those two have been after each other for a decade. If he hasn't scared her off by now, I have to say that I think it might work out in the end." He shrugged, his smug smile parting for a breakfast pastry that left a dusting of powdered sugar on his lips and doublet.

Elara glanced out the leaded glass window, smiling to herself as the steam from her teacup fogged up the frosty glass. The world outside was white, coated with fresh powder of its own, and the trees dripped with crystals. Peaceful.

The calm before the storm, she thought. She would savor it, this moment. Here, drinking tea and telling jokes with her fiancé and her friend. *Thalia would love this*. The rising hope of their imminent freedom tempered Elara's heartache over her family's absence.

Lysandra prowled in, her feline form tense, dark fur standing on end. Elara abandoned her teacup to scoop her up and sat on a velvet sofa, tucking her legs underneath a blanket and scratching the familiar behind her ears. Instead of Lysandra's usual chipper purring, Elara was met with a low hissing.

What's wrong? Elara asked silently.

Your family is gone.

Elara's brows knit together in confusion. *Yes . . . I know. They've been captive for months—*

No, they are dead, Elara.

Elara froze, her mind wrapping itself around those three impossible words: *"They are dead."*

You're wrong. Lord Stormrider swore an oath. The wedding . . .

Elara's eyes flickered to where Caelan and Sera were talking, their faces and hands animated, engrossed in their own conversation and oblivious to the turmoil going on inside Elara's head.

He knows, Lysandra said, the thought laced with sorrow. *Caelan knows. He's known since the start.* She placed a tiny black paw on Elara's arm, large green eyes shimmering. *I'm sorry.*

A searing pain ripped through Elara, one half of her heart sinking like a stone and the other choking her from inside her throat. She rose, sending Lysandra bounding to the floor. Elara took a sharp step back as the room swayed around her, gripping the edge of the sofa to steady herself, fighting to stay upright. Grief squeezed her chest, making breathing feel impossible—each inhale was shallow, ragged, and filled with sorrow.

Her skin grew clammy, her face and fingers numb. Her ears filled with a rushing sound, like a storm pelting the roof with hail and wind. Caelan and Sera were speaking to her, frantic and worried, but while their mouths moved, Elara couldn't hear the words. Caelan reached a hand toward her.

"Don't touch me!" she hissed, though she hadn't intended to speak.

The familiar numbness of loss washed over her, but not before tears welled in her eyes and trickled down her cheeks. She said nothing else while Sera and Caelan looked from her to each other, unsure what to do. Elara became a statue, cold and utterly still save for the tears streaming down her face and the shallow rise and fall of her chest.

Silence reigned, a suffocating blanket of tension heavy in the air, punctuated only by the occasional strained breath. The ground rocked beneath her, and she was grateful for the sofa she held fast to.

Finally, Elara whispered, "You knew." She pointed at Caelan with a shaky finger. "You knew that my family was dead this entire time?"

Panic flashed across his features.

Good, you should be afraid, she thought.

Sera placed a hand on her shoulder, giving her a gentle squeeze and a tiny shake. "I'm so sorry, Elara."

Elara slowly directed her gaze toward Sera, her eyes the only part of her moving. When they fixed upon Sera's face, Elara saw the shame and remorse etched into her features. She didn't care.

"And you . . . You knew too, didn't you?" The stare she set upon her so-called friend was bloodthirsty. "Did you help murder them? Did you torment their minds, or just erase them entirely until they were nothing?" Red coated her vision, her nostrils flared, and the chill that had descended upon her figure turned molten.

"Elara, wait, let me—" Caelan said.

"No. I knew better than to trust you—my enemy's son. To believe in us. I've never met a man who could turn down power for love, and you're no different. You *used* me."

And I let you. Elara turned the full force of her fury to Caelan, giving him a look that caused him to back up. A look that said, *Run.*

Caelan and Sera backed out of the room with infuriating composure, as if they thought Elara just needed some privacy to process and calm down. They were wrong. Once the door to her chambers closed and she was alone—though she guessed Caelan wasn't far and her guards were lurking outside—she let her stone facade crack. Her face scrunched up, her tears flowing more freely now and her nose dripping. Her hands balled into fists, her nails cutting into her palms and drawing blood before the moon-shaped slices healed almost instantly.

Elara stalked over to the window and gazed outside once more. Dawn arrived, painting the sky in shades of pink and gray. More snow fell softly, coating the courtyard in a cold dust. Any trace of greenery or the bright oranges and yellows of autumn had long since faded, leaving the scenery drained of its life.

I have to get out of here. With that one thought driving her forward, Elara donned a thick coat and wrapped a fur-lined cloak around her shoulders, pulling the hood over her head. She yanked on wool socks, well-worn boots, and gloves. Elara pulled her dagger out of the hidden place under a crooked floorboard and strapped it to her ankle.

While Caelan had schooled her in weapons, he hadn't offered to let her keep any. Just another reminder that she was, in fact, a captive who had gotten too comfortable with her captor. Thankfully, she'd had the mind to sneak the dagger into her room through the tunnel Lysandra had discovered.

Ready to be free of the suffocating room, she ventured outside into the courtyard. "Stay inside, keep warm," Elara ordered Felix and Silas. They looked at each other with eyebrows raised, startled by the command in her tone. She glared back at them when they didn't obey her and stalked behind her. "You can spy on me just as easily from the doorway or windows." Her definitive words hung in the air as she departed.

Elara wandered the courtyard until she found her destination: the garden. She sat on a stone bench, the snow crunching under her weight, and inhaled the freezing air. She pressed her hands against the stone, savoring its solidness as the chill seeped through her gloves. *Maybe this is another vision*, she thought. *Maybe I just need to be patient until I wake up.*

I'm so sorry for your loss.

Elara looked around to discover a speckled snowy owl perched on a nearby branch. She reached out and stroked Lysandra's soft white feathers.

Sighing after a few more slow, lip-chapping breaths, Elara resigned herself to the inescapable nightmare that was her reality.

Mama. With her sweet lullabies and ridiculous tea parties.

Papa. With his crinkle-eyed smiles and scary bedtime stories.

Thalia. Never again would Elara tease her baby sister about holding the reins wrong while out riding, laughing all the while.

Dead. Gone. Her family was lost to her. She cried until her eyelids swelled shut and her lips tasted of salt.

Elara's kingdom was under the control of a monster. And Caelan. He'd lied to her—she'd trusted him, and he'd betrayed her. She might have expected this from Sera, the monster's servant, but not him.

I loved him, she thought. *I gave him everything. And he took it all away.*

CHAPTER 39

Caelan

D AYS PASSED, AND ELARA still hadn't spoken to him. Not in any meaningful way, at least. Caelan, listless and dejected, wandered the halls of the palace, busying himself with routine tasks. He tiptoed around an apology, and Elara kept their conversations pointed, focusing on finalizing details for the wedding. *A wedding that might not even happen now—not in earnest,* he thought. The now-famous royal couple still linked arms in public and dined together. As far as the rest of Serendith was concerned, they were happy and in love. Keeping up the charade—and it was once again a charade—was harder this time, knowing what it was like to be loved by Elara.

Elara sat at the head of the breakfast table, book in hand, distractedly spooning porridge into her mouth. Caelan sat across from her, pretending to be interested in a piece of bacon. The table stretched between them, the steam wafting off the spread of biscuits and meats highlighting the chill in the air.

"Good morning," he said, the greeting stiff and awkward.

Elara's response was clipped and frigid, like all the others over the last few days. "Good day to you as well," she said, not bothering to look up from her book. She sipped from her steaming mug.

"Elara, please," Caelan said, the sound of desperation in his voice grating on him. "We can't keep going on like this." He gestured toward her and then to himself, demonstrating the physical distance between them. That space didn't even come close to matching the emotional distance in their relationship.

Elara marked her page, closed her book, and set it down on the table with care. She studied Caelan for the first time in almost a week, her eyes searching his face. He ran a hand over his disheveled hair and rubbed his unshaven jaw. He tugged self-consciously at his jacket, his fingertips sore from the nails being chewed halfway down to the quicks.

"Tell me why," she demanded.

Caelan blinked at her. He'd tried to explain himself countless times, each attempt met with the same cutting rejection from Elara.

"I was going to tell you." He raised his hands out in front of himself at her glare. "I was. Lysandra must have overheard me talking to Silas about it the night before you found out." He rubbed the back of his head.

"You mean the man you've had spying on me?" she asked, shaking her head. Caelan flinched. "Why didn't you tell me before?"

"I'm sorry. I know I don't deserve your forgiveness," he said.

"No, you don't." Elara folded her arms across her chest, eyeing her book like it was an escape hatch.

"But you deserve an explanation." Caelan's voice faltered, his faith in himself shaken. He'd convinced himself that he was doing the right thing, protecting her. But it was the same flawed logic echoing his father's beliefs—a twisted attempt to prove that the ends justified the means. The burning shame crept over him, making his face flush. A bitter taste filled his mouth as he acknowledged the truth he'd known all along: He wasn't worthy of her love.

Caelan looked across the table at Elara, realizing he was out of options. *No more secrets.* He braced himself and shared a tale that only one other person in the world knew.

"I—" He looked at her blankly, his words caught in his throat. He cleared it and started again. "I lost my mother when I was seven years old. She was the person I loved most in the world. She was warm and selfless. Beautiful. My father adored her, and we were happy together."

Elara's expression was unreadable, a blank slate giving away nothing of her inner thoughts.

"She grew sick suddenly," he continued. "She stopped eating, lost weight, and slept all the time. Her mind . . . She wasn't herself." Caelan shuddered. "The physicians thought it was poison. My father was relentless in his pursuit of the culprit. He suspected everyone—our allies, our enemies, our household staff. He didn't sleep for months. It drove him near madness, watching her suffer."

Caelan paused, drinking cool water from his crystal goblet. His hand was shaking as he placed it back on the table, and he silently cursed himself. Elara's eyes had softened—she knew the madness his father was capable of firsthand—so he kept going. "Eventually, there was no one left for him to blame and torment. Except me."

A flicker of pain and sympathy shone in her eyes. Brow furrowed and head tilted, a silent question formed in her expression: *Did he hurt you like he hurt me?*

So much worse, my love, he thought. His fingers traced the scars on the back of his opposite hand, one of many abuses. "I have been afraid of that man ever since. I am ashamed to say it, but that is the truth. I did not have the strength to defy him, not until I met you.

"When my father told me about his plan—driven by that wretched prophecy about our child—I didn't know what else to do but follow his orders. You have to understand, Elara, I was raised to hate your family. But when I saw you, *really* saw you, covered in dirt and then defending a servant, I realized you might be different. Then you healed, and I thought you were a liar. I was so confused and ashamed . . ."

"How? How did they die?" she whispered.

"My father slit their throats himself, the night you agreed to marry me." A fresh wave of nausea washed over him as she avoided his gaze. "Sera told me that they were still blinded—just in a peaceful darkness. They didn't suffer."

Elara was silent for a few moments, gazing down at her silverware. "Was it real?" she finally asked. "Us?"

"Yes," he said. "Elara, I came into this situation thinking you would be greedy and privileged. Then I met you and you asked for my help. You were so genuine and curious. I knew you were different from what I first thought. You were never my enemy, Elara, and I hope you can see that I am not yours either."

Tears pooled in her sapphire eyes, and Caelan hoped they were tears of relief as one slid down her cheek. He longed to close the agonizing distance between them and wipe it away—to wipe away all her pain.

"Why did you keep lying to me, then?" she asked. "You know what it's like to lose a mother. You knew what they meant to me, Caelan. Everything I have been fighting for was a lie."

"I didn't know how important it was to tell you the truth. You were already in such a terrible situation, and I didn't want to take away your hope," he said. *I know what it's like to lose all hope.*

Elara's face went pale, her mouth turning down in a frown. She squared her shoulders and leaned back, farther away from him. "Thank you for telling me about your past. I'm sorry about your mother." Her tone was even, almost clinical.

No. "Please, Elara, you must understand. I grew up in a world where lies were the only way to stay safe, to keep those I care about safe. I am still learning. Please give us another chance."

His vision was blurry behind tears of his own. His shaky hands were now balled into fists. *I can't lose her too.*

"I'm not ready, Caelan," she whispered.

Caelan's heart sank as they both rose from the table and she glided away, the silk of her train dragging on the floor behind her, whispering against the polished floor. As the last of the fabric slipped through the doorway, the searing pain of loss shot through him, bringing him to his knees.

CHAPTER 40

Elara

E LARA DRAGGED THE BACK of her hand across her forehead, using the linen wrap to catch beads of sweat before they stung her eyes. Alone, she gulped water from a delicate goblet that looked ridiculous in the filthy makeshift training room. Elara had once felt like she didn't belong here either, but with her messy hair, sweat-stained clothes, and a newfound confidence in her capabilities, she felt at home.

Dust motes floated around her, sticking to her as she continued hitting the hanging canvas bag. Each punch articulated her frustration. *Thump.* At Caelan's betrayal. *Thump. Thump.* At herself for trusting him in the first place. *Thump. Thump. Thump.* At her father for putting her family in danger with his schemes.

Elara recalled the last conversation she'd had with the king, when they'd argued about her attending the council meetings. Her knuckles cracked with the force of her final blow. *Maybe you were right, Father. Maybe I wasn't ready for all of this.*

Collapsing onto the floor, she lay back and followed the cracks in the painted plaster ceiling with her eyes. One crack split a woman's once-serene face into pieces. *I feel shattered too*, she thought. Elara and Caelan had spent the last few days putting on brave faces for the court, pretending to be in love once more. Even knowing about his childhood, she couldn't shake her bitterness and find it in her heart to forgive him. She couldn't even forgive herself for trusting him.

Instead of facing him, she threw herself into her studies. Her magic lessons had stalled—she'd hit a wall, unable to heal any other plants, and Ursa was unsure how to guide her over it. Elara continued to focus on her physical training. However, it only eased her mind for a short time. Research provided more relief, the comforting solitude of the library calming her as she anticipated their impending nuptials.

Lord Stormrider left Elara and Caelan alone to plan, only offering a few suggestions to make the festivities more politically advantageous. Elara hadn't cared when he hinted certain nobles should sit closer to the bride and groom. When he suggested escorting her down the aisle himself, while the king performed the ceremony, Elara balked. The thought of an illusion of her father taking part in the wedding made her stomach churn. Caelan miraculously talked his father out of that idea. A small mercy from the man who had broken her heart.

Elara stood, dusting herself off, and focused on her next solo drill. Grabbing a wooden short sword from the rack, she spread her feet apart and began shadow cutting. A step forward with a diagonal cut, followed by a step back with a mirroring cut to recover. Then a side step with a matching horizontal cut, followed by a thrust and guard check. On her last forward step, her foot caught on a loose floorboard. Her ankle twisted, and a loud snap echoed across the room.

She fell to her hands and knees, hitting the ground hard and gritting her teeth against the pain. Her face flushed, and tears filled her eyes. Even though she knew she would heal—although she wasn't sure what her magic's exact limitations were—she still felt the pain. Months of training had desensitized her to most common bruises and cuts—and a few broken fingers—but this was another beast altogether. She took a few deep breaths as the pain, then adrenaline, rushed through her and quickly yanked her foot to align her ankle properly before healing it. Searing pain assaulted her senses, providing a welcome blindness to her raw emotions. Ursa had told her the importance of setting bones and joints before her essence healed them in the wrong position. With her ankle aligned, Elara pictured the bone fusing, the torn ligaments and tendons tightening, and the swelling subsiding. In moments, her injury had healed completely. Drained by pain and magic, Elara slumped over from exhaustion.

She hugged her knees to her chest, and her tears flowed freely, as if the dam holding back her emotions had broken once more. A wave of all the despair she'd suppressed washed over her. Drowning her.

Before, Elara had been driven by her desire to save her family. Now that they were gone, her love for Caelan might have sustained her. But their relationship was tarnished now, like her mother's old silver jewelry. Heirlooms that would now pass to her. Just like the crown.

And there it was—she would become queen, with or without Caelan by her side. If her love for Caelan wasn't enough, then her love for her people would have to be.

As she released her pain, renewed purpose bloomed within her. She and Caelan would work together to defeat Lord Stormrider, and she would take control of the continent. As a Serathi, she would be no ordinary queen. She'd serve as a beacon of hope, a reminder of what was possible if the noble families united to find the Well and restore magic.

I won't let my family's deaths be in vain. I won't disappoint you, Father. Not again.

A hand brushed her shoulder, pulling her from her thoughts. Elara peered up at Sera, then unfurled herself.

"Are you all right?" Sera asked.

"What do you think?" Elara snapped back at her. Elara rolled up into a seated position on the floor, and Sera plopped herself down in front of her, crossing her legs. The motion looked at once graceful and ridiculous, given Sera's floor-length chiffon gown.

"Honestly? No," Sera said simply. "I'm sorry that I lied to you about your family. I know it doesn't make a difference, but I want you to know that."

"Why did you keep lying to me after . . . after we became friends?" Elara nearly choked on the word "friends" and fought back more tears pooling at the edges of her vision. She distracted herself by fiddling with a piece of fabric caught in a nail on the weathered pine floor.

Sera seemed on the verge of crying too—her lower lip and chin quivered, and her eyes were red around the edges. "I . . . I know it was wrong. To keep a secret like that from you. I can't make any excuses for that. But I promised Caelan that I wouldn't tell you. He is my oldest friend. I would do anything for him."

"Even betray your other friends?" Elara asked, raising an eyebrow.

"Yes." Sera didn't hesitate to answer.

"I can almost respect that. Almost." Elara sighed, rubbing her still-tender ankle. "How will I ever be able to trust you, Sera?"

"You love him, right? Even after he lied to you?" Sera asked.

I still love him, Elara thought, and her expression must have given her away, as Sera said, "Of course you do. And he loves you. I'm confident he will never lie to you again. He did it to protect you, and he knows now that he was wrong. So, I will never need to lie to you again."

"And he loves you—he'd never put you in a position like this again," Elara added.

Elara didn't like it, but the plain logic, and raw honesty, gave her a strange sense of comfort. She placed her hand in Sera's and said, "Tell me about you and Caelan growing up together."

Sera looked down at their interlaced fingers resting in her lap atop a pile of lilac skirts. Her blond hair was pulled back into a tight chignon, but a delicate strand had escaped and hung over her eye, making her look softer, younger.

"You know the scars on Caelan's hand?" Sera asked. Elara nodded, conjuring the image of the bubbled flesh in her mind. "He was twelve when it happened. His father forced another child to inflict that pain on him."

Elara grimaced. "Stars . . . I had no idea. That's horrible." After learning about Caelan's mother, and now the depths of his fear for his father, she understood. It didn't excuse everything he'd done to her—the lies—but she understood.

The two women sat on the dusty floor like that for an hour, Sera recounting more horrors before they were forced to stretch their legs. They walked, Sera talked, Elara listened. They settled in Elara's room, eating together as Sera told Elara more about what it was like for her and Caelan growing up around Lord Stormrider. Where Caelan had spared her some details—or maybe didn't know the extent of the abuses he didn't see—Sera was an open book.

"A few years ago, Caelan's father gave me this." Sera clutched the amulet around her neck. "You know what it does?"

Elara nodded. "It allows you to conceal memories, right?"

"Yes," she whispered. "It took months of practice, torturing his prisoners by twisting their minds. After that, I understood why so many hated my kind."

"I'm so sorry . . . No one should ever go through that." Bile rose in the back of her throat as she heard what Sera had endured. *Lord Stormrider is a monster.* It was enough. Enough for Elara to understand, to forgive the lies, to wrap Sera tightly in her arms and ask her to stay the night in her room so they wouldn't be alone.

CHAPTER 41

Elara

C AELAN WAS STANDING ON the bank of one of the larger
ponds on the property that hadn't yet iced over. The
snow had subsided, leaving the shoreline muddy and slick. Elara
approached silently, watching as he scooped up a handful of
pebbles. After the fourth one skipped across the water, she stepped
behind him and placed a gentle hand on his shoulder. He turned,
eyes widening with surprise and a shy smile brightening his
features. Caelan looked at her like a man who was dying of thirst
and she was a freshwater stream, finally found and able to quench
him. Elara held out her hand, palm up, and waited for him to pass
her some rocks.

She threw her first one, which soared over the pond before it
bounced off the surface once, twice, seven times. When it finally
sank, Caelan let out a hearty laugh. The sound made her heart
skip like the stones. Elara launched her second stone, but as
soon as it hit the water, it plopped under the surface with a soft
gulping sound. She looked over at Caelan incredulously while he
pretended to examine his fingernails.

"No fair," she said, bumping him with her shoulder. He stiffened at the friendly gesture, perhaps unsure of her intentions after suffering days of her aloofness.

"I think we took fair off the table a long time ago," Caelan said, suddenly serious. He didn't apologize again, and she was glad for that. Instead, he simply looked down at the water's edge as the ripples they'd created faded away and the surface smoothed over, as if nothing had disturbed the pond's peace.

"I talked to Sera," Elara said. "I don't agree with what the two of you did, but I understand it much better now." She took his hand in hers and brought his knuckles to her lips.

Caelan's eyes flashed to hers, burning with hope. "How can you forgive me? I've done everything wrong."

"I did everything right, and look where that got me. I think it's time we changed the rules of the game," she said. Elara had been waiting for others' approval, for others—men especially—to believe she was "ready." First with her father, then in her training with Caelan. Now, she had no choice but to step into her own power—to have faith in herself and take what was rightfully hers. She would reclaim the throne even if it wouldn't be how she'd imagined it. *And Father won't be there to see it.*

"Will you help me? Rule Serendith?" she asked. "It won't be easy—the crown is heavy. But we can't let your father have it."

"Our plan will work." He pulled Elara into his side, his warmth and familiar cedar scent filling her with longing. And trepidation.

Elara shrugged out of his embrace and stepped back. "It has to." Before he could say another word, she turned and left him alone at the water's edge. *No matter what becomes of us.*

E LARA KNOCKED ON CAELAN'S door as the sun rose the next morning, scattering buttery light on the floor through the colorful windows. A heavy thump sounded, like that of a boot being dropped to the floor, before the door creaked open. A shadowed eye peered through the crack in the doorway. Caelan flung the door open and beckoned her in.

"I wasn't expecting you," he said, blond hair mussed and one boot on, the laces still undone. He hadn't even buttoned up his shirt yet. Elara followed him into the room, closing the door behind her with a soft click. "It's good to see you," he said. Dark circles hung under his bloodshot eyes, and fresh bruises covered his hands.

Elara knew that the last few days had been rough on him, and a tiny darkness inside her was glad for it. But she did still love him, and it hurt to see him suffering like this. Elara had a plan coming into this conversation. She was going to stay calm, collected. Despite her willingness to move forward together, healing their relationship and rebuilding trust would be a lengthy process. The emotional wounds they'd both sustained would take longer to heal than his bruises.

Elara had intended for them to sit and have a cordial, if difficult, conversation about what had happened and their expectations for the future. That plan didn't stand up to the starving look in his eyes. Caelan looked so sad and sweet and irresistible.

Without saying a word to him, Elara flung herself into his arms. He gasped in surprise, then wrapped his arms around her waist and squeezed her tight. Elara looked up at him, and they locked eyes. She pressed her lips onto his and slipped her hands underneath his shirt, dragging her nails down his back with enough pressure to make him shiver. Caelan stroked her hair and released her lips in favor of her neck. He found her favorite spot, and Elara let out a soft moan.

Caelan traced circles into her inner thigh with his thumb. The circles worked their way up her leg until she was tingling with anticipation. His eyes roved down, then up—as if he was memorizing every inch of her. She was still fully clothed, but that gaze alone stripped her bare.

Caelan lifted her, and Elara wrapped her legs around his waist. He carried her, placing her on the bed like a prize. Where their first few times together had been near wild, this time was tame. They savored every touch, every whispered breath, the familiar scent of each other's skin a welcome balm after what felt like years of separation.

Elara gently cupped Caelan's face, her fingers tracing the line of his stubbled jaw. His golden eyes were no longer strained with longing, but softened with peace. The weight of the past seemed to lift as they both knew, with quiet certainty, that this was a new beginning. A light peck on his lips, then she nuzzled into his neck, the texture of his shirt rough against her cheek. With a sigh of contentment, he settled his chin on her shoulder.

They remained entwined with each other for a while before Caelan gestured to his lone boot—still on his foot. Elara laughed as he attempted to ready himself for the rest of the day. Before he could do much more than get his other boot on and start buttoning up his shirt, Elara stopped him.

"Wait," she said. "Do you have time for a bath?"

He grinned. "With you? Always." He pulled on a cord, ringing a bell to summon a servant. Soon, an older man Elara had never seen before prepared a bath for the couple. The attendant filled the cast-iron tub with steaming water, and the crisp fragrance from floral oils filled the room.

"Couldn't you do that for him?" Elara asked, concerned for the man's well-being as he lugged the last bucket over to the tub.

"Yes," he whispered. "But Phineas wouldn't appreciate it—he'd see it as an insult. Not everything needs magic as its solution."

The crackling fireplace cast a gentle glow throughout the small room. Caelan ordered some wine, along with a tray of fruits and cheeses, and arranged them on a three-legged wooden stool next to the bathtub. It all looked and smelled like heaven to Elara. But, cuddled against Caelan's chest in the water, the rest of the world fell away. She was home.

CHAPTER 42

Elara

E LARA WOKE TO SCRATCHY grass against her cheek and arm. A pair of beady eyes stared into hers, a forked tongue flicking out of the creature's mouth with a soft hiss. *Get up*, Lysandra pleaded. Elara exhaled in relief that the onyx serpent was her familiar.

Where are we? Elara asked silently, too unnerved by the circle of dense forest surrounding them to speak aloud. The massive trees loomed overhead, tall enough to block out the sky, and groaned around them. The forest was ancient and alive with a strange humming that she felt in her bones. The freshness of spring leaves masked the rot hidden beneath.

Step into the mist, Elara. She's waiting.

Elara tried not to cringe at the unusual feeling of scales against her skin as Lysandra curled around her arm like a gauntlet. Mist swirled at the base of the largest tree at one edge of the clearing. It glowed with an odd shimmering blue light. Elara crawled toward it on hands and knees, her head throbbing as she got closer. When the pain was so intense that she feared she might faint, she reached out her fingertips as if she could grasp the light.

The forest fell away, and the pain subsided as the mist swallowed Elara. She looked around, seeing nothing but endless softly glowing clouds.

"What do I do now?" Elara asked Lysandra.

Wait. Quiet your mind. She will come.

Elara's heart pounded against her chest. She counted her breaths, trying to fend off the panic clawing at her the longer she waited. After what felt like an eternity, the mist began to clear, and Elara found herself surrounded by more unusual trees. Head back as she gazed skyward to their vast canopy, her mouth fell open. These loomed over her like palaces, wreathed in gold and silver, fitted with stained glass windows of every color and lit from within. The jewel-toned leaves glistened in the breeze, sending a shiver down her spine. She looked around, her dread growing, and felt claustrophobic after staring at an open void for so long.

Lysandra slithered down Elara's nightgown before shifting into her raven form. The bird hopped a few paces, then flapped up onto a low tree branch. *There*, she spoke into Elara's mind.

Elara looked in the direction Lysandra's beak was pointing. A snow-white deer materialized between two trees and began striding toward them. Elara jumped as something grazed her shoulder.

"Hello, Princess." A voice as old and deep as time itself sounded directly behind her.

Elara turned away from the deer slowly, finding a slender hand upon her shoulder. A woman wearing a flowing white gown and a veil obscuring her face stood inches away.

"Tell me, child, what brings you here?" the woman asked.

"I'm not sure. Where is here, exactly?" She flinched as the deer's wet nose brushed her fingertips. The warmth of its breath against her palm comforted her, and it nudged her until she stroked its face.

"My familiar—Della." The shrouded lady nodded to the deer in introduction.

Lysandra cawed from her perch. Elara said, "Oh, this is Lysandra. I'm—"

"Princess Elara Evensong," the woman said.

"You know me?"

"I've been watching you since you were a babe." The woman moved her hand from Elara's shoulder to her cheek, the long sleeve of her gown rippling.

Elara steeled herself against the stranger's cold touch. Questions flooded her mind, but her lips refused to shape the words, as if she were in a dream, watching herself from just outside her own body.

Is this another vision? she asked Lysandra.

The raven cocked her head and blinked. *Yes. You're safe here, Elara. Calm your mind.*

Closing her eyes, Elara focused on one thought and forced her mouth to move. "Tell me what I am."

The woman sighed and stroked Elara's cheek before tucking a strand of hair behind her ear. Elara froze—the motherly gesture wasn't what she'd expected.

"Come with me, and I will show you what you wish to know. But I warn you, the truth is dangerous." She placed a hand on either side of Elara's face, pressing her cheeks firmly. "You must be strong, Elara," she said, her tone now more serious than somber. "Do not give in to temptation."

The woman touched her forehead to Elara's. A flash of blinding light transported Elara once more, landing her amidst pure chaos. Black smoke thick enough to shield the rising sun darkened the sky. Screams of pain washed over muck and piles of writhing bodies—a battleground. Mercifully, she couldn't smell the stench of the blood and excrement that had turned the earth to mud beneath her feet.

Familiarity dawned on her. "I've seen this before," Elara said, her voice somehow carrying over the din. "There's a tapestry in my home's library."

She stepped over a body, stooping to examine the filthy uniform. Emerald green. *Like Father's—my—soldiers.* The next of the fallen wore forest brown, a house color she was unfamiliar with. The woman's arms were covered in vine-like markings, reminiscent of Caelan's sigils but far more extensive.

"Who are they?"

"Your ancestors," the shrouded lady answered.

"No, the others." Elara pointed to the woman in brown.

"Your ancestors."

Elara stared at her, adrenaline racing through her veins. The shrouded lady pointed to one moment of stillness amongst the chaos of the battle. A brown-clad medic, denoted by a gray flag on the battlefield, tended to one of the fallen. The medic pushed the soldier so that he was lying prone, facing the sky. A wave of nausea overtook Elara as she beheld the gash across his face. Blood dribbled out of his mouth and over his broad chin. The cut was bone-deep, running from his forehead to his jaw over a now-empty socket where his eye had once been.

The medic kneeled at his side and wiped her bloodied hands on an already-soiled apron. She placed her hands on either side of his face with tenderness and sang. It was a lullaby that Elara recognized—the same that her mother had sung for her and Thalia hundreds of times as children. When the last sweet note faded into the roar of the ongoing fight, a soft glow emanated from the medic's hands, soon surrounding both her and the wounded soldier.

Elara leaned forward, disbelief sending a chill down her limbs. As the light faded and the medic slumped onto her side, exhausted, the soldier gulped in a huge breath and bolted upright. The gash was nothing more than a white-lined scar on his otherwise handsome face. Recognition colored his features as he beheld the limp woman at his side and cradled her in his arms, glancing around and preparing to run them both to safety. His gaze met Elara's, and though she knew instinctively he couldn't see her, she shivered. He had a new eye, as bright blue as a summer sky, while his other was a golden brown.

"How?" Elara asked.

The shrouded lady pressed her palm to Elara's forehead. Blinding brightness flashed before her eyes, and then the woman transported Elara again. Pots of tinctures bubbled on the stove, and a curtain of air-drying herbs hung on the far wall. This scene was intimately familiar to her—they stood in the infirmary back at the palace. She watched herself holding a cold rag to Caelan's forehead, willing him to survive after his father's assault a few weeks ago.

"You know how," the woman whispered behind her. "You have done it before."

Elara watched as her past self's hand glowed, just as the medic's had in the last vision, and, as she pressed the rag onto Caelan's forehead again, the light entered him. She slumped forward, her face pressed to his chest, unconscious. Lysandra, in her feline form, hopped up into her lap.

Elara shook her head. "I didn't know," she said in disbelief.

"You have the gift within you. You can call on it at any time to heal others. It is a simple matter of will, as you also have the skill." The shrouded lady pressed her palm into Elara's forehead once more. "There is one more thing you must witness."

Elara closed her eyes. When she opened them, she was standing outside the window of a strange cabin—the dwelling carved into a smaller tree than the gilded ones from her first vision. A fire roared in the hearth, boiling a cauldron of fragrant, earthy stew, and a little girl played with corn husk dolls at her father's feet. The father was unwell—he was too thin, his bones sticking out, visible even under the thick blanket draped over his shoulders. A woman—his wife—brought him a steaming cup, and he beamed at her. She smiled, the expression full of sorrow, and stroked his stubbled cheek.

The wife's grim face, as she turned to tend the fire, unsettled Elara.

"Can't she heal him?" she asked.

Before the shrouded woman could answer, a cup shattered on the floor. The girl shrieked, and the wife rushed back to her husband's side. His eyes stared ahead, unseeing. Dead. His wife placed her hands on his chest, the light of her healing glow forcing Elara to shield her eyes. The man came back to life—his black hair now streaked with white—and embraced his wife and daughter. Before Elara could rejoice with them, another young girl materialized in a doorway off the main room. She was pale as a ghost, and as quickly as she appeared, she dropped to the floor, lifeless. The healer and her husband fell to their knees, weeping. The sound of their despair etched itself into Elara's mind.

"Only death can pay for life," said the shrouded lady, bowing her veiled head.

Unable to control her impulse, Elara wrapped her arms around the strange woman. It was like embracing a statue—the shrouded lady had no warmth, no pulse, no life to her figure. Still, as the shrouded lady wrapped her arms around Elara's back, Elara felt a familiar warmth in the connection between them.

"Farewell, Elara, until we meet again. Use your gifts wisely."

A T LAST, ELARA RETURNED to her body in Caelan's bed, reaching out to his sleeping form beside her. She fitted herself against his chest, his heartbeat soothing her ragged spirit. Lysandra was waiting for her atop the blanket, lifting her feline head in surprise.

What did she show you? she asked inside Elara's mind. Elara dragged the back of her hand over her face, wiping the tears from her cheeks. Her mind was reeling with the violence, death, and life she'd just witnessed.

I have some difficult decisions to make. I'll tell you more later, she told Lysandra, hands shaking.

Lysandra blinked at her, then crawled over to her legs and nuzzled her shins. *Whenever you are ready.*

Elara couldn't help but smile at her familiar, reaching to stroke her fur with a trembling hand. *This changes everything.*

CHAPTER 43

Elara

E LARA TREMBLED AS IRIS's skilled fingers buttoned the dozens of pearls on the back of her wedding gown. The silken white gown dripped with crystals and embroidered red astilbes—matching the flowers decorating the binding marquee. A crown of crystalline branches formed a heavy headpiece. Bloodred coated her lips. She'd chosen the ensemble as a show of strength and inspiration to her people. When she'd selected the dress, she hadn't known that she would wear it this confidently, full of hard-earned strength and grace. She scarcely recognized herself in the mirror, her reflection that of a fox disguised as a dove. No longer a powerless prop, Elara was a driving force in her own future and the future of the kingdom.

"Have you heard anything from our contact?" Elara asked. As soon as she'd processed her vision with the shrouded woman, Elara had asked Felix to give Iris the name of a trusted contact at the country house where her family was allegedly being kept.

"She confirmed that their . . . bodies are still there. In cold storage," Iris said, sniffling.

Elara grasped Iris's wrinkled hand, squeezing it. The loss left both women with a deep ache in their hearts, a wound that wouldn't easily heal.

"Thank you, Iris." Elara's skin crawled at the image that flashed in her mind—her sister, mother, and father stuffed into a damp cellar to keep their corpses from rotting.

"How are you feeling, my dear?" Iris asked, pinning a last curl into place.

"Ready," Elara said. And it was the truth. Today, Elara would marry the man she loved and, in doing so, unite the two most powerful lineages in history. They would defeat Lord Stormrider and bring an end to generations of conflict, ushering in a new age of peace. Her reign as queen would bring hope—a tiny ember, glowing in the darkness, that Serendith could change for the better.

It all begins tonight, Elara thought, stomach fluttering.

Sharp knocks on the door interrupted her thoughts, and Sera strolled into the room. "Elara, you look . . . radiant," she said, eyes wide and nodding her approval. "Be careful this evening—every man in the kingdom will want you. And every woman will want to be you."

Elara chuckled. "Thank you. But I only need them to admire me enough to follow me when I'm queen. And the only man's opinion I care about tonight is Caelan's." She gave Sera a pointed look.

"Don't worry, we'll take care of him." The headpiece's hanging crystals tinkled as Sera's fingers brushed them. Her eyes traced

Elara's figure, soaking in every detail of her gown. "Stunning," she said, nodding her head in appreciation.

Elara smiled, stifling a snort at the thought that Sera could envy anyone else's appearance. "You too," she said.

They'd both chosen their armor well for the occasion. Sera wore a floor-length midnight-purple gown dotted with silver embroidery reminiscent of the night sky. Lace sleeves covered her arms in false modesty, as both the front and back of the gown cut low, showing ample tanned skin. The neckline plunged to her belly button and revealed a glimpse of her sigils—a pattern of smoky swirls across her sternum.

"Let's hope we can dance—or fight—in these," Elara said, lifting her heavy skirt with effort.

Sera popped her leg out of a slit that reached her hip. "I think I'll be just fine."

Elara opened her desk drawer and revealed her dagger. She tucked it into a pocket Iris had sewn into the gown, concealing it. "Hopefully I won't need it." If all went according to plan, there would be no battle, and Caelan would capture his father with ease. Elara gulped down her dread.

"He'll be fine, Elara," Sera said.

Jalin interrupted them with a loud cough, poking his head in the doorway. "May I come in?" he asked, hand covering his eyes.

Jalin? Elara's eyes widened. She had yet to see her former guard since Sera had restored his memories.

Sera rolled her green eyes. "Of course, Jalin. And you can look; it's only bad luck for the groom to see the bride before the wedding."

Jalin entered the room, his face flushing a deep shade of red. "Elara . . . Princess . . . You look incredible," he said in awe.

"It's really you?" Elara breathed.

He nodded. "Thanks to blondie here. I don't have long—Lord Stormrider will notice my absence." He rocked back on his heels, wringing his hands together. "I had to see you before—"

"I'm so happy to see you," Elara said, tears of joy brimming her eyes.

"Me too. I'm glad you're all right." A wide grin spread across his face.

"Any news?" Sera asked, brows pulling together.

"Everything is in place. We have the tent surrounded. Everyone will be hidden in plain sight—disguised. Caelan will confront his father after the first dance."

"Good. I'll be ready then," Sera said, clutching her amulet. "We'll only have a few minutes to subdue him and move him to the dungeon. If he breaks free, we will have to fight."

Jalin nodded again. Elara's stomach churned.

"If it comes to a fight, evacuate the guests as quickly as possible," Elara said. "Oh, and remind Caelan and the rest of our allies that I need Lord Stormrider alive."

Sera crinkled her nose. Jalin sighed and folded his arms. "Are you sure?" he asked.

"I know. I don't like it either. But we need him alive. Without a trial, our subjects' loyalty is at risk. I know what kind of queen I want to be." Elara squared her shoulders and raised her chin.

"And what will the trial be about, exactly?" Sera asked.

"Silas found several of Lord Stormrider's *proposals* for trade agreements in my father's study that qualify as treason. They'll keep Caelan's hands clean and prove the crown's justice is fair once more. The true nature of our engagement and my family's deaths must remain hidden," Elara said.

"And after the trial?" Jalin raised an eyebrow.

"We announce that my family fell ill again. That they weren't as fortunate this time, vulnerable from the affliction they recently faced." Elara looked down at her hands, the weight of her headpiece making the tiny movement challenging.

"And Caelan has been mending fences with several nobles, particularly those whose wives or daughters he was . . . acquainted with," Sera said.

Elara rolled her eyes. "I've been doing the same, sorting through the king's documents and identifying those who have unsavory agreements with him. I've assured them of the crown's ability to conclude those dealings. Any more talk of prophecies with his inner circle?"

"Nothing new. Lord Stormrider has been focused on the wedding night, telling them to celebrate the conception of 'the savior of essence,' " Sera said.

A red haze coated Elara's vision. She'd decided against telling Sera and Caelan about what she'd learned from Lord Stormrider about his true intentions—his desire to control essence and limit it only to the elite nobles of his choosing. Elara considered telling Sera about her new plan for Lord Stormrider—the real reason she wanted him alive. She searched Sera's eyes and found nothing there to dissuade her, but fear curled in her belly. Elara wasn't ready to admit the truth and wasn't ready to fully trust Sera again. Tonight, her primary goal was their survival and Lord Stormrider's capture.

"I have to go," Jalin said. "May the stars guide us." He slipped out the door as Felix entered, offering Elara his arm to escort her outside.

"It's time," Felix said.

Elara took a deep breath. *Time for my wedding. Time for my revenge.*

CHAPTER 44

Caelan

E VENING FELL, AND THE Cygnet Moon rose high above the
canvas city, its silvery-blue halo reflecting fractals of light
across the frozen pond and fresh powdery snow. The blanket
created a peaceful quiet, as it muffled voices and the footsteps
of people who occasionally wandered off the cleared pathways.
Nobles, merchants, and wealthy citizens gathered at the city center
in their warm coats. Many of the women carried fur-lined muffs for
their delicate hands, and fluffy hats perched on their heads. Caelan
didn't blame them. He stuffed his own hands deeper into his coat
pockets as his breath misted in front of him.

Caelan entered the tent and strode down the aisle. He smiled
and occasionally nodded to acknowledge a favored friend or key
ally. As the crowd settled in around him, no one spoke above
a whisper, but the excitement in the room was palpable. The
musicians played, and the crowd's energy rose with every chord
struck. Caelan took his place on the dais, hands clasped loosely in
front, chin held high. His squared shoulders rose as he took a shaky

breath in response to a shift in the music. The traditional bride's march filled the room, and his heart pounded against his chest.

The silks were pulled aside, revealing a bundled-up Elara. She stepped inside, and her attendants removed her hood and cloak. A collective gasp of appreciation arose from the crowd. Elara had selected a dress with red flowers. Iris had braided Elara's hair high, and delicate crystal strands hung from a crown of branches and fell over her face. Even as Caelan's breath left his lungs, a smile tugged at the corners of his mouth.

Many older attendees widened their eyes, appalled that she had forgone a traditional veil and modest gown. Her dress revealed an ample spread of skin from arms, shoulders, chest, and bosom. Caelan licked his dry lips, focusing his gaze on her beautiful face. She was no innocent, helpless woman being married off to a lord of a higher station. No, she was a queen with her crown, marrying the man she loved for the betterment of the continent. Caelan's heart swelled with pride. Elara refused to hide, to submit for the sake of tradition. He admired her boldness, and any who would question or challenge her would never have the courage to match hers.

Elara glided down the aisle, never breaking her eye contact with Caelan. A genuine smile, intended solely for him, brightened her features. Greedily, he took her in, and in that moment, the world faded, leaving him simply a man about to wed his love. He could almost forget the battle that was coming.

Almost.

As she reached the dais, Caelan shook his head to clear his mind and gather his thoughts before stepping down and offering her his arm. He helped her up onto the dais—he didn't know how she'd made walking in her heavy gown look effortless—and they stood facing each other. He wrapped his calloused hands around her smooth ones, interlacing their fingers. Their hearts pounded hard enough that he could feel her frantic pulse echoing his own.

This was the sort of love that inspired paintings and the songs his mother had sung. The nation would record this moment in its history, but Caelan would cherish it. One of his thumbs traced a circle on the back of Elara's hand, keeping him grounded, present in the moment.

"Silence, please. Welcome, one and all, to the sacred union of Princess Elara Evensong of Valoria and Captain Caelan Stormrider of Veilkeep." The officiant held his arms out wide, his long gray sleeves draping onto the ground in front of him. As he spoke, his tall pillar hat bobbed. He had a long white beard and hair to match, his eyes glowing with pride.

As the officiant continued his speech, Elara's smile fell and her eyes widened, tears pooling at their edges. Caelan traced her gaze to the front row, where Sera's illusions of her family were sitting beside his father. A searing pang of guilt and sadness struck him that her family couldn't be here to witness her wedding. Caelan squeezed her hands in reassurance.

"Hey," he whispered. "It's going to be all right. I've got you." He held her hand to his lips, and the audience's collective sigh washed over them.

"I know," she said, her smile returning, smaller than before. "I love you, Caelan, no matter what."

"I love you too. We can do this."

"All rise," the officiant boomed, and the audience stood in unison. "Your Highness, if you please?"

Elara held out her hand, palm up. With a slim silver knife, the officiant sliced the outer edge. She grimaced—putting on a show for the crowd—then squeezed her fist to encourage fat droplets of blood to fall into the wide brass bowl at their feet. Caelan was next, doing his best not to flinch at the knife's sting.

Tink. Tink. Tink.

The blood vow sealed his fate. One prison traded for another. Soon he would become the king of Serendith. The weight of responsibility settled onto his shoulders. But at least he wouldn't be alone. It was a good thing he never wanted to be free of her—his heart had been hers from the first time she'd punched him in the jaw in their filthy training room.

"By the mingling of your lifeblood, two streams have become one river. Before the stars, the realm, and all who bear witness here today, your bond is sealed. From this day until your last, you are bound not only by blood and oath, but by essence itself. May the stars guide you."

"May the stars guide us," Caelan and Elara echoed in unison.

The officiant lifted the bowl high to the cheers of the crowd.

After wrapping their hands in clean linen, the couple turned to face their guests. The royal newlyweds stood on the dais as the nobles lined up in the aisle, waiting for their turns to kiss the bride's cheeks and wish the couple well. Meanwhile, servants repositioned the benches, clearing a space for dancing. Caelan counted those among them who were in his ranks and double-checked the exit points.

Servers passed silver trays of drinks to those who had finished paying their respects to the couple, while the musicians indulged in a raucous melody. Elara was more patient than Caelan in managing the guests. She was kind but firm, fending off requests for audiences with the king or less savory favors.

"Not now," she'd say with a wave of her hand. "Let me enjoy my husband for the evening, and perhaps my father will hear your request during the next council gathering." With her dazzling smile outshining even her dress, it was impossible for them not to be enamored with her and walk away satisfied, even if they hadn't gotten what they'd wanted.

Caelan shifted his weight from one foot to the other, antsy from standing in one place for so long. He nodded amicably at each set of guests and even shook hands with those he was genuinely friends with. He pretended to be interested in the drinks and the conversation, but his skin crawled in anticipation. Caelan, though accustomed to attention at parties, found this unparalleled. He was used to the advances of beautiful women—and the occasional gentleman—but not the advances of politicians. Elara rubbed his shoulder, and he leaned over to kiss her on the cheek.

"Almost there," she said. "How are you feeling?" She scanned the room, no doubt wondering where his soldiers were stationed.

"Ready to get out of these ridiculous clothes," he said, tugging at his stiff collar. "And to get you out of that dress." Teasing her distracted him from his fear. Elara's blush gave him something to look forward to when this night was over.

Once they'd chatted with the last members of the line, Iris whisked them away to a private corner of the tent. A small table had been prepared with two of the place settings that Elara had chosen, plates overflowing with a selection of the food being passed around on trays and served with white gloves. Caelan stuck his finger into a saucy dish and brought it to his lips, then caught Elara staring at him and checked to make sure no one else was in earshot.

"All of my men are in place. Jalin and Kaz too," he said.

Elara nodded, the movement almost imperceptible in her headdress. "Sera and I are ready too. After our first dance, you and I will corner your father, and she will blind him."

"And I'll take care of the rest."

"If anything goes wrong . . ." Elara began.

"If anything goes wrong, my men will evacuate the tent, and I'll fight him." Caelan's knuckles turned white as his grip on a spoon threatened to bend the metal.

I won't fail you this time. His silent promise, a firm knot in his chest, gave him the courage he needed for the upcoming confrontation.

CHAPTER 45

Caelan

C AELAN WATCHED AS THE blood drained from Elara's beautiful face, her eyes wide and glassy. He followed her gaze once more to the illusions of her family. Her sister, Thalia, watched from the sidelines as the king and queen swirled around the dance floor—as was Serendithian tradition. Caelan's gut clenched. Was this what Elara had seen in her vision? *How horrifying it must have been when she found out they were really gone*, he thought, wrapping his arm around her and rubbing her arm to soothe them both.

"Excuse me for a minute," she said, wiping at her eyes.

"Of course," Caelan said as Sera rounded the corner and reached out to Elara.

"Come now, let's get you cleaned up." Sera offered Elara a handkerchief. "You might have to delay the first dance for a few minutes while we fix her makeup," Sera said to Caelan.

"Take all the time you need. They can wait," he said. Caelan scanned the room for Silas. He signaled for him to join them.

"Watch over them," he ordered. With a curt nod, Silas escorted the women out of the tent.

As the dance finished, the king presented the queen to the crowd amidst a roar of applause. Caelan took a deep breath, steeling himself for one final performance. He plastered a smile onto his face and tried to focus on how gorgeous Elara looked and the fact that she was his, now and forever. *Even if I don't deserve her. Tonight, I will make it up to her and set things right. Together, we will save Serendith from my father.*

"I believe the father of the lucky groom would like to make a toast." Caelan's voice boomed out over the crowd as he raised his goblet high and nodded to his father across the room. The crowd tittered with excitement and turned their attention to Lord Stormrider. He raised a brow at his son, a movement unnoticeable by anyone else, then beamed, raising a glass of his own and diving into a speech. Caelan heard none of it, anxiously monitoring the entryway for Elara and Sera's return.

Within a few minutes, Elara and Sera reappeared in the tent, calm and collected. Caelan would never have guessed that she'd been upset if he hadn't seen her tears himself.

Lord Stormrider concluded his toast as Elara glided onto the dance floor out in front of Caelan. With one hand holding hers and the other behind his back, his fingers itched to wrap around the hilt of his sword. *Soon,* he thought.

Music swelled over them, the melody sweet and slow and romantic. The crowd murmured and shuffled inward, closing the circle around the couple, eager to watch their first dance.

Elara followed his lead, matching him step for step and twirling gracefully as he nudged her waist or lifted her hand to maneuver her into a turn. The finale of the dance involved them stepping in a circle, facing each other with hands raised, but not touching. The tension in the small space between them was electric and more agonizing than when his fingertips brushed her skin.

The blur of the crowd and the flickering lanterns came into sharp focus. Caelan's muscles tensed as adrenaline pulsed through his veins. This dance was just a warm-up. He restrained himself, managing his strength with effort so as not to squeeze Elara too hard when he grasped her waist again. With one last twirl, he slightly dipped Elara, indulging in one last delicious look at her flushed cheeks and chest before his eyes searched the crowd. He clocked his father, holding his gaze. The elder Stormrider clapped along with the rest of the onlookers, bobbing his head once in approval.

Bastard, Caelan thought. The gesture felt like a slap. Now that he had his father's approval, it was the one thing that he despised the most, and he no longer needed it.

The crowd roared in applause as Caelan lifted Elara out of the dip and kissed her. Her lips were warm and soft, adding fuel to the growing fire in his belly. As they parted, she reached up to his face and dragged her thumb across his lips. It came away red.

"There," she said, smiling up at him. "It's time." Her eyes glistened in the flickering candlelight.

He nodded, then guided her off of the dance floor to face his father. Sera wove her way through the crowd, flanking Lord Stormrider as Caelan and Elara approached.

"You know what to do," Elara whispered to the little servant girl at her heel. The girl nodded and scampered over to Iris at the edge of the dance floor.

Lord Stormrider held his arms out to his sides. "Marvelous, my son. And daughter," he said, taking Elara's hand. Caelan resisted the urge to chop his father's hand off in front of the entire crowd right then and there. He scanned the room and recognized his men conducting crowd control, nudging guests onto the dance floor, distancing them from the quiet corner Lord Stormrider was now in. All the staff encircled the dance floor, gilded goblets in hand. With a nod, Iris dropped a tiny pearl into her cup, the others following suit. As each pearl hit liquid, columns of Sera's signature purple smoke billowed to the top of the tent, creating a wall of illusions. Cheers of delight sounded from within the smokescreen at whatever spectacle she had prepared for them with her potion.

"Indeed, a truly joyous occasion, Father." Caelan's skin crawled at the sound of his own voice, dripping with false appreciation.

"Congratulations to you both. Let us raise a glass once more to the future of Serendith." Lord Stormrider's glass halted halfway up as he tried to toast them. The sudden stop jolted the liquid within, causing it to slosh onto the ground. His eyes widened, then turned white—unseeing.

Sera walked forward and placed a hand on Lord Stormrider's shoulder, making his body go limp but still stay upright. The glass tumbled to the ground, landing with a thud against the carpet. "I can't hold him like this for long," Sera said, teeth gritted.

Caelan nodded, heart hammering. "Let's move."

As soon as Caelan tugged at his father's sleeve, a glint of gold encircling the man's finger caught his attention, and painful cold wrapped around Caelan's wrist. Ice rose from the ground, encasing his wrist and immobilizing him. *No.* Panic clouded his vision and stole his already-shallow breath. "Elara, run!"

A dark chuckle sounded, echoing in Caelan's mind. Lord Stormrider's eyes shifted back to normal—the same golden brown as Caelan's. A crooked grin spread across his face as he shoved Sera to the ground and stalked over to her.

"Did you really think you could best me with your illusions, child?" he asked her. "I practically raised you. I taught you everything you know. You didn't think I'd have a fail-safe for this?" He leaned over Sera and tugged at her glowing amulet. A knife appeared in his hand from beneath his cobalt cape. He shook his head. "I'm sorry it had to come to this, but I can't let your betrayal go unpunished."

Sera's eyes widened as Lord Stormrider held the tip of the dagger to her chest. Caelan lunged toward them, clawing at the ice holding him in place. He summoned a blast of water and aimed it at his father. But it was useless. The elder Stormrider blocked the blow as if he were brushing away an annoying insect.

"Please! Stop!" Caelan cried, trying now to coax the ice back into its liquid form to no avail. Sera was his oldest friend—they'd survived so much together at the hands of his father. Hot tears rolled onto Caelan's cheeks. His throat tightened, and fear like nothing he'd ever known swallowed him whole. He should have said his goodbyes to Sera, to Elara. They were all going to die at his father's hand, because of his failure. This was what his life amounted to—his last moments, his final breaths—losing all the women he'd ever loved.

Fury, pure and fiery, coursed through Caelan's veins. Elara had looked upon their situation with hope—that they would survive this and rule together. He looked at his father with nothing but hatred. And he knew in his heart which one of them was stronger.

Lord Stormrider pressed the tip of the knife into Sera's chest, drawing blood. "You must really think me a fool, child," he murmured, shaking his head. In a flash, he threw the knife. The world around Caelan slowed to a halt as he watched helplessly. He tried to stop the blade with another blast of water, but he was too late. The blade shimmered, flying end over end until it embedded itself in its target.

His father's knife was nearly hilt-deep in Elara's stomach.

CHAPTER 46

Elara

As if blooming outward from the injury, a purple mist enveloped Elara's body, and she shifted into Sera. Her hands flew to her wound. Blood seeped into the white fabric, her vibrant skin paling to a dull gray. She folded over, knees hitting the ground with a sickening sound.

"No!" Elara screamed, rushing forward to catch Sera's falling form. The illusion Sera had cloaked Elara in vanished too. Elara cradled Sera's head in her lap. "It was supposed to be me," she whispered. Lord Stormrider was supposed to attack Elara, disguised as Sera. It was a safeguard, designed to help Caelan if he faltered. None of them had anticipated that Lord Stormrider would so fully resist Sera's blinding magic—or see past her illusions.

Sera's breaths came fast—wet, gurgling. A mix of blood and bile gushed from her mouth.

"I'm so sorry," Elara said, stroking her friend's silky blond hair—still so beautiful despite the blood staining its ends as more flowed from Sera's mouth and down her cheeks. Sobs racked Elara's body as Sera's emerald-green eyes fluttered shut.

Lysandra soared overhead, cawing in agony. *Don't, Elara. You're not ready.*

But it was too late. Elara tugged the blade from Sera's abdomen and swiftly pressed her hands to the wound with all her strength. *I can't let her die.* Elara sent the thought to her familiar.

In the corner of her vision, Elara saw Caelan, still trapped. His eyes were slits of rage as he glared at his father. Silas, Felix, and Kaz moved in to protect Caelan, swords raised.

She couldn't hear what any of them were saying, diverting all of her focus to helping Sera—to keeping her alive. Death wasn't just hovering in the tent—it placed its feet solidly on the ground near Sera's body as she took her shuddering last breaths.

Movement flickered in Elara's periphery, and armor clanked behind her. "Come with me, Your Highness," a gruff unfamiliar voice commanded. A rough hand grasped her shoulder. She whirled on him, dagger clutched in her bloody fist. Adrenaline coursed through her, and a primal snarl escaped her lips. In an instant, her blade found its target—the weak point in the scale mail at his elbow. Her vicious slash caused him to drop his sword, and she clambered for it, the fabric of her dress ripping underfoot. Sword in hand, she swung with all her might, the pommel slamming into the man's helmet with a sickening thud. The force of the blow vibrated up Elara's arm as the man slumped over, unconscious.

Panting with effort, she rushed to shove her hands back down onto Sera's wound. The bleeding had already slowed to a pitiful trickle.

Help me, she begged Lysandra. *That's part of this, isn't it? You need to help me.*

There was another caw as the raven landed on Elara's shoulder, her claws digging in painfully.

Yes, Lysandra said, and Elara sensed her familiar's reservation. *We can try together. Breathe, Elara. The same way you imagine essence knitting your flesh and bone back together, send it through hers.*

Fiery white light burst forth from Elara's palms, searing them. Gritting her teeth, she let the wounds remain open as the essence flowed from her hands into Sera's failing body. The two women connected—the light serving as a bridge to transfer the magic between their flesh.

"It hurts," Elara gasped. Sera's pain became her own. Her abdomen felt the blow of the knife, as if from a hard punch, knocking the wind out of her. The pressure turned into burning as her nerves became overwhelmed. Her muscles clenched around the phantom injury, and a wave of nausea threatened to consume her. Ringing sounded in her ears.

I know. I feel it too. Focus, Elara. Stay with me. Lysandra dug her claws into Elara's shoulder even harder.

After what felt like hours of agony, the pain faded, along with the light emanating from Elara's palms. Sera's eyes snapped open, and she inhaled sharply as she bolted upright. Elara sagged in relief, a black halo forming around Sera's shocked face as the edges of her own vision faded.

"Elara!" Caelan's voice sounded far away. As she stared into his familiar golden-brown eyes, Elara realized she was going to die. She had nothing else to give. All her energy, her essence, and her life force left her. Colors blurred and sounds muted, until the world around her dissolved into a silent void.

I love you. Elara's unsaid last words echoed in her mind.

A COOL HAND BRUSHED her cheek, and Elara found herself in the forest from her vision. "It's you," she said as her sight returned and she beheld the shrouded lady.

"Indeed, Princess. Shh," the woman cooed. "All is as it should be. All will be well."

"What happened?" Elara asked.

"You pushed yourself too far," she said, now stroking Elara's hair. The featherlight touch could have almost soothed her to sleep.

Elara fought to pull her last moments to the forefront of her mind. "Did it work? Is Sera alive? Is Caelan—"

"Hush, now. Here, see for yourself." The shrouded lady knelt to the ground, pulling Elara down with her, and dipped her finger into the earth. A shimmering pool of water formed, rippling out from the detritus of the forest floor and filling, crystal clear. As Elara gazed into it, her reflection morphed into Sera's face.

"Wake up!" Sera was shaking Elara's shoulders, trying to rouse her.

"What is this?" Elara cried, rising before the shrouded lady's slender hand wrapped around her wrist, gripping tightly and pulling her back to the vision pool.

"Watch, Elara."

"Caelan, she's gone!" Tears streamed down Sera's face. She rose, healed but still covered in blood. With a fierce determination in her green eyes, Sera lifted her arms, and the onslaught of Stormrider's men halted, their eyes milky white.

Elara watched in horror as the vision pool revealed her own unconscious body lying on the ground. *No, not unconscious. It's my corpse.* Pushing down the sickness that somehow swirled in her phantom stomach, she turned her attention to Caelan, his wrist still encased in ice. His face, etched with a deep sorrow that mirrored the ache in her own heart, caused her heart to sink. She squashed down her own pain at the thought of losing him, worry for his safety taking the forefront.

You can do this, Caelan. She prayed he could find the strength he needed to win this battle—for himself, for the kingdom.

Elara's heart dropped as Lord Stormrider cut down Silas, clearing a path in the chaos to his trapped son. Caelan stilled. Panic washed over Elara.

Don't freeze. Come on! she silently begged him.

Caelan's shoulders rose, and his chest expanded. In a flash, he launched a torrent of water, aimed at his father's chest. Lord Stormrider blocked it with a wave of his own, chuckling.

"Really, boy?" he said. He stepped backward, falling into an offensive stance, preparing to strike back. His lips curled up, revealing his canines.

"Really, Father," Caelan hissed. "Go ahead, kill me!"

"You ungrateful . . ." Lord Stormrider's sneer turned into a grimace as a whip of water left a red welt across his cheek.

Caelan grinned. "Come and get me, old man."

Eyes narrowing, Lord Stormrider rushed Caelan, charging forward with his sword now raised. Caelan drew his own sword and blocked the blow, the deafening sound of metal colliding ringing through the air.

Elara's throat constricted as Caelan lowered his blade, allowing the tip of Lord Stormrider's weapon to find his chest. "You won't kill your only son. Especially not one who is king." Caelan held his free hand out to the side, dropping his sword, the clattering mocking his father.

Lord Stormrider searched his son's face, considering. "It's a shame about the girl," he said, jutting his chin toward Elara's body. "We'll have to find another of good breeding to warm your bed tonight."

Caelan's gaze swept across her body, and he shook his head, eyes flashing with grim determination. He raised his hand and launched a thin jet of water, this time directly above himself to one of the hanging lanterns. The water sliced the delicate chain, dropping the lantern onto Caelan's trapped hand.

The glass shattered, and oil coated the ice and Caelan's flesh. Flames licked at his hand, the ice steaming and crackling.

Elara watched as, for a moment, the little boy behind the man came to the forefront. The fear and pain and betrayal he'd felt when his father had first melted the flesh of that same hand twisted his features. But Caelan wasn't that little boy any longer. With a yank, he pulled his smoking injured hand from the remnants of the ice and threw the full weight of his body against his father, knocking them both down.

Lord Stormrider's eyes bulged as he tried to catch his breath, and Caelan reached for the stag's head pommel of his sword. A geyser erupted between the two men as Lord Stormrider launched Caelan off of him. Caelan reeled, landing on the ground an agonizing distance from his weapon. He sputtered, salt water dripping from his hair and clothing. Shards of ice flew from his father's fingertips, slicing into the flesh of his arms and cheeks. Caelan raised his hands, and a sphere of water engulfed Lord Stormrider's head. His father clawed at it, his face a blur of gurgling agony behind the water. Caelan's eyes blazed with rage.

Don't kill him, Caelan. Don't let him make you a murderer.

Lord Stormrider fell to his knees, and Caelan released him. Lord Stormrider coughed and choked down gulps of air. Caelan shoved him back onto the ground and ice of his own making encased his father's arms and legs, trapping him.

Exhausted from the effort and pain, Caelan slumped to the ground, the muscles in his arms and legs trembling.

Elara's heart soared. *You did it, my love. But . . .*

"I . . . died," Elara said to the shrouded lady. "How am I here?" She gestured to the surrounding forest. "Are you dead too?"

The woman nodded. "I passed centuries ago. This"—she gestured to the trees around them—"is the Veil. The place between the world of the living and the dead. Few are permitted to reside here, and far fewer still are those who can pass back and forth between the two realms."

"Druids," Elara whispered.

The woman nodded, her covered face eerie in its expressionlessness. "You, Elara, are no mere druid." She lifted her veil.

Elara's eyes widened, and her jaw slackened. She was looking at . . . herself. The woman was Elara's twin, identical in every way except for their hair—Elara's was dark, while the woman's was like spun silver.

"Great-granddaughter of the ages, you are the heir to a powerful and dangerous legacy. You must return to Serendith, reborn." Her ancestor's cool lips brushed against Elara's forehead in a ghostly kiss.

EVERYTHING WAS INKY BLACK and warm—thick. She was swimming, kicking for the surface, where the light, where Caelan, where life awaited. Elara gasped, air flooding her throat, back in her body in the tent. Gilded lanterns and crystal garlands floated above—she'd never realized just how intricate they were. She tried to sit up, bracing her hands on the rug beneath her, but Caelan lay on her chest, sobbing. At the sound of her breath, he raised his head and wiped the tears from his eyes.

"You're alive," he said, disbelief and relief warring across his features. He put a hand on her chest, smiling at her heartbeat, sure and steady.

"You did it. You saved us." Elara's voice was raspy. She sat up slowly, cupping his face. He placed his injured hand over hers.

"Here." She took his melted flesh and held it to her lips. Their hands glowed, and when her light faded, his skin was smooth once more, the fresh burns and scars alike gone. Pride swelled in her chest. She had journeyed to the Veil and back. Not a human, not a druid—something different, something *more*.

CHAPTER 47

Elara

A FEW WEEKS PASSED, marked by the slow but steady crystallizing of the trees. After the wedding reception, Felix and Silas—healed by Elara—had dragged Lord Stormrider to the dungeon, imprisoning him in the very cell he'd furnished for Elara. As much as Caelan had wanted his father dead, Elara was grateful that he remained alive, awaiting his trial.

Thanks to the servants and soldiers on their side, along with Sera's illusion magic, none of the wedding guests knew what had transpired that night. As far as the court was concerned, Elara and Caelan spent a blissful evening dancing the night away, celebrating their love.

The following morning, the city had buzzed with the shocking news: Lord Stormrider had been arrested for high treason. The official decree highlighted Elara's discovery of an illegal stockpile of artifices—weapons intended for a coup. In one week, she would preside over his trial in full regalia, beneath the vaulted ceilings of the great hall, showing the whole of Serendith who she would be as their new queen.

Her palms started sweating at the thought of planning funerals soon too. She had already announced that the king and queen had succumbed to their new mysterious illness, paving the way for today's celebration. She squared her shoulders, breathing through the weight in her chest. *There will be time for grief. Later,* she reminded herself.

Lysandra hopped up onto the king's—Elara's—desk, almost knocking over a bottle of indigo ink.

"Hey!" Elara scolded the feline, then shook her head, a small smile tugging at the corner of her lips. She reached out to stroke her familiar's silky fur. "We've got a big day ahead of us, don't we?"

Lysandra looked up at her, green eyes shimmering. *I found this.* She opened her mouth, and out plopped a glowing moonstone the size of a robin's egg. *It's from* her. *Wear it today. Make your ancestors proud.*

Elara palmed the gift from the shrouded lady, the gem warm against her skin. "Thank you," she whispered.

T HE THRONE ROOM DOORS groaned open, revealing the silent crowd, hundreds strong. As Elara stepped through the threshold, her gown billowed around her, whispering against the marble floor. Her skirts were a cascade of tulle and silk feathers, each of them white as the snow that fell outside the giant arched windows. Raven hair cascaded down her back in soft curls. It hung simply, with no adornments save for the thin golden circlet with a singular moonstone—her ancestor's gift—that hovered just above her brow.

Her eyes found Caelan, who was waiting with the eldest magi atop the dais, in front of two thrones. His charming smile was warm and genuine, the skin around his eyes crinkling. He'd dressed for the occasion in his family colors—deep cobalt blue and sea gray—but despite the quality of the fabric, the plain-cut attire symbolized deference to Elara. While they would both be crowned sovereigns this day, the court knew Elara Evensong was the true ruler of Serendith.

After her long promenade, she reached for Caelan, grasping his hand as he guided her up onto the dais.

"You're shaking," he whispered, lacing his fingers through hers.

"Only because I know what these crowns cost us," Elara replied.

"I'm here. You can do this." Caelan squeezed her hand.

They stood side by side, facing the magi. He lifted a simple silver crown for Caelan and began the rite. Caelan kneeled. The weight of the crown flattened his wild golden curls, taming them. Elara knew the weight was heavier for him, the sacrifice he was making for her—to rule by her side when he wanted nothing more than to flee the stifling palace for the open sea. He caught her eye, and she was thankful that there was no resentment in his gaze, only fierce devotion, and her heart swelled.

Then it was her turn. The magi lifted a bejeweled golden crown far more ornate than Caelan's and turned to her, waiting.

Instead of kneeling, she turned and settled into her father's throne, smoothing her skirts on her lap with steady hands.

"Your Majesty," the magi whispered, confused. "It is customary—"

"I am not a customary queen," she said, voice like steel cloaked in silk.

A ripple of gasps moved through the chamber.

Caelan stood taller before her, saying nothing, but pride burned in his eyes like firelight.

To his credit, the magi recovered quickly, pivoting and hurrying over to the side of her throne, placing the heavy crown on Elara's head. The crown did not eclipse her circlet, but embraced it, its gilded arcs hovering like guardians above the stone at her brow.

Elara remembered the first time she'd sat here—a toddler bouncing on her father's knee while her mother cradled a giggling Thalia in her arms beside them. A flower crown she'd crafted from weeds and daisies with fingers sticky from honey buns had rested on her tangled hair. *I wish you were all here to see this.* A bittersweet ache and a knot of anxiety twisted in her gut as a mix of emotions warred within her.

"All hail Elara Druidborne Evensong, queen of Serendith!" the magi declared.

At the title she'd requested of the magi, the audience broke their silence, murmurs rippling out amongst the gathered nobles and merchants.

"Druidborne? Impossible."

"I've heard rumors about the Evensongs—"

"They haven't had an essence affinity in ages—now she's claiming to be descended from druids?"

In the front row, Sera smirked, her arms folded across her chest. Elara had shared what had happened when she'd been in the Veil—how she had met a druid ancestor who'd resurrected her.

The soft roar of the crowd almost engulfed the second announcement. "All hail Caelan Stormrider, king of Serendith!"

Caelan sat beside her. Elara reached over and placed her hand atop his, resting on the arm of the second throne. She then grasped his hand and held both their hands aloft in a sign of unity. Caelan's eyes widened in amusement. After a moment, he threw his head back in delighted laughter.

"I love you," he said.

She squeezed his hand. "Then rule with me. And never let me forget who I am."

The crowd erupted into applause, but Elara barely heard it. Her gaze drifted to the towering stained glass windows, their kaleidoscope of color blinding in the morning light. Beneath them, surrounded by stone and shadow, Lord Stormrider waited.

Her hand tightened around Caelan's. She didn't deserve his joy. *Not yet. Maybe not ever.*

Let them celebrate. Let the court believe this day marked a fresh start.

But before dawn, she would set aside her crown and descend into the darkness. Not as a ruler. Not as a sovereign.

But as a sister.

And she would do what only one reborn under the Cygnet Moon could do.

CHAPTER 48

Elara

ELARA STROKED CAELAN'S BARE shoulder, pressing a kiss onto his warm skin. He breathed deeply and evenly, not responding to her. *Good*, she thought. *Lysandra?* The black cat lifted her head, uncurling from her dozing spot on a nearby plush chair. *Will you stay with him and let me know if he stirs?* The cat nodded. *Thank you.* Elara smiled at her familiar and rolled out of bed. After dressing, she headed to the infirmary. She drifted through the silent halls, only pausing to accept a quick bow from a guard or servant. No one questioned what she might be doing roaming the halls in the middle of the night—at least, not out loud. One of the perks of being queen, of being free.

The door to the infirmary creaked as she pushed it open, and Elara glanced around out of habit to ensure the noise hadn't alerted anyone.

"No need for that, child," Ursa said as she stepped into view, her face lit up by a lantern seated on the large wooden table. Elara exhaled and stepped into the room, closing the door behind her quickly.

"You're not the one who has to do it," Elara pointed out.

Ursa clicked her tongue. "If you weren't ready, you wouldn't have spent so much time gathering the ingredients." She placed a soothing hand on Elara's forearm. "You can do this, my dear. You've done the research, and this"—she pointed a crooked finger to the moonstone circlet—"will do the heavy lifting."

Elara touched the cool moonstone on her forehead. Similar to Sera's amethyst amulet, the gift from her ancestor would allow her to channel her healing essence into something far greater. At least, she hoped it would. Sera and Ursa had finally translated more of the Druidic sections of the journal, which was the basis for the upcoming ritual.

Elara took the linen sack that Ursa offered her and cast a worried gaze over the cloth-covered figure on the table.

"Don't look yet," Ursa warned. "I'll see you soon, my dear." She hurried Elara back through the door. "Good luck."

Elara wound her way down the alabaster halls until she reached the staircase that led to the dungeons beneath the palace. The sound of her footsteps echoed, bouncing all around the stone walls. She pulled a small lantern, enchanted by the flamewards to stay lit, from its mount near the entrance and walked to the cell at the end of the line. Though victory was assured, a growing shadow blanketed her heart.

A small huddled figure wrapped in a dark wool cloak perched in one of the chairs in the ridiculously decorated cell. Lord Stormrider looked up, his chains straining. His hands were encased in metal, gauntlet-like shackles at the ends of those chains, immobilizing his hands and fingers—preventing him from using his essence affinity.

"Well, well," he said, standing up and dragging himself to the iron bars. He pressed his face to them, his cheeks already grimy after many nights in the dungeon. "Look who's come to visit—Queen Elara. Though I think it would be more appropriate for me to call you 'daughter,' don't you? Seeing as I am your only living parental figure."

Elara balled her hands into fists, almost burning herself on the hot metal lantern. It was no matter, since her flesh would mend better than her heart. His words were the only weapon he had left to wound her with, and they certainly hit their mark. His attack refocused her purpose, eliminating any lingering doubts about her plan. She had weighed it carefully, mindful of the pain it might cause Caelan. Despite the hard nature of their relationship, Lord Stormrider was still her husband's father.

"You will not be living for much longer," she said, with more confidence than she felt.

He shrugged his broad shoulders. "You may have been able to beat me in this battle, but I still have many allies. The trial will show my innocence—"

"There will be no trial. At least, not a real one." Elara sat, crossing her legs under her long skirt, on the damp stone in front of his cell, just out of his reach. She opened the bag Ursa had prepared for her and spread the items out in front of her.

"Did you bring me a picnic, child? How sweet," he said. His tone, however, was less sure than before. He was losing his bravado as Elara cryptically placed her items in a circle. "What do you mean about the trial?"

Still, she said nothing. Instead, she opened several canisters and mixed the contents together in a miniature cauldron the size of a mortar bowl.

"What are you doing?"

At that question, Elara looked up from her craft. Lord Stormrider's eyes grew wide as realization crossed his filthy face. "I heard you proclaimed yourself 'Druidborne.' Does that mean . . . ?"

She smiled grimly, nodding. "Yes. You were right, Lord Stormrider, about your prophecy. You just weren't looking for my child. Your translation was inaccurate. The savior of essence wasn't to be *conceived* under the Cygnet Moon, but *born*. When I healed Sera, I died and passed through the Veil. When I returned, I was reborn."

He backed away from the bars as if she'd slapped him, all the blood draining from his face. Pressing his back against the far wall of the cell, he tried to place as much distance between them as he could. "Impossible," he hissed. "You're a Serathi? And you're descended from . . ."

"Druids," she finished for him.

Lord Stormrider sputtered a few moments before composing himself enough to ask, "What exactly is your power?" He must not have seen her heal Sera in the chaos of the battle.

"I am a healer," she said, finishing her arrangement and rubbing her hands together. "And tonight, you will make me a killer."

Lord Stormrider fell to his knees, begging Elara not to kill him. "Please," he sobbed, his words breaking through between shaky breaths. "I can't undo what's been done, but—"

"But I can," Elara interjected. "That's the problem, Lord Stormrider. I see no reason to spare you for all of your vile deeds, when I could trade your deplorable life for another's. I can have one piece of my family back. The family that you broke."

At that, he stopped talking, knowing that nothing he said would change her mind. Elara lit a match to set the concoction in the cauldron ablaze. The dancing flame was an unnatural blue, flickering with an eerie, silent intensity. A flicker of renewed determination shone in Lord Stormrider's eyes as they grew larger.

With the fire made, Elara took a deep, calming breath to prepare herself. She stood and leaned forward, reaching her hand through the bars of the cell. "It's time," she said, "Give me your arm."

Lord Stormrider stared at her, and she could see the wheels turning in his mind as he struggled to find a way out.

"If you try to harm me, I will simply heal, and we will begin again," she said softly.

The wheels stopped spinning. Lord Stormrider stepped forward, reached out a trapped hand, and placed it into hers.

"Why did you lie to Caelan? About his mother?" Elara asked, her lingering curiosity about the matter bubbling to the surface.

A puzzled look crossed his features. "He told you about that?" Elara nodded.

"I . . . I didn't want to admit that her death was my fault. It was easier to let them all think she was poisoned than tell anyone about the bracelet—the cost of her visions."

"Is there anything you'd like to say? To Caelan, maybe?" she asked.

"I'm sorry," he breathed, tears welling in his eyes. The shadow of sorrow that crossed his features was genuine.

"I'll tell him," she promised. "Thank you for bringing him to me. And thank you for your life. I will use it well."

A single tear streamed down his cheek.

Elara wrapped her hand around his forearm, closed her eyes, and felt for his life force with her essence. A burst of energy flowed through her arm and into his, up to his shoulder, his head, his heart. She searched until she found the light at the core of his being. In her mind's eye, her essence was like a serpent, so she opened her fanged mouth and swallowed the light. Lord Stormrider gasped and slumped to the floor as she withdrew. Elara placed her hand into the azure flame, searching for another's soul through the portal to the Veil and making the trade.

Ignoring the chilling stillness of Lord Stormrider's body, she stood from beside the cell and didn't look back. She felt the weight of holding the soul inside her as she walked back to the infirmary, where she would complete the ritual.

"Stars above," Ursa whispered as she beheld the glow of Elara's power emanating from the bare skin of her face and hands, as well as the moonstone.

Nodding toward the figure on the table, Elara said, "Please remove the sheet."

Ursa bustled over to the table, gripping the edge of the white sheet with trembling hands. She pulled it down enough to reveal the face and shoulders of a woman's corpse.

Elara let out a sharp exhale. "Thalia," she croaked, holding back her tears of sorrow and rage.

Her little sister's face was gray, sunken in, even rotting in some places—a gaping hole in one of her cheeks, allowing her teeth to peek through. A garish slash split the flesh of her throat. Elara swallowed, fighting a wave of nausea. To Ursa's credit, the seasoned physician paled but didn't get sick.

With effort, Elara pulled her focus back to the task at hand. She stood by Thalia's head, inching the sheet down farther so that she could set her cauldron of flame on her sister's chest. Elara placed one hand on Thalia's forehead, pressing the serpent of essence into the still body.

It felt worse than being inside a living person, like Sera or Lord Stormrider. The remaining blood had coagulated, and the joints and muscles were stiff. No light, no darkness, just an empty vessel. She reached the dormant core and opened her serpent's mouth, freeing the light of her sister's soul. Cell by cell, the light and Elara's healing essence spread, awakening the organs, filling the lungs with air, pumping the heart.

It seemed as if, by sheer will alone, Elara was reviving her sister. Elara risked pulling the sheet off all the way so that she could watch the healing progress. The bones thickened, the joints loosened, the arteries and veins filled with fresh blood. The muscles softened, and fat filled in the sunken in spots. The skin turned from a dull gray to a healthy pink, like that of a newborn baby. Even the hair became full and bright again. Rotten areas—several more than just the cheek—knit back together with new flesh, not leaving a single scar.

With the ritual complete, Elara held her breath as she waited for her little sister to wake.

When Thalia's eyelids finally fluttered open, her bloodcurdling scream ripped through the silent room.

EPILOGUE

*A*T LAST. *A* DRUIDBORNE. *The one born under the Cygnet Moon.* A sinister grin tugged at the corners of her ruby-red lips. She pulled her slender finger from the fountain where she had summoned the vision. The last of the ethereal glow faded as the ripples tickled the edges of the copper basin.

The little human queen perched atop her throne. *So innocent. So unaware of the power coiled beneath her skin.* It pulsed like a newborn star—bright, wild, and unclaimed. At that age, Helene had had the same naivety and untapped potential.

The druid queen now paced in her lush garden, crunching the gravel beneath her heeled shoes as she floated from one carved planter to the next. She occasionally stopped only to pluck a bloom, examine it, and squish it in her fist. The latest flower to fall victim to her frustration was a white rose—a desdemona—and its thorns bit deep into her flesh. She hissed at it, examining the fat droplets of blood that formed in her palm.

"Are you all right, Your Majesty?" one of her servants asked. The queen glared at him. He flinched and scurried away.

Years ago, the bleeding would have stopped already, and the skin would have healed completely. No longer. Their remaining essence was fading, faster now than ever before. Helene's only hope to restore the Well after hundreds of years of waiting was a human child, now enthroned in Valoria.

Elara Evensong. She should hate the girl. Should want her dead. But the Well had chosen Elara, and Helene had never been able to defy its will—not truly.

The queen's scouts had reported on the recent Serendithian coronation, a show of unity and hope for peace within the human realm. Helene had scoffed at their foolishness and thrown her breakfast plate at the poor messenger.

"Bring her to me," she'd commanded, her voice like broken glass.

A war is coming, Elara. And you, my dear, are on the wrong side.

"Join us, Druidborne," she said, voice low as she pressed her bloodied palm to the fountain's edge. "Or perish."

Crushed white petals floated to the ground, only to be smashed under the druid queen's stride.

THANK YOU FOR READING

I'd be incredibly grateful if you took a moment to leave an honest review—either where you purchased the book or on your favorite review platform. Reviews help new readers discover the story and ensure they know exactly what to expect when they pick up a new book.

Real feedback from real readers makes all the difference for indie authors like me. Even a simple star rating (no written review needed) goes a long way. Thank you for helping me continue creating books for readers like you.

COMING SOON

Elara and Caelan's journey continues in the next exciting installment of The Serendith Saga—*Into the Druid's Keep*—coming soon!

STAY IN TOUCH

Sign up for Jennifer's author newsletter and follow along on social media

authorjenniferladams.com

instagram.com/authorjenniferladams

facebook.com/authorjenniferladams

pinterest.com/authorjenniferladams

GLOSSARY

CHARACTERS

Caelan (KAY-lin) Stormrider: Name means "Warrior"; Son of Eamon Stormrider; Guard Captain

    Della (DEL-uh): Name means "Noble"; Familiar

    Eamon (AY-mon) Stormrider: Name means "Protector"; Lord of Veilkeep

    Elara (eh-LAH-rah) Evensong: Name means "Princess, Light"; Princess; Daughter of Evadne and Reginald Evensong

    Evadne (ee-VAD-nee) Evensong: Name means "Good"; Queen of Serendith; Elara's mother

    Felix (FEE-liks): Name means "Lucky"; Stormrider guard

    Geoffrey (JEFF-ree): Palace guard

    Helene (Heh-LEEN): Name means "Shining Light"; Druid queen

    Iris (EYE-ris): Elara's maid

    Isoldea (ih-SOHL-dee-uh): A woman of the court

    Jalin (JAY-lin): Name means "Calm, Strength"; Elara's guard

    Kaz (kahz): Name means "Peace"; Elara's guard

Lorian (LOH-ree-in): Stormrider soldier

Lysandra (lih-SAN-druh): Name means "Liberator"; Shape-shifter

Malcolm (MAL-kum) Ashfall: A Son of the Sky; Magi

Meg: Young servant girl

Narissa (nuh-RISS-uh): Seer

Phineas (FIN-ee-uss): Stormrider servant

Reginald (REJ-uh-nuhld) Evensong: Name means "Ruler"; King of Serendith; Elara's father

Rurik (ROOR-ik): Embrathi; Caelan's childhood friend

Seraphine (SER-uh-feen) Greythorn: Name means "Burning One, Heavenly"; Nimireth; Caelan's childhood friend; Caelan's lover; aka "Sera"

Silas (SYE-lus): Stormrider guard

Thalia (TA-lee-ah) Evensong: Name means "To Flourish"; Princess; Elara's younger sister

Ursa (UR-suh): Royal physician

PLACES

Celestial Summit: In the Stormspire Mountains

Emberreach: Home to the Embrathi and Tharven; City carved into a volcano's caverns; aka "The Molten City"

Serelia (seh-RAY-lia): Lies deep in the Verdant Forest

Serendith (seh-REN-dith): Continent; Kingdom

Shadowed Isles: Home to the Moiren and Nimireth

Stormspire Mountains: Home to the Children of the Sky; a mountain range in the northernmost part of Serendith; aka "The North"

Valoria (vuh-LOR-ee-uh): Seat of the monarchy in Serendith

Veil, The: The place between the living and the dead

Veilkeep: Caelan's home; At the southernmost tip of the Shadowed Isles

Verdant Forest: Ancient home of the druids

OTHER DETAILS

Aether (AY-ther): Drug-like substance from the mines of Emberreach; aka "Stardust"

Artifice: Magical device inspired by ancient relics

Children of the Sky: Arcanists; Energists who can create and manipulate electricity

Council of Magi: Serve the monarchy and govern Serendith

Cygnea (sig-NEE-uh): Constellation; "The Swan"

Druid: Race

Druidic: Language of the druids

Embrathi (em-BRAW-thee): Elementalists; Flamewards who can create and manipulate fire

Essence: Magic imbued in all living things

Iskren (IS-kren): Language

Mabine (MAY-been): Holiday celebrating autumnal equinox

Magi (MAJ-eye): Mage; Individual who serves on the council

Moiren (MOY-ruhn): Elementalists; Watermages who can create and manipulate water

Nimireth (NIM-i-reth): Arcanists; Illusionists who can manipulate the senses to alter one's perception of reality; aka "Sorcerers"

Pyrael (pie-REE-ull): A flame as tall as five men; Part of the Thal'Sira

Relic: Ancient artifact imbued with essence

Serathi (seh-RAW-thee): Arcanists; Gifted with healing magic

Shattering, the: The last war

Sigil (SIH-jil): Magical brand received during the Thal'Sira

Sylari (sihl-AH-ree): Elementalists; Windbinders who can create and manipulate wind

Thal'Embra (tal-em-BRAW): Tournament rite; fire magic

Thal'Moira (tal-MOY-raw): Tournament rite; water magic

Thal'Sira (tal-see-RAW): Initiation ceremony

Tharven (THAR-vuhn): Elementalists; Stonesmiths who can manipulate earth and metal

Well, the: Source of all magic in Serendith

ACKNOWLEDGEMENTS

Like many worthwhile things in life, writing a book is not a solo journey. I am deeply grateful to my family and friends who supported me—and only occasionally looked at me like I was a little crazy—as I brought my first novel to life while raising a toddler and working a full-time corporate job.

To my incredible husband, Branden: thank you for your unending love and support. Elara and Caelan's story would never have come to life without your encouragement to follow my dream.

To my parents, Charles and Sheila: thank you for helping me build this big, beautiful life and for giving me the gift of resilience. I am so proud to be your daughter.

To my baby girl, Sylvie: thank you for choosing me to be your mama. You remind me every day that the world is full of magic—if only we know where to look.

To my grandmother, Mary Alice: thank you for encouraging me to read and write as a little girl. I'll never forget typing up my first stories on your ancient computer.

To my friends Brad, Michael, Dani, Enrique, and Aeyla: thank you for being excellent beta readers. Your feedback was instrumental in shaping the plot and characters within these pages.

To my father-in-law, Chris: thank you for helping me feel beautiful in my author photos.

To my editor, Natalia: thank you for weaving your magic into this story, strengthening it and helping me grow in my craft.

To the team at Miblart: thank you for creating such an incredible cover—I still want to cry happy tears every time I see it!

To my pups, Duchess and Roman: thank you for the snuggles (even when they distracted me from writing!)

And lastly, I thank God for allowing me to do the very thing I feel I was made to do.

ABOUT THE AUTHOR

Jennifer L Adams writes emotionally rich fantasy filled with flawed heroines, powerful magic, and themes of love, loss, and reclaiming personal power. When she's not writing or spending time with family, Jennifer is likely watching Survivor, snuggling with her dogs, or hosting game night with friends in Phoenix, Arizona. A lifelong lover of puzzles, strategy games, and meaningful stories, she believes that the most powerful journeys often begin with one small spark of belief.